praise for justin robinson

"No one writes hard-boiled weird like Justin Robinson. Whether in his retro *City of Devils* series, or here in *BlankAnon*, his breakneck pace and wise-cracking heroes always make me happy. Bob Blank's attempted redemption from the world's biggest mistake is a grimly gonzo journey through conspiracy land USA, loaded with plot, pathos, delightfully demented characters, and lovely crunchy sentences that sizzle and spark like a mouthful of pop rocks."

— *Nathan Long*

praise for Mr Blank

"The smart-aleck narrator of this sassy crime caper is an agent who uses so many aliases for his work in the information underground that his real name is never certain... Robinson (*Undead on Arrival*) keeps the action fast and the banter between characters light."

— *Publishers Weekly*

"To read Justin Robinson's *Mr Blank* is like following some self-deprecating, white rabbit into a sprawling, L.A. noir wonderland on a 100-MPH, nerd culture-fueled rollick."

— *Fanboy Comics*

BLANKANON

JUSTIN ROBINSON

Candlemark & Gleam

For information, address:
Candlemark & Gleam LLC,
2523 Solstice Trail, Chapel Hill, NC 27516
mes@candlemarkandgleam.com

Library of Congress Cataloguing-in-Publication Data In Progress
ISBNs: print 978-1-952456-31-2, ebook 978-1-952456-32-9

Cover art by Kate Sullivan, Athena Andreadis, Alastair Motylinski
Editors: Athena Andreadis, Melissa Scott
www.candlemarkandgleam.com

For the Owl and the Turtle

contents

chapter
one

MIKHAIL LEANED INTO THE MIC, and in his best NPR voice, read off a list in measured, hypnotic Russian.

Despite living with him for a year and my long and storied association with the Russian mob, I spoke the language about as well as one of those chimps that bored researchers teach sign language to. The thing is, you pick up languages through context, and the unconnected string of numbers and nouns Mikhail read every few hours didn't have any. Could have been a roster of spies, could have been a shopping list, could have been the cast of *The Great Muppet Caper*. Beat the hell out of me.

It was late. Mikhail's shack was more hole than aluminum siding, so the night didn't so much bleed in as remind me that the difference between inside and outside was largely philosophical. Up here in the hills it could get pretty cold. Well, as cold as Los Angeles ever got anyway. I lay on my cot that wasn't much more than a web of rust and stared up at the sparsely starred sky through the holes in the ceiling, listening to the coyotes yip-yip-yipping through the hills. It was enough to drive a guy to drink. Lucky for me, it was a short ride.

Mikhail was on the other end of the room by what a generous visitor might call a front door, perched on a squeaking old office chair in front of the bank of antique radio equipment. Muddy light shone from consoles and dials, illuminating the spectral figure of my roommate and the only person who didn't hate the sight of me. He had long, pale limbs and round belly, and the kind of eyes that implied cannibalism was only a single lean winter away. The wild hair and matching beard made him look like he should be living under a bridge and pestering crossers with his riddles three. He was dressed only in a yellowed pair of jockeys. Mikhail might have owned other clothes. Anything's possible, I guess.

Mikhail had been up here for a while. I met him years ago, in my first life as every conspiracy's errand boy. His number station was working for somebody or other. I couldn't remember. Communists maybe, or some double-black cell in the FSB. Hell, he could have been working for the Cat Fanciers this whole time and I'd never know, sending coded messages about who wants chicken, who wants liver.

Mikhail didn't have much of a life. He did his broadcasts, grew a tiny bit of food, and spent an inordinate amount of time on that chemical toilet watching the buzzing helicopters with a wistful gleam in his eye. Once a week, he threw on a poncho made of plastic blue tarp and went down the hill to Tacos el Chido and ate his weight in mariscos. Point is, he was the one person I knew who didn't have enough of a life to be disturbed by the ongoing fascist coup, so he was still talking to me. As much as he talked to anybody, that is.

I got up. Everything hurt, but that was pretty normal considering my lifestyle. My limbs creaked, and I damn near swooned. I wore an old undershirt that looked like it had lost a fight with Mothra and a pair of shorts that used to be a pair of pants. I had shoes. I swear. Couldn't tell you where they were. If I was really lucky, they weren't inside a coyote.

I staggered past the rat's nest Mikhail slept in for a few fitful hours during the day, and out the front door. Well, door*way*. We didn't have a door. This wasn't Beverly Hills.

A chill breeze wafted through the hills of Griffith Park. I was cold, but fuck it. Cold wasn't going to kill me. I don't even think it was trying to anymore, which was as disappointing as it sounded. Below our hovel, the city lights twinkled in the perpetual twilight of an LA night. The dirt was soft under my bare feet. I needed a walk. Wasn't like I could sleep anyway. I'd mostly given that up. It's an easy habit to break if you fuck up your entire life and the lives of everyone you care about.

A tarp crinkled, sometimes blowing up just enough to reveal weathered tires. The hulk of steel farming dust under the tarp was almost nineteen feet long. It sat on the leeward side of the shack, partially shaded beneath a corrugated metal roof. I moved past it, not even wanting to look. That dust covered up memories, so it was good for something. The thing about memories is they never listen when you want them to leave you alone.

My phone was plugged in along with several of Mikhail's devices, on a makeshift charging station he'd built in part out of discarded car batteries. I took it, telling myself I wouldn't look at the pictures, that I wouldn't read the messages.

I was lying to myself, and I knew it.

I ambled past the chemical toilet Mikhail had thoughtfully put downwind, and to the still, which he had not. Old metal barrels of corn liquor that smelled like paint thinner and tasted worse were lined up like terra cotta soldiers. I grabbed an old empty Coke bottle from where I left it next to them and filled it up to the neck. It was like getting lemonade from a cooler, but even better because this lemonade could kill brain cells at twenty paces. I didn't even have to wash out the bottle; if anything was living in there it would be dissolved soon.

I stopped by the little garden plot and yanked an ear of corn off the stalk. No, it wasn't good. Yes, it made my teeth hurt. I gnawed on it anyway because someone had to.

I'd gotten to know the game trails around Mikhail's shack pretty well. I had to walk aimlessly somewhere if I was going to contemplate how badly I'd fucked everything, and I had nothing but all the time in the world to do it in. When I first moved in, I thought maybe if I wandered around long enough, that mountain lion who lived out here might take pity on me and sharpen its claws on my skull. But he'd been put down after eating poisoned coyote meat. Lucky bastard.

It was dark enough to turn the world into looming shadows, and it was only a combination of memory and the bulletproof certainty of drunks that kept me on the path. I swigged deeply from the bottle of shine and gnawed on the musty corn. I didn't have a destination in mind. Destinations were for people with goals, hopes, stuff like that.

The moonshine had kicked in once the shack disappeared behind the bends in the trail. The world started to heave like I was on the deck of the *Titanic,* and everything got that fuzzy feeling like I was wrapped up in shag carpeting. Oh sure, I'd wake up later and find feet all cut to hell from rocks and thorns, but I couldn't feel a damn thing right now, and that was what was important.

Right on cue, the phone whispered to me. Not literally. I wasn't that far gone. The pictures, the messages, both of which I should have deleted, begged to be looked at. So I did, because I'm a chump with all the willpower of a soggy sponge.

The pictures were easier to take. The contentment in them was only sad in the context of my present state. And let's be honest, it's damn near impossible to keep a drunk from staring longingly at pictures of his gorgeous ex. It's what we do, as inevitable as running into things or assuring a frightened friend that we love them. It's hard to say how old exactly the pictures were. At least a year. I hadn't taken any since the last one. What did I have anymore that I wanted to remember?

Mina, in what had been our kitchen. She was giving me that smile that was only for me, somewhere in that warm spot between loving, amused, and long-suffering. Her face was partly in shadow, the sun streaming in behind her. I could hear her laughter, running up my spine. And then, I could hear her voice, all the love stripped out of it, saying the last thing she ever said to me: "You've done enough."

Truer words were never spoken. I had in fact done enough, and it led me here. Mina wasn't the only one not talking to me. Some of my friends made sure to tell me in person to fuck myself. I had a fancy new scar running down the right side of my face courtesy of Sir Guy d'Guy of the Knights of the Sacred Chao. And before you think it was a cool dueling thing, he actually carved it with a broken Yuengling bottle. Bigfoot told me on no uncertain terms that I'd never see him again. I didn't even have the courage to talk to my closest friends. Oana Constantinescu would hate me—she was Mina's best friend, after all. Lara Hernandez had to think I was lower than worm shit. I'd done enough. I didn't have the stones to see the disgust in their eyes, though. So now I wasn't doing a damn thing. It was the one way I could think not to fuck the world up with yet another memetic virus.

The pathway I was on ran along the upper part of a slope, going from flat area to narrow track and back again. Fat bushes and trees clung to the dusty hill. I'd passed out under a lot of them in my time here. They looked comfortable now, but I knew from experience waking up on them with a head hollowed out by a nighttime bender, that they were not. I leaned against one, the wobbling shadows of the hills menacing in their nearness.

"Just fucking do it," I growled. There was no response. I'm not a religious guy, as a rule. It's hard once you meet actual gods to maintain any sort of sublime awe. I wasn't sure who I was talking to. It was everything, all muddied up: the world, my mistakes, and that part of Mina that hated me for the best reason there was to hate anyone. "I'm here. Either do it or...I don't know. Use me. Point me in a direction."

I swigged the shine, looking down at the base of the trunk and wondering if it would be the site for the evening's night terrors when I heard a sound like an enthusiastic proctologist making an upsetting discovery about an elephant. I gripped the tree to keep from falling, balancing on the heaving deck of the hill. I could swear I saw little sparkles in the edge of my vision. That was the fun part about the moonshine—powerful enough to be a hallucinogen, so I got to grapple with literal avatars of my mistakes from time to time.

The noises were coming from a short way up the path. I'm a polite sort who never wants to keep a nightmare waiting, so I lurched my way over there. I'm pretty proud to say that I didn't fall down once. I rounded a bend in the path and found the source of the noise in the middle of the path.

It was a chupacabra.

Anyone who's ever encountered one of these little horrors knows how dangerous they are. Sure, they're technically only *goat*suckers, but spend any amount of time around them and you discover just how elastic the word "goat" can really be. They're about three feet high, and get around like the bastard offspring of chimpanzees and sugar gliders. They're covered in bristly black fur with a line of silver spines going from the crowns of their heads down their backs. Their faces are a bit like your classic Grey alien crossed with Nosferatu, and their hands sport some truly vicious claws. They're also at least twice as strong as a human being. Meet a chupacabra, and prepare to run or become a cautionary tale.

This particular chupacabra was elbow-deep in a goat carcass, messily slurping up every drop of blood it could get its greedy little mouth on. It cracked bones and chewed flesh. Its hands and face gleamed wetly in the moonlight.

I sat down on a rock next to the creature. The meaty smell was overwhelming. He glanced up at me, and I swear a look of confusion clouded his monstrous face for a second or two. The thing was, I knew something he didn't.

"Hey," I said.

The monster's serpentine tongue ran along his bloodstained lips, as though he were contemplating adding me to its feast. A decision flickered through his crimson eyes, either deciding I was anemic or I would serve as a light dessert. He dipped his head back into his gory meal.

"I'm Bob."

The chupacabra burped. It echoed in the goat's chest cavity.

"You're probably wondering what I'm doing here. Griffith Park, maybe. Or possibly Earth. Maybe you're wondering why I'm talking to you. Probably don't get a lot of conversation. The thing is, you're a better conversationalist than Mikhail. I mean, you'd have to be. You have better table manners at the minimum."

The chupacabra removed its head from the goat carcass. Its vertically-slitted pupils were wide, making it look like I was staring down two Saurons. My DNA frantically tried to warn me that I was talking to a predator and pled with me to pick either fight or flight.

"Anyhoo, I live up here. Been a year, I think, maybe longer, not really sure. When you drink as much as I do, it's easy to lose track." I toasted the chupacabra and tossed back another gulp of engine degreaser. "I live over...there, someplace, with Mikhail. He said his last name is Bakunin, but I'm about 90% sure that's a lie. Technically, I lied to him about my name twice, so who am I to judge, right?"

The chupacabra yanked out a glistening lump of something and extended the morsel to me with a weird hissing sound.

"I'm good." I showed him the ear of corn I'd been gnawing on.

The chupacabra sat down and chewed on the lump. It was a liver. Was he making a joke? If he was, it was the best joke a chupacabra ever told.

"You know? You're okay," I said.

The chupacabra growled at me.

"Right, right. I keep losing the thread here. I'm pretty drunk, and that's on top of whatever long-term damage to my noggin. Yeah, so things used to be going pretty well. I was a fixer. You know what a fixer is? I do whatever anybody needs. I worked for any conspiracy that would hire me, which was most of them. Life was good. I had a house, the most amazing girlfriend you can imagine, and for once in my life, people respected me. Mostly dangerous maniacs, but maniacs are people too."

I sucked on the bottle, hoping it would burn out the memories I was relating, but knowing it wouldn't. "So one day I get this job. It's a dead drop, anonymous. Some of them were. I took some, didn't take others. This job really didn't seem like anything. I've done some heinous shit in the past. Not killing anybody, I mean, not directly, but I've done shit. This is the Information Underground, you know? They play for keeps. Not *every* job was dissolving a corpse in acid, but enough of them were. Starts to give you a cockeyed view of the world. So this job, the one that fucked everything up, didn't seem like anything. It was posting. Posting! Do you know what an image board is?"

The chupacabra slowly blinked his blood-red eyes. I laughed. "Do chupacabras have image boards? A place where you can post racist memes and attempts to get other chupacabras to kill themselves because you have a slightly different opinion on a movie?"

"Glah," the chupacabra said finally.

"Let me back up. Do you know what the internet is? It was a thing that used to be amazing. A million sites, each one catering to one person's unique brand of beautiful insanity. You could find anything you didn't even know you needed until the exact moment you found it. But then, you know, capitalism spurs innovation, so now we have like four sites and they're all your most racist uncle at Thanksgiving dinner telling you the real problem with immigration. Anyway, there's these image boards—we call them the chans for a long dumb reason I'm not gonna get into—whose whole thing is free speech. And the thing is, unfettered free speech turns into Nazi shit and kiddie porn. It's a chemical reaction. Inevitable."

"Burrrap."

"No, you're right. Free speech as a principle is a good thing. But there's no universe where 'We should go kill all Jews' or 'We should take sex pictures of kids' qualifies. It's a fucking dodge used by perverts and Nazis so they can do perverted Nazi shit. Where was I? Right. So anyway, I get an envelope at one of my drops, and here's the job: make up a conspiracy. Invent one. Just start posting about it on this one image board. The worst of the worst, or it was at the time. That's it. That was all! And the money in that envelope was the kind that doesn't make you ask too many questions.

"So I go to this board, and it's the dumbest crap. Just a bunch of assholes trying to shock each other with ironic racism that's only ironic if someone takes offense. There's another dodge. I spend some time reading it, and there are already conspiracies on there. This community is cooking stuff up all on their own. I mean, one glance and you know they're pretenders, but it's a whole thing on the boards. People pretending to be insiders and posting about these vast plots. The thing is, no one asks why someone who actually was involved in some kind of secret conspiracy would post on a damn image board. That'd be like wondering how come we never see a toilet on the Millennium Falcon. And nothing that they're saying is new. It's all..." I trailed off.

The chupacabra stared at me. Then, almost like a human, he put his fist to his heart and gave a thunderous belch. It stank like a slaughter-house in July.

"Thank you for that. Do you know what *The Protocols of the Elders of Zion* is? Right, you don't read, and if you did I'd hope you'd pick something good, as opposed to racist hoaxes from Tsarist Russia. So, the *Protocols* is a bullshit tract that's supposedly the minutes from a secret meeting from the Jewish masters of the world plotting to do evil things. It's utter nonsense and was probably cooked up by the Tsar's secret police. But racists don't need logic to convince them to be racists, so people bought it because it gave them the excuse they needed to steal from their Jewish neighbors. That stuff got wrapped up in the blood libel, which is another bullshit conspiracy theory about Jews eating Christian babies."

"Glah?"

"Don't look so excited. Here's the thing about conspiracy theories. They seem like all fun and games on the surface, but dig a few inches and they're all about hating people, and it's almost always Jews. They'll dress it up in other terms to give themselves plausible deniability, but there it is. It's always about ginning up fear against a minority group that's somehow simultaneously in control of everything, but also weak and inferior. And that's what I'm seeing on these boards. It's like watching a bad cover band. Okay, I'm kind of lazy, so instead of coming up with a whole new conspiracy, I just looked at what was already there and I fed it back to them. I told them that the government had been infiltrated by the Cabal. Boring name, right? The Cabal is an entirely fictional group of rich and powerful people who harvest a drug out of the blood of frightened children that they traffic. See? Just blood libel only I've basically switched out Jews for Democrats."

The chupacabra really seemed like he was taking this in, chewing thoughtfully on goat organ meat. It was almost funny. There were no goats in Griffith Park. This was, I supposed, my subconscious trying to fool me. Like I said, I'm kind of lazy.

"I took the oldest conspiracy crap in the book and grafted it on to the community's political enemies. That was it. The laziest shit ever. I didn't think anything of it. It was a job. A well-paying, easy-as-hell job."

The chupacabra had paused in its eating. Then, quietly, it said, "Kuurrrr." I took that as "Go on."

"You ever want something to catch on, don't be creative. People fucking loved what I was doing. And...do you know what cold reading is? Sure you do. Well I was doing that. I made the vaguest, most inconsequential predictions that it was possible to make, and then flat-out told them that disinformation was part of the act. So that any time I was wrong, they could point to that post and stay happy that I wasn't challenging their overall belief system in any way. And the thing was, the theory was carnivorous. The mythology was vague and elastic enough that it could eat up other theories. Oh, you like that little bit, tack it on. It'll fit. That one too. Didn't even matter what I said after a certain point. Do you see what I'm saying here?"

The chupacabra uttered a low hiss.

"Exactly. So the dumbest, laziest, most clichéd nonsense I could shit out took off. People believed it and they held rallies and they voted for people who believed or pretended to believe. And here's the other thing. You know how we get fascism?"

"Hurk."

"Conspiracy theories. When the world isn't working like people are told it should be, they need an explanation, and they're always going to pick the one that means it's not their fault and they don't have to change in the slightest. That's always going to be a conspiracy theory. There's no real ideology to fascism, so they're left with nonsense. So I got hired for a job and instead...I kind of made a fascist movement. Grifters latched onto the whole thing and started interpreting me like I was some kind of crappy Oracle of Delphi. They made t-shirts. *T-shirts.* I made some money and fascism made fucking t-shirts."

The chupacabra sucked on a lump of meat thoughtfully. The sound it made felt like a question.

"No, I didn't get anything from the back end. That's not the point!"

I swear the goddamn thing shrugged.

I took a swig of moonshine. It didn't burn any clarity into me, but I felt warmer. "So...you can imagine that when you spark a fascist movement, and that fascist movement takes over the government, your friends who *aren't* fascists stop talking to you. They kick you out of their house. Your house. Well, jointly-owned...it doesn't matter. They tell you that you aren't the man they fell in love with, that looking at you makes them sick to their stomach. You say you can fix it and they say you've done enough and you know they're right. So you go. Nobody else will take you in."

The chupacabra shoved the meat into its mouth and moistly masticated.

"I *couldn't* work. How the fuck do you work after a job breaks the world? How do you pull that trigger? You don't. You do the only rational thing, which is to get yourself a good substance addiction." I toasted him with the moonshine. It—he—looked concerned. Weird look on a chupacabra. "And you crash in a shack with the one person who doesn't hate you."

The chupacabra stuck his claws in the goat and rummaged around. It sounded a little like a gorilla third baseman enjoying a good chaw.

"Do? What am I supposed to do? I don't even have control of it anymore. That's the best part. Right when the whole conspiracy-fascism thing was taking off, the guy who ran the image board stole the conspiracy out from under me. I needed his cooperation to post anonymously but have the veneer of authenticity. And then suddenly, I couldn't. He took it away. And he's bad at it! I know that shouldn't upset me, but it does. He's a hack. But you wanna know the funniest part? After he took over, it got even more popular. I mean, you've seen the news. You know what happened. What's still happening. Homegrown terrorists fighting to put a boot on their own necks for the sake of freedom."

It was almost funny, so I laughed, but even through the drink, the sound was chilling. The chupacabra yanked his hand out of the carcass, and like Mola Ram, was clutching the goat's heart. It wasn't still beating, of course, and I was slightly disappointed when it didn't catch fire. He held it out to me. At first, all I saw was the organ meat, but as I stared at the glistening lump of muscle, I started to see the chupacabra's meaning. Or my subconscious's meaning through the little monster, because granted, it was a stretch of an idea even for a creator of backyard fascism.

"You're saying that if I kill this guy, I can take the whole thing back and break it? Cut the heart out of the conspiracy. That's brilliant." I had the inspiration of the inveterate drunk on me now. For the first time since I could remember, I was inspired to do something other than slow suicide with the bottle. Sure, it was *homicide*, but that's an improvement. Right?

I stuck my hand out to the chupacabra. "You got a name?"

He hissed at me in response.

"Uh... Ramon? Milhouse?" I thought about it. "Pud Galvin?"

The chupacabra hissed and his eyes widened. That looked like a yes to me.

"Pud Galvin. Nice to meet you." I stood up. "Let's go, Pud. We're gonna kill a man."

chapter
two

YOU DON'T SET out to commit murder without a little bit of prep work. And since the man I wanted dead wasn't in the shack I'd been "living" in the past year plus, I was going to need wheels.

I returned along the path, with Pud hobbling along beside me. A man and his chupacabra felt like a suitably epic beginning.

"I didn't mean to get your dander up. The only thing I know about chupacabras is that they're shockingly good at killing people, and I assume you like it. I hope that's not offensive. Now, when I say we're going to kill somebody, we have to find him first."

The chupacabra growled.

"I know someone who might know. So that's our first stop."

"Burrap."

The sun was rising as the shack came into view, the light stabbing the raw edges of my burgeoning hangover. I took the last swig of my moonshine, trusting that to blunt the blades of brightness. The shack was almost pretty, with its scrap metal antenna on the roof, its walls a patchwork of aluminum, wood, and repurposed trash bags. That chemical toilet was almost a throne looking out over a powerful fief. Oh yeah, I was drunk all right.

Real double takes aren't common in the wild, so when they happen, it's best to savor them. Mikhail glanced up as Pud and I walked inside, went back to staring at the dials on his radio station, then snapped his body around to stare in horror at the chupacabra in the center of his living space.

"Ебена мать!"

"Pud Galvin," I corrected.

"Bobby, there's a monster in the house!"

"Don't worry. He's not a real monster." I gave Mikhail a reassuring smile. He recoiled. "He's my spirit guide."

"What?"

"He's my spirit guide. If this were a normal chupacabra, he'd be killing both of us."

"That's what I'm afraid of."

"Yeah, that'd be pretty scary." I frowned at the nest of blankets and dirty pillows where I'd been sleeping. "Hey, Mikhail...I'm gonna be gone for...I don't know how long."

"What?"

I snapped my fingers. "Right, yeah." Pud and I went back outside, to the betarped shadow rustling in the morning breeze. Pud glared at the rising sun with deep suspicion. I grabbed one end of the tarp and unrolled it, revealing the 1959 Cadillac Eldorado beneath. Its snazzy seafoam and white paint job used to gleam, but now was tarnished under a layer of dust. Even the alien pinup girl winking saucily on the side looked sad. The Roswell Belle had seen better days. "Don't worry, doll," I told her. "Like herpes, I'm back."

Pud hissed. Mikhail came out as far as the doorway, hiding behind as much of the jamb as he could, watching Pud with open terror. "What are you doing?"

"Q!"

"What about it?"

"I'm going to go kill it. Him. The whole...thing." I flailed my arms in what I hoped was a grandiose enough manner to convey the import of my task. I slumped, regarding the car. "You think this'll still start? I'm pretty sure the powerplant is nuclear, so it should be okay? The half-life is in millions of years..."

"Kill Q? Q's an idea. You can't kill an idea!"

I advanced halfway around the car, and judging by the fear in

Mikhail's eyes, I must have looked like something feral. "Can't I? You can kill anything with the right attitude and fire. Mostly fire."

"This is crazy," Mikhail said without much conviction. Or maybe he was nervous about taking a stand. I couldn't blame him. I was in a mood and also drunker than Dean Martin at the Friar's Club.

I opened the car's back door, and it uttered that heavy creak that only classic cars can manage. The remains of my last bed were in here. Really, just an old hospital sheet and an inflatable duck. I picked up one of the pails of corn and dumped it onto the back floorboard. I was going to get hungry and I wasn't made of money.

"Bobby, you're acting weird."

"Am I, or am I acting so normal that it just seems weird?"

"Look at this rationally. You're going to hurt yourse—" Pud hissed and Mikhail yelped, recoiling more. I don't know how he was keeping upright. At this point he just looked like a cartoon character peering around the side of the doorway. The rest of the Scooby gang could stack up over and under him.

"I need fire," I announced. My desire had not produced a flamethrower among the junk littered around the shack.

"Where are you going?"

"Okay, so maybe I can't kill an idea, but I can kill a man who stole an idea. That's a normal thing to do."

"You are drunk and you have a monster. If you do not get eaten, you will be thrown in a dark hole for the rest of your life."

I laughed. "Already there, Mikey. I feel great. Better than I've felt in a long time."

"I'm happy for you?"

I filled my bottle up with moonshine, and then, what the hell, a few more from the mismatched collection of plastic water and soda bottles. Those went in the front seat. I'd need easy access if I was to prevent the specter of sobriety from derailing this particular train of thought.

"You know how in *Frankenstein* the mad scientist makes the monster, and so it's his responsibility to kill it? That's what's going on here."

"You know what happens in the end of that book, yes?"

"There's a giant party at a ski lodge after they save the rec center?"

Mikhail stared at me with a combination of fear and concern that was almost heartwarming. "I think maybe you should sit down. Actually, I think you should get rid of your monster and then you should sit down. You're not making much sense."

"Nothing makes sense, Mikhail. Not this place. Not what you do with your life. Not why we've never gotten a *Jurassic Park* movie where Christians get replaced by dinosaurs and only a cloned army of Teddy Roosevelts can stop them."

"Bobby..."

"I'd call it *The Velocirapture*." Mikhail stared at me, his brain struggling through a reboot. I grinned. "Thanks, Mikhail. If you hadn't given me a place to crash, I don't know what I'd be doing. Not this." I opened up the trunk and found my shoes. An old pair of Converse All-Stars that had seen better days, these things had been on my feet for the kinds of capers that most people never even dream of. I have to admit, when I laced them up over my bare feet, I felt a little jolt. I was back, kind of. I had a mission. A real mission. One that mattered.

"Get in," I said to Pud. The chupacabra hopped in the back, noticing the inflatable duck immediately and hissing a warning at it. I opened the front door and paused. "I'll see you around."

Mikhail emerged like a groundhog hunting for his shadow, watching Pud shuffling around in the backseat. He looked at me, his eyes big with a fear I didn't recognize. "I can't talk you out of this."

"Nope." I slid into the front seat, and the warm leather cradled me like old times. The keys dangled from the ignition. I hoped I was right about the car's powerplant, otherwise this was going to be a short and embarrassing trip. I turned her over and the Belle gave a bass rumble undercut with an unearthly hum that said she was good to go. I hit the gas and she spat up some dust and gravel behind us, and we swerved onto the downhill dirt road out of Griffith Park. And yes, this was all technically illegal. Squatting in the park, driving in the park, drunk, having an unlicensed chupacabra in the park, super illegal. By the standards of the Information Underground, however, Mikhail was supposed to be there, so it was fine.

I found the paved road and headed for the exit. Before long, I merged onto Vermont Avenue, and I was in the city. Along with the lingering aridity in the air, and the abundance of tinsel and reindeer decorating the streetlights, I made a deduction. "Hang on, it's Christmastime?"

"Glah."

"I didn't think you had a calendar or anything. Before or after?"

Pud leaned over the backseat and made either a purring or a growling sound at me depending on how charitable one was being about his intent.

"Where are we going? Let me give you some background. Funny story. The thing about right wing grifters is that, down to the individual, they all want to make it in legitimate entertainment. You know, comics, or screenwriters, or actors, that kind of thing. But that shit's hard. You have to be extremely good and lucky, or you have to know the right people."

I turned the car north, taking us between the Santa Monica mountains and into the Valley. The Belle is two and a half tons of Aldebaran steel, so it was basically a battleship with fins, and once I got her onto the highway, she was humming. Pud wasn't buckled up, but I didn't know how you got a chupacabra to do that. In the event of a collision, he'd probably be happier being thrown clear ready for action anyway.

Once the horns died down from my merge into traffic, I went on. "This particular grifter we're going to see today was not even slightly good, and he's too oily to make the kind of impression you need to make. So he wouldn't even get on the B-movie circuit."

"Glah!" Pud said.

"Oh, there's no way anyone would let him do porn." I swerved into another lane while the other cars gave me a two-horn salute. "So this guy, Sander Siegel, I knew him from my second life. He was a gofer for the local Thule Society, but I'm pretty sure he stopped returning their calls when he hit it big with this internet radio thing he does now. Not that they mind. He's doing more for them now than he ever did for them then."

"Burrrap."

"The Thule Society is one of the explicitly Nazi groups out there. They pay well, but hoo boy are they assholes. Last time I ran into them, their enforcer, this real piece of work by the name of Kirk Shelley tried to frame me for a murder he committed. I blew up his car and got him sent up the river instead, so fuck him." I swigged shine from a Gatorade. Maybe my body would confuse that with hydration.

"Grrrm."

Horns followed another impulsive lane change. The other cars sure were moving slow that day. Not everyone was out to change the world, I suppose. I rolled down the window and whooped. It felt *good*. Then I swerved to keep from hitting the car in front of me that might as well have been stopped. Pud hissed.

"Sander? He figured out Q was a grift pretty damn quick. He was just pissed that I was horning in on *his* grift. So he was out there beating the drum that the whole thing was a LARP. Live Action Roleplays are usually more wholesome than this...getting out to a park, bopping a fake orc on the head with a padded sword, y'know, healthy nerd type shit. Now it means to pretend to be an insider on image boards to create an interactive conspiracy theory for bored fascists to decode."

"Hurgh."

"Decode, as in 'make shit up'. They call it baking, because the posts are breadcrumbs and these dinks never made a loaf of bread in their lives. And get this, every decoded message magically decides that whatever the post said, it agrees with their fascist politics. It's kinda like religion in that way."

Pud settled back in the seat, pondering whatever it was chupacabras pondered. Perhaps goats with fifty percent more blood. The noise he made next was almost a question. I was beginning to understand the little guy.

"Anyway, Sander doesn't like Q, and he doesn't like Paul Mallon, but he moves in exactly the right circles to know where Paul might be hanging his head. Oh, sorry. Paul Mallon owns the boards where I used to post and where the shit still is. You and me are just going to scare Sander a little. Make him tell us what he knows. You up for that?"

Pud bared his teeth.

"I love you, spirit guide."

Sander Siegel lived one of those parts of Burbank that looked like a more weathered version of the neighborhood in *Edward Scissorhands*. It was a little on the nose, considering his politics, but I figured what the hell. The fact that he couldn't recognize a cliché that he was living inside of pointed to the fact that he'd never make it as a writer. Then again, who was I to judge? I lived in a shack.

The street was straighter than a Johnny Unitas flattop and just as reactionary. Every house was decked out in Christmas cheer. Inflatable Santas laughed from rooftops, lawns that had never seen snow were occupied with ceramic Frostys, and poinsettias were epidemic.

Sander's house wasn't hard to find. The Blue Lives Matter flag hanging up by the door gave up the game. Other than the fascist signaling, it was a nice place. It had kind of a forest cottage look to it, like elves might make wooden toys inside. Horrible, pro-police brutality toys, but y'know, still toys. A bigleaf maple tree covered the lawn and walk with shed leaves. The only thing that made the house stand out, other than the flag, was the satellite dish on the roof. It wasn't for cable, either. It was an old school alien-hunting satellite dish, vomiting Sander's sweaty lies out to his hundreds of thousands of subscribers.

A few steps down the street, a pair of crows feasted on a spilled Burger King combo. Whoever had gone there for lunch had thrown the whole thing into the gutter. The crows didn't react to me or Pud, continuing their croaking meal of empty calories.

At the head of Sander's walk, I squared my shoulders and shook out my arms, expecting to have nerves. I wasn't a heavy, after all. I was never the guy they sent to shake anyone down. If I scared people, it was always a third party sort of scare. The old ringing telephone bank, or the terrified interview, maybe your occasional Bob Lazar special. I was good at those gags.

I wasn't scared at all. Everything was bright and clear the way it hadn't been for a long time. I reached back into the car and withdrew the bottle of shine. A gulp of that degreased my insides and sharpened me like the handle of a toothbrush ready to be thrust into a prison informant.

"C'mon, Pud. Let's scare the shit out of this turd."

I strode up the front walk. His welcome mat said "THIRD AMENDMENT" in calligraphy. That was almost enough to stop my forward momentum. Almost. I kicked the door right by the lock. I'm not especially strong, but I was that day. Maybe it was the booze, maybe it was the purpose, but I kicked that door in with a righteous fury.

"Yoohoo, Sander!"

Sander's home was decorated in the kind of kitsch that's almost never meant ironically. It looked like a Washington DC gift shop but somehow tackier than that implies. The walls were wood-paneled with display cases for yet more tawdry junk. I had the rock-solid certainty that once upon a time, the decor had been different. Maybe some pictures of family, a few tchotchkes of cats or penguins or something—nondenominational shit. But Sander, in a fit of patriotic fervor or severe lapse in taste, bought a ceramic eagle heroically dry humping an American flag. Then, over a period of weeks, months, years, it had spread, taking over all the other pictures and objets d'art, leaving only this. A manifest destiny of kitsch.

The living room was empty of people. The house was silent. If Sander wasn't home, I was going to be slightly sad about wasting my entrance, but waiting creepily and eating the entire contents of his fridge had some appeal. Just as I was warming up to the idea of a bologna sandwich on white bread with a side of mayo, a panicked scrabbling crawled up from the back of the house. The rat was frightened already. Good.

"I hear you, little fella! Come on out, I just want to talk." I wasn't doing Jack in *The Shining*, but I maintain it's impossible to say something like that in a situation like this one and not kinda be doing Nicholson.

I didn't wait for a response. I wanted him to hear my footsteps, heavy and even. Even if he never saw one of those movies, we know what Michael Myers or Jason Voorhees sounds like. They'd preyed on our ancestors, and thus, a terror of the masked killer exists on our genetic code. It'd been since my exile since I saw any movie. They still had slasher flicks, right? I tried to remember to ask Sander.

A hall extended down the length of the house, and that was where the panicked rodent sounds were issuing from. The pictures hanging from the wood paneling were all of Sander. Sander holding a gun, Sander making an "okay" hand sign with a bunch of beefy white guys, Sander posing with third string political operatives, Sander holding a machine gun and desperately trying not to look terrified. I paused at one of the pictures. It was Sander posing with Kirk Shelley. Small world.

"Hey, Sand—"

The gunshots were thunder. The door next to me sprouted some new holes while a couple of the pictures on the opposite wall shattered and fell to the floor. I watched them with interest. The air was heavy with cordite and my ears gave me a busy signal.

"Intruder! I'm calling the cops!" Sander's voice sounded like a cartoon mouse sending a meal back to the kitchen for being underdone. It was the kind of voice that woke up the bully in everyone, even those of us who didn't know such a beast lurked in our ids.

"Hey Sand—" I tried again.

More gunshots turned the clapboard door into so much sawdust. The whine in my ears found a new, even more painful pitch.

"Would you knock that off? This is really bad for our hearing!"

"Bob?" Sander squeaked.

I turned the corner and moved the door—now merely a shroud of dusty lace—aside. The room was Sander's indoor studio. The walls were covered in foam, and those were festooned with American flags and all of their fascist variants, more eagle memorabilia, and, confusingly, a head shot of Gil Gerard with the eyes removed. I had zero plans to ask what that was all about. Standing right next to his computer monitor, just out of sight of camera but where Sander could see her, was a blonde anime schoolgirl figurine, her hands demurely clasped behind her.

Sander had a pair of desks set up in an L-shape, with a desktop computer, small soundboard, and a microphone. A camera at the far wall was pointed at where he would be sitting if he were in the middle of a screed. He had crammed himself partway under his desk, pointing a pistol at the door with trembling hands.

Sander was a little guy, with dirty blond hair, abundant freckles, and pale brown eyes the exact color of a loose stool. He and puberty had largely been ships passing in the night. His black turtleneck and jeans implied a Li'l Fash section at a department store: for all your reactionary sixth grader's sartorial needs.

"What the hell are you doing here?"

"Are we on?" I gestured at the webcam aimed at Sander's now empty chair.

"Yeah, I was in the middle of my show."

I peered into the unblinking eye of the camera as I approached it, which I would learn to regret. I yanked it off the shelf, the cords falling away. Then I did my best Nolan Ryan. The camera exploded into plastic and metal shrapnel.

"What the heck, Bob? Those things are expensive!"

"You can afford it."

"Not with these California taxes," he whined.

Sander was just beginning to pick himself off the floor when I squatted over him, getting right into his pinched, weasely face. He recoiled. "What the hell are you doing, Bob? Jeez, you stink! When was the last time you took a show—"

I flicked him in the forehead. "Paul Mallon."

"What are you, gay? Get away from me."

I slapped him. "Paul. Mallon."

He brought the gun up. "I have a gun."

I snatched it from his hand and pointed it at a wall. Click, click, click. I tossed it away. "Paul Mallon, Paul Mallon, Paul Mallon."

"Bob, what are you doing?" I think this was right where Sander started to get what was happening. Maybe he saw something in my eyes, or smelled something on my breath, or finally registered that I looked like I'd spent a year living in Griffith Park. His squeaky voice developed a quaver, and his eyes started rolling like a sheep who's heard the first wolf howl.

"There it is," I murmured. I didn't mean to say it, just think it, but it came out anyway. "I'm going to ask you where Paul Mallon is, and you're going to tell me."

"You don't look so good. You want a Coke or something?"

I nodded to myself. I was going to have to make a stronger impression. I wrapped my fists in his turtleneck and hauled him to his feet. "Sander, I want you to know that I'm not enjoying this."

"Enjoying what?" He was scared, and I hate to admit that felt pretty good. Sure, Sander was one of the most bullyable people in existence, but it wasn't all of that. He was every mistake I'd made in the past year. I couldn't hurt them, but I could hurt him. His forehead was about level with my mouth, and he was standing on his tippy toes. I kissed him right on the brow furrows, then heaved him over the desk. His legs ragdolled against his computer as he went tumbling. The schoolgirl figurine clattered to the floor next to him. "Tiger J!" he yelped.

"Where the hell is my booze?" I asked the room. It had to be around here somewhere. I was definitely carrying it when I came in, and I needed another drink.

Sander, for his part, was sobbing and swearing, crawling across the floor for his gun, clutching the girl to his chest. "You can't just break in here and beat me up!"

"Isn't that the cornerstone of your entire political philosophy?"

"You liberal thug!"

"Not a liberal, and the Thuggee never actually let me in the organization. Something about doubting my commitment to either Kali or Sparkle Motion. I can't remember. Seriously, have you seen my booze?"

Sander popped up like a jack-in-the-box, the gun leveled somewhere in the vicinity of my head. He cradled the figurine like she was Fay Wray and the way he was smirking felt like it was for her benefit. "Reach for the sky, you fucker." The curse fought him on the way out, his mouth unused to making the sounds. I'll be honest, I don't trust anyone who can't curse. It points to a weakness in character.

"I'm not kidding. I came in here with a bottle. Mostly clear, smells like industrial disinfectant?"

"I have a gun!"

"An unloaded gun." His eyes went big, and he bolted for a shelf, rummaging around, looking for bullets I was guessing. "Hey, Pud?"

"Don't call me that!" Sander whined.

"I'm not talking to you." Pud loped in. I wasn't sure where he'd been, but he was wet now. "I was talking to him."

It probably won't surprise anyone to know that I've read a lot of H.P. Lovecraft. In those stories, whenever a character sees a monster, they go a little bit insane. I always thought it was exaggeration, just Lovecraft's inherent xenophobia manifesting itself in that drama queen way of his. As Sander turned and beheld a living, breathing chupacabra in his house, I got to see it in real life. The fact that Sander himself was really racist was a coincidence. Maybe. He turned white as a ghost at a country club, gibbering and pointing at Pud with a nerveless finger, his whole body wracked with tremors. It was honestly a little funny.

"Wassamatter, Sander? Never seen a monster before?"

Pud launched himself across the room, throwing his arms wide and letting the multicolored flaps beneath catch air. Sander screamed and the room suddenly stank like an outhouse. Pud landed on Sander and took the screaming little fascist to the floor.

"Don't kill him," I said. Pud made a disappointed noise. Sander held the girl in front of him like a cross for a vampire, but chupacabras aren't scared of anime. As though to prove it, Pud snatched the figurine from Sander and stuck it in his mouth experimentally.

"Tiger J, no!" Sander cried.

"Blah!" Pud said, spitting the girl out.

I walked around the desk and knelt beside Sander. Between what he'd done in his pants and Pud's breath, this section of atmosphere had become decidedly fragrant. I smacked Sander in the staring moony face lightly a few times. "Hey, you still in there, big guy?"

"That's a monster!" Sander hissed, like this was news to me.

"Yeah, we carpooled here. Now listen carefully. He won't eat you, but only if you tell me what I want to know. Understand?"

Sander gave me a pathetically eager nod. He stared into Pud's eyes, and I think I knew what he was seeing there. "Yeah. Yeah, sure."

"Okay. I want to know where Paul Mallon is."

Now Sander looked at me, frowning. "Why would you want to know that?"

"Doesn't matter. All that matters is that this monster isn't going to eat you if you tell me."

"Paul retired. Whatever you think he did, he didn't do."

I sighed. "Sander, you were so cooperative just a second ago."

"Look," he said, his voice quavering, "I think we got off on the wrong foot. Let's get up, and we can talk about this like civilized people."

"You want to debate me?" I sneered.

"Don't be ridiculous. You're clearly drunk and maybe you're not thinking clearly. I'm trying to help you."

"What do you know about me?"

"You're white? You're a man?"

"You'll need to go a little deeper. You and me met when you were still working for the Thule Society. You remember that?"

"I never—" he snapped, then as Pud growled, Sander slowed his roll, dropping his voice to a scandalized hiss. "I never worked for the Thule Society! I might have done favors for a few *members* of the Thule Society here and there. I wasn't on their membership rolls. I wasn't a member myself."

"You know you're not on camera, right? You don't have to deny that you're a Nazi."

"I'm not a Nazi!"

"Yeah, sure pal." I frowned at Sander. "Okay. Well, I worked for a lot of conspiracies in my time. Pretty much all of them. And on one of those jobs, I *invented* a conspiracy out of whole cloth. Just pulled it right out of my butt. And that conspiracy's name is Q. You getting this?"

"You're telling me that you're Q."

"Yeah."

"Q claims to be high ranking military intelligence."

I laughed. "I've told people a lot of things."

"I knew it!" he crowed, then as Pud leaned in, more quietly said, "I knew it."

"Yeah, because you're smart." Massaging Sander's fragile ego would take me a long way. He styled himself as an intellectual, despite the fact that his ideas basically all ended up as "How about colonialism again?" The words did the work, and I watched him react. "Mallon took Q away from me, and he and I need to have a talk. Only he's not returning my calls anymore. So I need to know where he is."

"If I tell you, you'll leave? And you'll take... Where did you get a monster?"

"I got secrets, motherfucker." I flicked his forehead. "Yes. I will leave. You'll never see me again, unless I need some lunch money."

Sander looked up at Pud, who loomed over him, making a barely audible hiss. Sander calmed. Something about a chupacabra's hiss. Probably needed it to keep from scaring goats. "Like I said, he's retired. He has a little compound off of Zzyzx Road. You know where that is?"

"A compound, huh?"

"You can't miss it."

"C'mon Pud. We're not eating him today." We walked out of the room, and there was my bottle, sitting next to a sad spider plant on an end table in the hall. I picked it up and poked my head back into Sander's studio. He was getting up, resentfully wiping chupacabra spit off the figurine. I waved the bottle. "It's okay. I found it."

"Great," he said, giving me a flat smile.

Pud and I returned to the car. A woman out walking her dog screamed when she saw Pud. I waved to her. It was a good day so far.

DESPITE ALL OF my big talk, I'm not a killer. I can barely fight. I only beat up Sander because he's a tiny man who couldn't win a fight against shame. So the reality was, I couldn't kill Paul Mallon no matter how much I wanted him dead. Fortunately, I knew a lot of people who killed professionally. *Un*fortunately, there was only one of them who might not want to kill me once I explained the situation.

I drove into North Hollywood, hoping he'd still be in the same crappy apartment I'd helped move him into. It had been a while. Truth was, it had been a while since I'd seen *anyone*. All I could do was cross my fingers that he hadn't moved and still liked me enough to kill a human being at my request. At least this guy could be paid in moonshine.

North Hollywood is a criss-cross of narrow streets, and blocks upon blocks are devoted to huge stucco apartment buildings that all manage to look equally depressing in entirely different ways. It's a triumph of architectural design.

The building I was looking for was supposed to be white, but exposure to the toxic atmosphere of Los Angeles had dyed it the color of a smoker's teeth. Blue trim went all around a building the shape of a Tic Tac box. It was sandwiched between one with a half-assed tiki theme and another that looked like the kind of living spaces designed for the needs of divorced men looking for a quiet place to drink themselves to death.

As a peace offering, I scooped a full bottle off the floor of the car and got out. Pud made to follow me, but I stopped him. "Sorry, pal. I don't want to scare this one. Wait here and I'll be right back. And...uh...try to stay out of sight." I had a brief image of the LAPD surrounding the car with guns drawn. That wouldn't end well for anybody.

Pud gave me a reproachful look and slumped down on the car seat. I made my way up to the building, putting my back to the wall next to the locked glass doors. After a couple minutes a resident emerged, and I slipped inside. I took the elevator up to the second floor, had a momentary panic attack that I'd forgotten which apartment was his, eventually figured what the hell and trusted my gut.

I knocked on the door I was pretty sure I remembered, which opened on the face of a stranger. He was a white guy with sleepy eyes and facial hair that was still deciding if it was going to get its shit together long enough to be called a beard. His shirt featured a screaming Invader Zim.

"Yeah?" he said.

"I'm looking for Hasim?"

"Come on in." He shambled back inside, calling, "Hey, Hasim! You got company!" The guy plopped himself down on the nearby couch and unpaused his game. It was some Mario thing I hadn't heard of what with living on a hill and all.

The combo living room and kitchen of the apartment was cleaner than I was expecting, just based on this guy and of course what I knew about Hasim. Everything looked to mostly be where it was supposed to, and no large mystery stains pooled on the countertop, no lines of ants poking around looking for something to eat. In short, this was cleaner than any apartment I had ever lived in. They even had a Charlie Brown Christmas tree by the window.

A door opened and the man who stepped out was Hasim Khoury, but it took more than a minute to square what I saw with what I remembered. If he hadn't been wearing a red and blue Blake Griffin jersey, I might never have recognized him at all. His curly hair was short and stylish, his beard was neatly trimmed. He looked...*healthy* was the best way I could describe it, and after a year or so of only seeing Mikhail, it was jarring. Hasim didn't always look that way. When he was drinking, he let the exercise or the sleep lapse. When he was really drinking, it was both of them.

He squinted at me. "Bobby? Is that you?"

"It's me!" I said, faking some devil-may-care attitude.

"What happened?"

"Therein lies a tale." I jerked my thumb at the roommate, who was industriously working the Nintendo controller in his hands. "Is he an Assassin too?"

Hasim's eyes widened. "Dude, no."

I laughed. "Did you move in with a Templar? That'd actually be a good sitcom. Quality shenanigans. It's a thousand year war over who takes out the garbage."

The roommate looked up from his game with a confused frown.

"It's cool, Jake," Hasim said. "Bobby's got a weird sense of humor."

"I don't know about that," I said. "I think anyone would laugh when a fascist shits his pants. Have I got a story for you."

Hasim stepped closer to me and recoiled. "Dude, you don't smell so great."

"I haven't really been showering."

He pulled me over to the door, not entirely gently. "You gotta keep a lid on it," he hissed, "Jake doesn't know anything. He's a civilian."

"Oh shit." I winced. "Sorry!"

"What the hell happened to you?"

"That's a long story."

"Let's take a walk." Hasim grabbed his keys off the counter, pocketed them, and escorted me out into the hall.

"It was nice meeting you," I called to Jake, who gave me a distracted wave. "He seems nice."

"Yeah, he's cool." We got into the elevator. When Hasim spoke again, it was halfway between concern and confusion. "You were gone for...I don't know how long, and you come back...you don't look so great."

"I *feel* great."

The elevator dinged open, and soon we were out on the street in front of his place. Hasim looked around, and satisfied that the few strug-gling actors and assistants out walking dogs were far enough away, got to the point. "What happened?"

"Yeah, okay. A story." I told Hasim the whole thing, top to bottom. I told him that I was Q, that I might have broken the world a little bit, and if nothing else, I was a testament to the impact a single person could have. I was George Bailey in reverse. Hasim stared at me the whole time, his brow furrowed as he took everything in. When I was finished, I waited for the riot act.

Hasim chose his words carefully. "You know, it hasn't been easy looking like me or having a name like mine lately."

The disappointment in his voice was worse than a kick in the guts. All I could do was mumble, "I know. I'm sorry."

He nodded, considering some more. "It hasn't been easy for a while."

"Yeah. I kinda figured."

"I've been thinking about forgiveness a lot lately, you know?"

"In like...a religious sense?"

"Kinda, but it's more than that. I'm not going to let anger poison me," he decided. "You fucked up, but I can't forget what you did for me. The thing with the monkey's paw. Nobody else would have gone to the mat for me like that. You're not forgiven, but...I think I can help you figure out a way to get there."

I shrugged. Seemed like the thing to do at the time. Besides, I felt bad that Hasim had known me under a fake name for so long. He adapted to calling me "Bobby" in record time. He said I looked like a Bobby. "I was happy to."

"Making amends is important," he said, putting a hand on my shoulder. "What do you want, Bobby?"

Yeah, it wasn't the words that boogied though my fantasies, but they were the softest ones I'd heard in too long. I had spent however long I'd been up in the hills playing the same recriminations in my mind, over and over. I believed them. The words might as well have been etched in my bones. I felt them reaching out now, threatening to take hold of me. If I started now, I'd never stop. I must have showed this one my face because Hasim wrapped me up in a hug. Right at that moment, the flood that had been building was dammed. It hurt, but I locked it up tight. Now wasn't the time for that.

I gently pushed away. "That's it. That's exactly it," I said. "Making amends isn't saying you're sorry. It's doing something to try to fix the harm."

"And that's why you're here."

I nodded. "Are you still an Assassin?"

He looked embarrassed. "Not really. I mean, I didn't turn in my membership card, and I know where the house is and everything."

"Do you still kill people for money?"

"I really want to stop, but it's hard for someone like me to get a real job. So it's been more of like a gig situation. Assassinations pay better than those ride-sharing things."

"Yeah, their big innovation is 'hey, what if we ignored labor laws?' So you're still a professional killer?"

"A little. I don't want to be. Why?"

"I need you to kill someone for me."

"What?"

"I told you. I fucking broke the world, and if this asshole is in the ground, then things start getting put right. Only I'm not a killer. I could psych myself up, but I know I'd bitch out at the last minute."

"There's a high potentiality for that kind of thing your first time. Although you shouldn't use the b-word."

"Fair. But are you willing to do it?"

"Who is it?"

I explained who Paul Mallon was. You know, owner of image boards where Nazi shit gets posted, that kind of thing.

"This isn't the best time to be a Muslim in this country," Hasim said in response.

"You're a terrible Muslim!"

"Please, don't tell my mom that."

"Hasim, when would I talk to your mom?"

"You implied one time you dated her."

I couldn't remember the exact circumstances of that remark, but I could more or less put together what I must've been talking about. "I wasn't serious. I was insulting your mom."

"How is that insulting her? You're like twenty-five years younger than she is, and at the time you had a job. You've always seemed pretty respectful toward women, and you know, she's a widow. She could do worse."

"What?"

"Sounds more like you're insulting yourself."

I rubbed the bridge of my nose. "I don't know your mom."

"Do you want to meet her? She's in Beirut, so that might be a problem. You'd also need to clean yourself up a little."

"Hasim, I'm not going to date your mom."

"Your loss, dude."

"Regardless, I'm not going to tell your mom you're a terrible Muslim."

He let out a relieved sigh. "Thank you."

"I was thinking more how silly it is that someone would want to keep you out of the country."

"They think I'm a terrorist."

"When you're an Assassin."

"Exactly!"

"I need you to be an Assassin, Hasim."

"I told you, I can't. I've been trying to keep my nose clean."

"While still doing assassinations."

"Only when I'm short on rent."

"This guy I'm talking about, he's a bad guy. He's a racist. He ran a site that hosted child pornography."

Hasim winced. "Don't tell me that."

"It's true. This is the kind of guy that you have Assassins for. You take this person out of the world, and it's a better place."

"Bobby, I can't. I'm trying to live in this country without cops busting my door in, and murdering a rich white man is pretty much the one thing that's actually illegal here."

I looked Hasim in the eye. It would be a stretch to call us friends, but we'd always been friendly. I put this in my mind, to call to it, to draw those feelings into my plea. "I'm begging you. Some of the shit you're dealing with is my fault, and I want to put it right somehow. The only way I can think to do it is to pinch this thing off at the source. And that means killing a bad man. Normally, you look at something like this, and you have to pay a terrible price, but here, we're looking at a win-win. This fascist movement eating the country—hell, the world—goes away, and a truly shitty person stops poisoning hearts and minds. I'd do it myself, but we both know I'd fuck it up at the last minute. You've had to have killed at least a couple people in your time you feel guilty about. Well, not this one. This helps balance those scales too."

It was a shitty thing to do to Hasim. I'll cop to that. The way he squirmed when I brought up his death toll confirmed I'd hit a nerve. I'd feel bad about it later. If using Hasim's guilt helped me fix the world, well, I'd pay the price for it once Mallon was in the ground. Maybe Hasim would hate me. He could join the damn club.

"Okay," he said.

"You'll do it?"

"I'll do it."

"Yes! Hey, to celebrate, I brought a little something. Now, it tastes like brain cell solvent but also, there's a negative side."

He looked at the bottle in my hands with unmistakable hunger. Hasim was a drinker. This conflicted with the Muslim faith of his fellow Assassins, so it was something he kept on the downlow. I have no idea if his mom knew or not, but I was thinking not. I used to meet him at this bar in Eagle Rock all the time.

"I'm an alcoholic," he said.

"Me too! That's why I thought this would be so much fun."

"No, Bobby. I'm an *alcoholic*. I'm in recovery."

"What? When did that happen?"

"Seven months ago when I admitted I was powerless over alcohol."

"Did you get in to therapy?"

He laughed. "I can't afford therapy. I have a regular meeting."

"Oh. Congratulations?"

"Thanks."

I took a big swig from the bottle. "Is it going to be a problem if I drink?"

"A little."

"Bummer," I said, drinking.

He sighed. "So where is the dead man?"

"Zzyzx Road. It's a bit of a drive."

"I'm going to put on some real clothes, then, and I have to get my knives." He looked me over. "And if I'm gonna be in a car with you, you need a damn shower."

"Fine." I followed Hasim up to his place and he pointed me in the direction of the shower. I washed the worst of my stink off, leaving a hell of a ring around the tub. I pulled on my old clothes and had a gander at the wild-eyed maniac in the mirror. I still looked like a decorative hermit, but I could no longer be smelled at ten paces, so that was something. By the time I was done, Hasim was dressed in jeans and a t-shirt and carrying a black leather roll bag. He said goodbye to Jake and we made our way out to the Belle.

Maybe fifty feet distant, a strange figure loitered at the corner. I couldn't quite make out his features, but he had long white hair in a neat ponytail, and he was dressed all in black, like Dr. Evil at a funeral. My attention snagged on him for a moment, and I swear he looked back at me. I wanted to get out of there for no reason I could name. Something about the man made me want to run.

I tried to staved off the dread with a long pull on the bottle. Didn't quite work.

"Are you okay to drive?" Hasim asked.

"Feels like a philosophical question." I said, getting in.

He slid in on the passenger side. "More like a practical one."

Pud leaned over the backseat. "Glah!"

"Holy shit! What's that?"

"That's Pud Galvin." I looked over at Hasim to emphasize what I said next. "My spirit guide."

Hasim couldn't decide who he needed to stare at with wide, terrified eyes. "You got a spirt guide. That's great, man. I'm really happy for you."

I jabbed a finger at Pud. "Don't eat him. That's Hasim. He's a friend."

I think Hasim was about to say something, but he didn't get it out. I stomped on the gas, and we were on the road. The man in black was gone from my rearview, but I didn't feel any better.

<h1>chapter
four</h1>

ROAD TRIPS ARE THE SAME, whether they're with your family or an Assassin and a chupacabra. You talk when you can, play the radio when you can't, and pull over as much as possible for snacks and bathroom breaks. Fortunately, Hasim and I had a lot to talk about, once he got over the fact that I had a chupacabra in the backseat. I don't think he ever really cottoned to the idea that Pud was actually a spirit guide and thus technically not a chupacabra. In any case, this was the first road trip Hasim spent with monster breath wafting up over his shoulders.

Hasim and I had basketball in common, but we'd split on either side of the Angeleno divide. I like the Lakers, Hasim likes the Clippers. So we spent a good chunk of time going back and forth over which was the better team. Here's what they don't tell you about conversations like that. If you're the Laker fan in the equation, it's basically the sports equivalent of kicking a puppy. Eventually, the Clipper fan is left calling you a frontrunner because it's all they have left. This time he had a small advantage in that I hadn't seen a basketball game in like a year, but still. The Lakers being better than the Clippers is inevitable, like the tides or stepping on the one wet part of your floor when you're wearing socks.

I found out that Hasim didn't have much of a taste for raw corn, and there was a time in my life I wouldn't have found that surprising. I polished off the last of the shine on the way, and had to make do with suicides from gas station soda fountains after that. Hasim wouldn't even let me spike them.

The ride took the afternoon, and along the way the road turned into one of those southwestern paintings that's all purples and oranges. The highway shimmered like a river, taking me to an oasis. Creatures roamed at the periphery of my vision. They probably came from the same place that had birthed Pud. I took it as a good sign, that whatever had set me on this path was giving me an eldritch thumbs up. That it did it with barely-glimpsed Lovecraftian horrors was perhaps troubling, but I'd take it.

Zzyzx Road is a turnoff on the desert highway stretching between Los Angeles and Las Vegas. You could say it's halfway between sins, but the truth was, there was a whole lot of nothing out there. From time to time, cults set up shop around the artificial lake in the middle of baking wasteland. I can't prove it, but I'm pretty sure it was just the name. Had they kept the old one, Soda Springs, it wouldn't be nearly as popular among the wingnuts. Every time I passed it on the way to Vegas, I thought I should go, but I never did. That was probably a common impulse.

This time, I turned off the main road between a fold of purple rocks. Creatures slithered just out of sight, congealing in the soft shadows. Hasim's roll bag sat on his lap, and he drummed his fingers on the dull buckles. Maybe he was getting nervous.

"Where is this place?"

"Sander Siegel said I couldn't miss it."

"Wait, *Sander Siegel*? You know that piece of shit?"

"Hasim, I know most pieces of shit in the greater Los Angeles area. It's kind of my thing."

"You know what that guy says about...pretty much anybody that's not white?"

"Yep. He was the only one who might know where to go."

Hasim shook his head. "Why didn't you ask me to kill *him*?"

"You want to? I got no plans."

He sighed. "Keeping my nose clean. I don't want to go back to Beirut."

"You know, the fact that you'd pick *here* over anywhere kind of illuminates how bad it is there."

"I don't know that good and bad are the way to judge. It's more the specific kind of good and bad you're into."

"Maybe I should move to Beirut."

"I don't think that would work out."

I had to laugh. "You're not wrong."

The road branched, leading up to a bluff, and I saw what Sander meant. Crowning it was a collection of old signs, some neon, some dancing Vegas lights, all glittering in the technicolor sunset. "Sander wasn't kidding," I said, turning Belle up the road.

"Kidding about what?"

"That place is lit up like Christmas Day."

"Do you celebrate Christmas?"

"Uh...yeah. I mean, in a secular, kind of cultural, I should buy things for people kind of way. Why?"

"Because it's the day after tomorrow."

"It is? I knew it was coming up but..." I might have hit pause on my existence, but the world hadn't. It kept spinning on, knocked off kilter by what I'd done.

"You okay?" Hasim asked.

"Yeah, sorry. My...uh...my last girlfriend liked Christmas."

"The redhead, right? She was nice."

"Unless you start a political movement antithetical to her entire belief system, yeah."

"Oh." He thought it over. "Oh, *shit*. Well, once this guy is dead, maybe she'll take you back."

I stopped the car and turned to Hasim. Even Pud stopped his subvocal growling, looking from one of us to the other. "This isn't about her, okay? She's not going to hear a peep about this. She's just going to find out one day that things got fixed and she's going to be happy and never know why or how. Understand me?"

"Yeah. Yeah, I understand." He paused, and I could see him thinking over his next comment and the moment he decided it was too good. "My mom wouldn't want you two-timing her anyway."

"I'm not dating your mom." I pulled back onto the road and made my way to the signs.

"How do you know this is the place?"

I pointed at the giant arrows leading the way to a gate straddling a turnoff. "Seems like a good sign to me."

"Okay…" Hasim said, frowning. Poor guy didn't have a complete picture. I could hardly blame him for that. Assassins had a reputation, sure, but they could be naïve at times.

I drove right up to the gateway as brave as you please. "Hey, Pud. Maybe hide under some clothes for a little while until we get the lay of the land here."

Pud made a grumbling sound, followed by rustling as he burrowed beneath the detritus of my time living out of the Belle. I slowed on the way up the dirt track until I could hear the individual rocks crunching beneath the tires. As soon as I was close to the gate, two figures freed themselves from either side. At first, I thought they were ghosts, with their pale, drooping features and billowing white robes. Ghosts don't usually carry AR-15s, though.

One of the ghosts waved me to stop and I obeyed, which is my usual tack with both ghosts and armed men. He came over to the driver's side window while the other one watched the car from the front.

"Hi there," the ghost said happily. I realized that she was a woman, and she had a decidedly Midwestern accent. She looked like a mom. "Need directions to town?"

"I'm here to see Paul Mallon."

The tiniest frown clouded her features. "The Prophet didn't say anything about visitors."

"I'm sorry, prophet?" I shook that off. I could deal with this later, or even better, not at all. "Tell him Bob Blank is here to see him. He'll talk to me."

"Wait here, please."

Hasim drummed his hands on the roll bag, and his head was darting around like a pigeon. "I don't like this. White people, desert, and guns is not my favorite combination."

"Plus…is it me or does she remind you of Edie McClurg?"

"Is that one of your exes?"

"I wish."

"Look, I appreciate you trying to reassure me," Hasim said, "but I'm bringing knives to a gunfight, and let's just say that these are the kind who might not be too happy to see me."

"Yeah, but they haven't gotten to know you."

One of Hasim's hands slithered into the roll bag. Had I not been paying attention, I wouldn't have seen it at all. The guy was smooth.

As for the two robed whatever-they-were, they convened for a talk, then the one who hadn't spoken to us moved away, producing a walkie-talkie from his robes. I heard only the whisper of static and a few mutters as he spoke into it. Then he and Edie talked and she returned to the window.

"It's your lucky day. The Prophet said he will see you. But as you know, his time is valuable, and the next little bit is spoken for. While you wait, can we offer you an early supper?"

"I could eat," I said, which was an understatement.

"Wonderful! Now, Calvin will direct you to where you can park."

"Thank you so much, Edie."

She frowned. "How did you know my name was Edie?"

"In another life, we were in love."

The frown came back. "Just follow Calvin."

The other ghost waved us through the gates. The thing about a good compound is there's no other word to describe it. This one had the usual—a single building that looked like it had been built there with intent, made of things like wood and plaster and stone. Then it was surrounded by a selection of shacks and tents, most of which were big enough to be communal. A pen of pigs made the air fragrant. More ghosts wandered the area, all cradling firearms.

Calvin waved us to a section by the gates that might charitably be called a motor pool. A couple sedans, a battered Army jeep, and an old VW bus were parked shoulder to shoulder. I pulled in ahead of them.

"Bobby, what the fuck?" Hasim hissed.

"I can't parallel park here."

"What? No. This situation is seriously fucked up!" Hasim's eyes were bigger than his head. I hadn't seen anybody that scared since...well, since Sander filled his pants.

"Aren't you hungry?"

"We're in some kind of paramilitary cult! You said we were going to kill one guy and now we're surrounded by armed white people. This is not going to end well!"

"The plan, such that it is, hasn't changed. All we need to do is get Mallon alone, and you...do your thing that Assassins have done for a thousand years, and we get out. Tell his secretary or whatever that he doesn't want to be disturbed. That'll buy us enough time to get back to the Belle. Trust me, I saw what they have, and only that jeep could *maybe* keep up with a real Caddy." I paused, making sure Hasim understood what I was saying. "The Belle isn't a real Caddy. She's..." I pointed at the night sky, "built. Understand?"

"Okay, okay. It's just that this morning I wasn't planning on killing anybody, let alone a road trip."

"It's weird, the order you said those."

Hasim slipped a sheathed blade out of the roll bag and tucked it into the waistband of his pants at the small of his back. "Let's go."

I got out of the car. Calvin had the mean face of a middle school vice principal. He pointed at a tent in the center of the camp, not too far from the pigpen. I smiled at him and made a Voorish Sign with my hand. He wrinkled his nose, keeping his distance as he led the way.

I rubbed my hands together on the way to the tent. The smells weren't what I'd call particularly good, but I'd been living in a shack for a year. My mouth was watering as I thought of all the bland, underseasoned food a bunch of desert dwellers had to offer.

The inside of the tent featured the kind of wooden picnic tables you'd find in a park. Judging by the graffiti scratched into them, that's probably where they'd been liberated from. Another ghost, this one a sad-eyed young woman, with hair long, straight, and brown enough that it could only have looked at home on a folk album cover.

Calvin said, "These two are here to see the Prophet. See they're fed." He gave me one more scowl, leaving the tent.

The young woman was far happier to see us, or maybe she faked it better. "Welcome! Please, have a seat. I hope you like casserole!"

"Sure," I said. The truth was, she could have substituted any noun there, and I probably would have been just fine with it. Hasim and I plunked ourselves at a bench, Hasim facing the entrance flap, and the young woman bustled over to the kitchen area.

Hasim leaned in and whispered, "This ends with you sewn into a bear."

"You're just paranoid," I said. "You'd have to go all the way to the Strip to find a bear."

Hasim shook his head. The young woman returned with a pair of metal plates piled with some form of unidentifiable cuisine. She set them in front of us, and returned a moment later with two tin glasses filled with water. The food was a bland lump, but it was sufficiently heavy and I could probably use it.

"You got a name?"

"I'm Beth," she said, standing nearby and making no attempt to sit down.

"Bob," I said, pointing at myself. I almost introduced Hasim, but I didn't know how well his name would go over. "Tell me something, Beth. What's this whole...compound...thing about?"

She smiled. "I'm surprised you don't know, what with you being a friend of the Prophet's."

"I haven't been around much lately. And I'm a friend of his from way back."

"Were you in the war together?"

Paul Mallon had never fought in a single war. "Yep," I said, "the war. I saved his life from a mortar."

She frowned. "He was a pilot."

"A really accurate mortar." I tried to show her what might have happened via hand gestures, but it was going as well as you'd think, so I stopped. "Anyway, yeah. We haven't talked much lately."

"What prompted you to come out here?"

"I had a vision," I told her completely honestly. "I was on a mountain and my spirit guide appeared to me and told me to find Paul. So I interrogated a false prophet, found an apostle of my own, and here I am."

She nodded. "That's how it happens."

Out of the corner of my eye I watched Hasim stare at us in

increasing terror. Poor guy. "But my spirit guide doesn't talk too well," I said. "So I'm still not entirely sure what all *this* is."

"We're a like-minded community," she started in standard cults-peak. "We want freedom of religion, freedom of speech, and the right to bear arms. We want the right to live as the founders intended."

"In a small, agrarian settlement stolen from Native people with an enslaved labor force?"

"What?"

"This casserole is delicious."

She smiled without much warmth. "We farm the iguana ourselves."

Hasim coughed. "Iguana?"

"They call it el pollo de los árboles," I said.

"Where do they call it that?"

"I get it," I said to Beth. "You're a...back to basics kind of community."

"Did you know that the United States government is actually a corporation?"

"Sure. I mean, not literally, but you let enough lobbying money in there—"

"No, the government was legally abolished and replaced by admiralty law. That's why courts have flags with gold trim on them." She went on talking, but I knew where she was going now. These folks were Sovereign Citizens, a particular subculture of far-right wing narcissists that essentially believed if you learned the right magic words, the government couldn't do anything to you legally. Drag them into court for doing any number of crimes they inevitably got up to and they'd spout legal-sounding nonsense like they were trying to cast a hex with subsections on the judge. The fact that this never worked a single time never seemed to dissuade them. I waited patiently until she was done with her spiel, packing away my iguana-and-potato casserole.

"Okay, that all makes sense," I lied, "but I've seen a lot of believers in that sort of thing. They don't usually set up communes."

"This isn't a commune! Those are evil!"

"What's this place?"

"It's an oasis where like-minded people can work for the spiritual and political liberation of our great land. We all contribute how we can. None of us are freeloaders!"

"What do you think a comm...never mind. How did it get started?"

"I first saw it on a friend's page, this place where I could go, the one place where real American values were being practiced. We weren't going to be replaced by immigrants or forced to tolerate non-Biblical lifestyles. When I came here, I was welcomed with open arms. God blessed the Prophet with a lot of money, and he wanted to use it for something good, so he built this place and we found it, one by one."

"None of that really adds up to 'prophet'," I said, then, hastily, "Great man, sure. But prophets need something more."

"Oh, well, we're all waiting for the Lord Jesus Christ to return from the Hollow Earth and rapture us to the Elysian Fields on Z'ha'dum."

"There it is."

"Are you two thinking about joining?"

"Sure are. I've been kind of adrift for the last year, and I think this vision is God's way of putting me on the right track."

Beth smiled. "I'm so happy that you found your way to us. What about your friend? He's pretty quiet."

Hasim looked at me in terror, and then in the worst southern accent I've ever heard, he said, "I'm just overcome by the Holy Spirit." In response to my incredulous stare, Hasim offered a barely perceptible shrug.

"We're so happy to have you here. I just know that whatever you're looking for, you'll find it with the Prophet."

"We're in complete agreement there," I said.

Calvin stepped through the folds of the tent. Outside, I caught a glimpse of the monsters that had been dogging us all the way from LA. "The Prophet will see you now."

"This was lovely," I said to Beth, rising. Beth clutched her hands and smiled at us. I think she was going for motherly, but since she couldn't be older than twenty, she topped out at babysitter.

Hasim and I followed Calvin across the compound to the one building that looked like it had been erected without any foresight. Abruptly, I saw it alone, perched on this hill, before the rest had grown around it. It looked almost hilariously suburban, that Mid-century

Modernism that would always read as tacky to me. I could imagine the person who built the house did it as an exaggerated white flight, leaving the cities so far behind they'd found themselves in the middle of the desert.

Calvin stopped at the doorstep where a pair of sunbleached plastic flamingos had been driven into the sand. "Go on in," he said, his tone making it clear that he didn't think either Hasim nor I should be there. I hate to agree with someone like Calvin, but he was absolutely right. Hasim looked from the house to the car, clear across the compound, and I'm sure he was measuring how far he'd have to go for something approaching safety.

"I cracked the windows, right?" I asked.

"Uh... I think so, why?"

"Pud's gotta breathe."

"Does he?"

I shrugged. "I mean, maybe." Do you crack a window for your spirit guide? The books were never clear on the subject.

I knocked on the door. "You just go in," Calvin said.

"How delightfully egalitarian."

I opened the door, which led into a wide open living room and a floating staircase to the upper floor. While the shag carpeting, the boxy furniture, the wood paneling, and the elbow-abrading stucco all said 1970s, the more temporary decor pointed to something that I would characterize as Modernist Anime Hoarder. The sour scent of old food left out in the sun hung in the air.

A door opened at the other end of the room and Paul Mallon stepped out. He had the look of someone overindulged. His skin was pale and waxy, and he wasn't carrying the weight he'd put on well. He looked like he was unaccustomed to standing, and doing his best to hide how uncomfortable he was. He'd grown a wispy van dyke, and his hair was thin, gray, and falling to his shoulders in defeated strands. He wore white robes like his converts. Had they all been together, they would have looked like a church choir.

"Bob, is that you?" he said in a voice that was probably intended to be booming, but cracks were obvious at the edges.

"It's me."

"Imagine my surprise when one of my flock comes to my door to tell me Bob Blank is back from the dead. A regular Lazarus."

"Back from the dead?"

"Figure of speech. I hadn't heard from you in a long time."

"Since you stole Q from me, you mean."

Paul's smile crystallized. "Why don't you come into my office?" He stepped into the room.

I briefly thought he'd be fetching a gun to put a bullet through anyone stepping through the door. I found out I was wrong when I found him sitting behind his desk with tented fingers, looking like he was imitating powerful men from TV and movies. He gestured at some chairs. "Have a seat. Who's your friend?"

"My attorney, Lionel T. Bandersnatch."

"It's a pleasure to meet you, Mr. Bandersnatch."

"Pleasure's all mine," Hasim said in the same awful southern accent.

We took our seats. "So what brings you to the desert with an attorney?"

"We were on the way to Primm. Thought we'd stop in. Things sure have changed, haven't they? Last we talked, you never mentioned anything about a cult."

"A cult? Those are hurtful words, Bob. You should be more sensitive."

"Sorry, I thought you were still into that whole free speech thing, where you're just really mean to everyone for no good reason."

He laughed. "Same old Bob. To answer your question, the people living here are a somewhat new addition. People are looking for meaning all over, and some have been lucky enough to find it here."

That was it, right there: People were looking for meaning. Paul wasn't wrong about that. All the grifters knew it, and that's why they were coming out of their caves and looking to gorge themselves. "The world doesn't make sense, and so they come out to the deserts and raise iguanas."

"Something like that."

"Z'ha'dum, Paul? You couldn't put more effort into it?"

He spread his hands. "What? Who doesn't like *Babylon 5*?"

"Apparently these people, since they didn't know you're making up scripture from '90s sci-fi TV."

"*Great* '90s sci-fi TV."

"Be that as it may."

"Would you be less angry if I called it Mount Olympus? Valhalla? Heaven? It doesn't matter what you call it, it's just a name. The answer is the *feeling* that it gives these people, not whether or not I happened to take something from TV."

"You're using them."

"Am I? They wanted somewhere to belong, and I gave it to them. Go on, ask them if they're happy here. They'll tell you that they are."

"That's how cults work."

"That's how religions work. The only difference is PR and time."

Hasim shifted in his seat. Hasim might not be the best Muslim in the world, but as far as I knew, he was entirely genuine in his faith. This couldn't have been the most comfortable conversation to be a party to. Of course, the particular beliefs of Hasim's subset of Islam, as codified by Hassan-i-Sabbah, had something to do with killing for grace. Based on what he'd intimated earlier, he might have had a shift in his faith. I looked over at him in horror. *Was I going to have to talk to him about religion?*

"What?" Hasim said.

"I'm sure you didn't come here to talk about my flock," Paul said.

"No, I didn't. I came here about Q."

He smirked. "And you brought your lawyer to intimidate me into handing the account back to you."

"Something like that."

"It's gone."

"What do you mean it's gone?"

"It's *gone.*" A sadistic light sparked behind his eyes as he leaned forward to really hammer the nail in. "I called it quits. You can read the post yourself. Q served its purpose, and the heat got a little too hot, so I ended it. I told all the Anons to go home. We were finished."

"You can't just *do* that. These people believed in an all-powerful cabal of child-devouring Satanists. Some of them believed in literal demons!"

"Some of them believed JFK Jr. was still alive."

"They took over the whole goddamn country! They're running the FBI and CIA and every other alphabet organization according to their insanity! They've started doing purges!"

"That's not my problem."

My voice had been steadily rising and now it was decidedly in shrill territory. I hadn't even noticed it happening, but I was standing now too. "Not your problem? *Not your problem?* You ruined lives with this bullshit! You broke the country!"

"Calm down, Bob." He was quiet, but his voice carried the menace of being protected by a cadre of cultists with machine guns.

Hasim put a hand on my arm. There's little more infuriating in the world than being told to calm down, especially by a sociopath who was scolding you for getting in the way of one of his little games. I sank back into my seat, shaking with impotent rage.

Paul smiled blandly. "It was an amazing thing you created. That's why I had to have it. Your mistake was putting it on *my* website rather than one *you* controlled. But now it's over. They got everything they wanted. They'll find the enemies they made up and they'll keep finding them."

"I can't believe this."

"Do you know the funniest thing? I called it off early and I found something interesting. Even without one of us feeding the mill with those ridiculous posts, they're still doing their thing. Still coming up with excuses why the Satanic kiddie-eaters haven't been arrested. Justifying why everything happened the way it did.. They didn't need us to wind them up. They were ready to go. And now they have everything they ever wanted. The most powerful military in the world, ready to chase their ghosts."

"Monsters don't ever get full, you know that right? They'll keep eating and eating and eating and sooner or later they get to you."

Paul smiled and I wanted to hammer his face. "I don't have a lot of time left, Bob. I'm an old man. I bet that I'll die before they even think to come for me, and in the meantime, I can live here, surrounded by people who adore me."

Hasim looked to me. "You want me to do it?"

"You can serve your legal briefs all you want," Paul sneered. "There's nothing provable in court. If they'll even convict one of their own."

Hasim pulled the blade, the metal glittering in the dim light. "I'll make it quick."

"That's how you do me? Bring a Mexican in here to kill me?"

Hasim got up. Paul gripped the arms of his chair, fighting the urge to cower. He forced a laugh out. "Fine. Do it. But it won't accomplish anything. Hell, they'll take my death and wrap it up in the whole theory, maybe kill ten or a hundred to take revenge for a patriot. I was killed by the Cabal because I gave a home to Q. Go ahead. Make me a martyr. That's the one thing my followers are missing. You like that idea? Put that knife in me and I'm immortal."

"Stop," I said.

Hasim looked to me. "You sure, dude?"

"What's the fucking point?" I got up. Paul broke into a wide grin. He knew he'd won.

Hasim spun the blade in his hands and it vanished like a magic trick. We made for the door, Paul's mocking voice following us. "There's no point! Never was! Go back and hide under whatever rock you've been under! The world doesn't need you and never did! Oh, and real nice lawyer you got there!"

chapter
five

IF YOU PLAY cards in Vegas, they let you drink for free. Makes good sense: the more you drink, the more your judgment is impaired, and the more money you bet. The thing is, I have good hands. Always did. I'm no Richard Turner, but I know my way around a deck of cards. That's the short version of me telling you to never play cards against me. I cheat, because that's the real game. I just never tell the rules to the other guy.

"Are you almost done?" Hasim asked.

"You should sit down for a hand or two, these marks don't know an ace from an acehole." The other card players, an old tourist couple, a well-dressed man, and a couple of college kids, shot me a glare. They thought I was easy prey when I sat down, some crazy desert dweller who lucked into a small roll. Most of their money was in front of me in chaotic stacks of chips. They probably wouldn't have let me sit down if I hadn't showered at Hasim's and they certainly wouldn't if he hadn't loaned me forty bucks to get started.

"Bobby, I'm an alcoholic," Hasim said.

"The drinks are free here."

"That's the problem!"

"Oh, right." Maybe it was my...I had lost count, so I'm going to say twenty-third gin and tonic for old time's sake. The point is, I was feeling sympathetic. "Maybe we should just have beer."

"Dude!"

A hand clamped down on my shoulder. I knew that feeling. That's "Sir, we need to talk to you in this airless room for a little while until you figure out precisely where you went wrong and promise never to do it again." I'd been waiting for it as soon as I started palming cards. Hell, I'd been begging for it.

"Sir, if you would come this way?" The words I was expecting—the voice I was not.

I turned around, and I did know the face. A little older, sure, a little rounder, but I knew him. He was a white guy, with a shiny bald head and a beard with more gray than I remembered. He was big, and though I think he'd put on weight since I saw him last, he looked diminished in his shiny pit boss suit. Really, after plate armor everything is gonna look small on you.

"Quentin?"

He blinked and looked closer at me. "Bob, is that you?"

"Yeah! It's good to see you. You want to grab a drink or something?"

"Sure." He looked to the dealer. "Cash him out."

I smirked at the relieved sigh one of the college kids gave. I took my chips, tipped the weary dealer, and followed Quentin over to one of the many bars dotting the casino floor. Like everything else in Camelot, the bar had a fake Knights of the Round Table kind of decor. It reminded me of Medieval Castle back home, probably because they were owned by the same company. Quentin was a Templar, or at least he had been.

He ordered a drink for me, a water for himself, and noticed Hasim. "Does your friend want something?"

"Oh shit. My manners. Quentin Cross, Hasim Khoury, Hasim Khoury, Quentin Cross." They exchanged a handshake and mild pleasantries, and soon we were all drinking—don't worry, Hasim was having a Roy Rogers. I noted with some displeasure that I was the only one killing brain cells. "What are you doing here?" I asked Quentin. "Last I heard you were King's Champion over at Medieval Castle."

Hasim's eyes widened. "He's a Templar?"

"Oh yeah. Templar, Assassin, Assassin, Templar."

Hasim and Quentin stared at each other like gunfighters. The tension was thick enough to rest my drink on. I was a little curious about what might happen if things went the way they usually did between those groups. The Assassins and the Templars were the Sharks and the Jets of the Information Underground with a beef going back to the Crusades.

Quentin's shoulders sagged. "I'm barely a Templar these days."

"Holy orders don't just go away," I said.

"Dude, are you trying to get him to throw down?" Hasim whined.

"They don't, but it seems to me all this *particular* Assassin is doing is chaperoning a drunk cardsharp through my casino. Far as I'm concerned, he's doing good work."

Hasim sighed in relief.

"Fine. Be boring," I said. "What the hell happened? Back in the day, you'd have been swinging your broadsword around and you would have already dropped at least a couple zounds."

"Things change, Bob. The Templar aren't doing so well, financially speaking I mean."

"Your conspiracy was founded by having a ton of money."

"The Knights of Malta got most of that in the schism," he said. "We ran out a long time ago. The thing is, no one wants to join the Knights Templar anymore."

"I'd think that relitigating the Crusades would be huge right now."

Quentin shook his head sadly. "Even the kids who come in to perform at Medieval Castle, used to be they'd join up eventually. Now? They think the whole thing is funny. I was telling this one kid about the history of the Templars, and do you know what he said to me? 'Okay, Boomer.'"

I laughed. "That's messed up."

"I'm not even a Boomer! Smack dab in the middle of Gen X! I've seen R.E.M. live three times."

"Yeah, I know what he's talking about," Hasim said. "If it wasn't for those Assassin's Creed games, nobody'd be joining up. And once we tell them that boats aren't really a part of anything, they're out the door."

Quentin nodded. "Yeah, it's like conspiracies are something their parents do. It's not cool anymore to be a part of a millennium-old secret society."

"Sorry about that," I said.

"What are you gonna do? So now instead of being a knight, I get to work in a casino that the Templars don't even hold a controlling interest in anymore."

"At least they kept the decor."

Quentin uttered a noncommittal grunt. "Listen, why don't the two of you take in our Cirque du Soleil show? People love it." He pulled a pair of tickets from the breast pocket of his suit and set them on the table. The image was a pair of Mardi Gras performers tied into meaty knots.

"Thanks," Hasim said.

"Don't mention it. Keep him," pointing at me, "away from the tables, all right? He pulls that stuff again and I have to bounce him."

"Will do."

Quentin got up to go, leaving his soda water and lime behind. He thought of something and turned back to Hasim. "Listen, if you want to, find me later. Maybe we could do a fight to the death for old time's sake."

"Wait, what?"

"You can have the front desk page me. There's a patio area up on the sixteenth floor that nobody goes to. We could have a good, old fashioned Assassin/Templar battle. Each one of us a champion for our faith and it ends with one of us bleeding out from a fatal stroke administered with such artistic precision it would make William Marshal himself weep." Quentin's eyes went distant. "That would be the way to go, wouldn't it? You Assassins actually have values. You have a code."

"I don't want to kill you, dude. You've been pretty chill so far."

Quentin smiled sadly. "Well, if you change your mind, my armor still mostly fits."

A small shape hobbled into my field of vision. It was Pud, though barely recognizable as he was now dressed like a sex criminal from the 1970s, in a trenchcoat, fedora, giant aviator shades, and a scarf. "Hey, Pud," I said.

Quentin barely looked. "Oh, there are three of you," he said, and put another ticket on top of the other two. "Think about it," he said to Hasim, and then to me, "and no more cards." The Templar lumbered off into the crowd. He was fed and dressed well, but I'd never seen anyone so defeated.

Pud climbed up onto the stool next to me and plopped down. "Glah!" he said.

"Where'd you get those?" I asked, fingering the coat.

"Brrrap. Hrm." Pud slapped the bar once. A drink slid into his waiting talons. It had to be rehearsed.

"Can we head back?" Hasim asked. "I'll drive. You can sleep it off."

I snorted. "Head back? Why? The fuck's back there?"

"Our lives?"

"Oh yeah, that's been going really well for me lately."

"Maybe we can figure out a way to get you some help."

"Help doing what exactly?"

Hasim shrugged. "Maybe we figure that out first."

"Nah, fuck that. Let's use these tickets. I'm in the mood for some weird eroticism."

I don't remember actually getting to the show. Dave Attell described this kind of drinking as time travel. The trouble was, you could only go in one direction. Believe me, over the past year I'd thought about time travel a great deal. Going back and just not taking the job. Easiest fix in the world, and it wouldn't lead to the Nazis winning World War II or the South winning the Civil War. That kind of shit seemed to have happened anyway. No, when the job offer and the envelope showed up in the dead drop, I'd just...not do it. Then I'd still have everything. Still have my life. The world would be less fucked by a pretty significant margin. A fascist movement minus its Great Excuse just isn't the same.

I stared at the picture on my phone, the shot of Mina in our kitchen, sun streaming in behind her. I wanted to yell at her, *"It didn't look like anything special!"* It was just an envelope, a request. Make me a conspiracy. *Make me a conspiracy.* So I did. I'd done so much worse, so much *obviously* worse. It was unfair that this, of all things, was the job that ruined everything.

The next thing I knew, two of the most attractive people I'd ever seen, these balls of sexy muscle, were apparently engaged in some intense frotteurism while balanced on giant metal hoops. Hasim sat on one side of me, Pud on the other, and both man and chupacabra were riveted.

"What the fuck?" I blurted.

A few angry looks came my way. Hasim shushed me. "Dude, be quiet."

"Where am I?"

"We're at the show you wanted to go to."

"Those nymphs clearly work out."

"It's Cirque du Soleil."

"Ohhhh, right. It's okay," I reassured the angry woman on Hasim's other side. Now that I was sure I hadn't wandered into a pornographic production of *A Midsummer Night's Dream,* I could enjoy myself. The more I watched, surrounded by an audience of middle-aged tourists, the more I felt like the show would have been less sexual had there been actual fucking on stage.

Maybe I was feeling prudish after a year of having absolutely no sex drive. Zip. Zilch. I had a dead zone right around my crotch. It's hard to get hard when you hate yourself to the degree that I did. See, there are those who dabble in self-loathing, but I'd had a chance to marinate in it. I knew every nook and cranny of my solipsism and had grown to despise it as only an intimate can. *Hard-ons are for closers*, I imagined Alec Baldwin growling at me, and frankly, that's enough to never get aroused again.

See, when you're in love, like I was, and the person you love tells you in all sincerity that the sight of you sickens them, well, it's tough to get into the head space that even approaches sex. Or at least it was for me. Any attempt to reclaim that part of my psyche couldn't be done until I'd made amends to the world. It was like Hasim's twelve-stepping, only in my case I wasn't trying to apologize. I was trying to delete an entire delusion. A feat that, as far as I knew, had never been done in the history of the world.

I didn't know if I could blame myself for Paul's cult out in Zzyzx. I knew it wasn't *not* my fault. Paul had made a lot of money on my hoax. He'd been raking in the dough as soon as I started the whole thing, and he took over the instant he realized he didn't need me when he could do it himself. It's called vertical integration, or so I've heard. A marketing-friendly version of Monopoly. Point is, Paul no doubt used some of his Q money on his little cult, so it was kind of my fault there too.

If I could time travel, I'd step in my phone booth and I'd go back the couple hours until I was standing in front of Paul again, the arrogant bastard. That smug look in his eyes when he told me Q was no more rankled. The juice was no longer worth the squeeze, so he'd stopped the grift. Only that doesn't move all the pieces back to square one, not to butcher a metaphor. Everyone who believed still believed, and they were now unfettered by whatever tiny lever of control we had exercised as architects of the hoax. They were all still out there, enjoying the fascist takeover of the United States and in many cases actively working for it. They were still preying on Asians, on immigrants, on trans people, on anybody who wasn't the perfect picture of whiteness. Anybody who fit the loathing in their hearts. A premade justification glistening in their gray matter.

Now I know what a lot of people are thinking: There are tons of people of color in the various fascist movements. There are prominent gay members too. There sure are. Look up the story of Ernst Röhm. He was a Nazi and super gay. He was also murdered as soon as he was no longer convenient. Fascists love to have cover from accusations of racism, homophobia, misogyny and all that. And the absolute second that they no longer need that cover, they purge all the useful tools like Röhm and his ilk.

I didn't have any delusions in this regard. I wasn't to blame for fascism. Just this corner of it. Fascism thrives on conspiracy theories, always has. I'd provided the most convenient one. Convince someone that their political enemies are hurting children and you give them license to commit the violence percolating in the stickiest parts of their consciousness.

Paul was right. Killing him wouldn't do a damn bit of good and might actually do some harm. What was next? I couldn't go back to the shack in Griffith Park and listen to Mikhail's numbers broadcasts. I had to do *something*. That's what these two fairies simulating vigorous sex on this trapeze were trying to tell me—even if something looks impossible, by God, you get in as deep as you possibly can and you rub and rub until someone finishes. Even if it was futile, I had to try. These alluring and sinewy elves didn't get where they were by not trying. No, they woke up every day, ate and exercised like maniacs and dreamed up ways of giving grandfathers from Duluth the strangest erections of their lives. It was inspirational.

I had to give the world a weird boner.

No, that's the booze talking, I reminded myself. I needed to kill an idea. Sure, it hadn't been done, *that I knew of*. It could have been done many times in the past. Could have been done millions of times. And as I watched these lithe sylphs climbing long bolts of arousal-red cloth, hanging like the tentacles of a colossal seabeast, I realized exactly what I needed to get it done.

I leaned over to Hasim, whispering, "We need to back to LA. I have an idea."

"Cool. I...uh...I can't get up yet."

"Just enjoy it, buddy. You've earned it."

chapter
six

WE DROVE BACK to the city through the wee hours of the desert night. It was freezing outside, but once we hit the city limits, it turned into a good LA December, pretty much a mild fall morning anywhere else. I'd ran out of the moonshine somewhere around Barstow, but the visions in the landscape still haunted me. I figured they'd be there until I finished this whole thing, made solid by my pineal gland the same way Pud Galvin was. So while Hasim dozed in the seat next to me, and Pud muttered in the backseat, I munched on corn and enjoyed the show.

I pulled off the freeway in Pasadena. Merry Christmas and Feliz Navidad all picked out in tinsel hung over the streets. More green and red tinsel snakes wrapped around the streetlamps. I stopped off at Lucky Boy and dropped the last of my meager Vegas winnings on some break-fast burritos. I needed to make peace with someone, and a Lucky Boy breakfast burrito was the only thing I could think of that might work. Plus, I was hungry for something that wasn't raw corn.

I got back in the car and Hasim roused himself as the door clunked shut. He sat up, sniffing and rubbing his eyes. "We're back home," I told him.

"Did you do your idea?"

"Phase one. You eat pork?" He nodded sheepishly. "Bacon, sausage, ham?"

He picked bacon and I handed over one of the calorie lumps wrapped in yellow butcher paper with "bacon" scrawled barely legibly over the top in black Sharpie. He sighed happily as he bit into it, and I did the same, eating as I pulled onto the freeway heading back into downtown. Pud leaned over the backseat and I handed a burrito back to him.

"Don't make a mess!" I scolded the chupacabra. He made a mess.

I drove into the part of downtown no one ever went, as far from the cluster of skyscrapers that made up the LA skyline as it was possible to be and still be downtown, maybe because no other neighborhood wanted to claim it. It was the part that used to look like the set of one of those '80s movies about a crime-ridden city gone feral. But shit had gotten worse. Somehow.

It no longer looked like Baseball Furies and C.H.U.D.s prowled these streets hunting for the unwary. This place had been forgotten. Deliberately so. Collectively, we had turned our heads from it and willed it out of existence, patiently waiting for the denizens to wither up and die.

The buildings were crumbling, the rusted-out hulks of cars ignored, and the trash had been mashed so flat onto the concrete that it was as much of a terrain feature as a sidewalk. Even the graffiti looked perfunctory. Shanties, built from tents, tarps, discarded scraps of wood, cardboard, and street signs, clogged every sidewalk. The people in them looked at me and Hasim with confusion. We weren't supposed to be there because no one was.

As we walked, Hasim emptied his pockets of cash, handing over something to everyone who was awake and within arm's reach. Pud loped along beside us in his Vegas disguise.

Our destination was a brick building that smelled even more strongly of urine than it had in the past, and this was a place that had always smelled more like piss than piss. The walls were ready to cave in if someone gave them a hard look. It had been entirely burned out at some point in the distant past, all the windows broken. The graffiti here was of a decidedly more occult bent, though some of it resembled swatches of computer code. And the one thing that should make anyone worried: the nearest tent was at least twenty feet away, and none of the residents got anywhere near it. There might as well have been a repulsion field around the place.

The door was open. Wasn't like there was a lock on it anyway. Eyes were on us as we slipped in, and I swear they were filled with pity. The urine scent faded inside, which was another good sign that this place was dangerous. Divine power pulsed three stories below my feet, a hum in my bones, calling to me in its senseless slurry of words. Maybe it already knew what I had in mind. Maybe it was eager.

A staircase led down, surrounded by more graffiti scrawled along the concrete walls. Occult signs, picked out in venom green, dripped down to the filthy floor.

"Hey, Bobby? I don't like this place."

"Yeah, it's not great."

"Why are we here?"

"The only thing that can destroy an idea is a god."

"God doesn't destroy ideas."

"Not God. *A* god. Different being."

"I might not be a shining example of my faith, but that's not... uh..."

"Trust me."

Pud made a soft keening sound in his throat, but followed us down the stairs. A sound like a dot matrix printer rattled through the echoey building. A sound—more of a feeling—came below it, like the heartbeat of words. The graffiti in this hallway had obliterated whatever paint, dirt, or smoke had stained these walls. Information, in its own way, rendered into madness by squalor. You know, like an image board in real life. I was heading down into the gullet of knowledge without context, of facts without understanding, and it wanted me to know I was welcome. And boy, I did not want to be.

The ceilings were a collection of rusting pipes. Doorways on either side opened into rooms filled with more machinery gathering dust. It was the kind of basement where Freddy Krueger hung out with the Alien and discussed which John Carpenter movie they were going to crash. Hasim and Pud were no protection; all three of us were the most sexually adventurous co-ed at camp and we were all ready to split up to find a missing cat.

The hallway terminated in a door decorated with a thirteen-pointed star etched out in bleeding paint. This one was shut, but a sickly green light bled all around the border. That's when I realized it was pulsing in time with my heartbeat. That wasn't a good sign. The worst part was that I think I knew what it meant. For a moment, I had fed the creature like no one else had, I had created something in its virtual space that bled out and became real. It was welcoming me.

You've done enough. That's right, I had, and here was my confirmation. The eldritch god of information was happy to see me. You never want to be a member of a club that will accept you as a member, well, it's worse when the only other member is Cthulhu.

I paused at the door and looked to Hasim. He stared at it, trembling. "Don't worry. It's going to be fine," I assured him. I think I sounded convincing.

"It can't hurt me?"

"Oh it can. I don't think it'll notice we're here. You're about to see the embodiment of all human knowledge, incarnated into a physical form by the dumbest motherfucker alive." I sighed. "The same motherfucker whose help we're going to need, so I should probably be nice. You're nice. How do you manage that?"

"My mom always said that everyone is a person, and people want to be heard and respected."

"Your mom sounds like a remarkable lady."

"She's single."

"Stop it. Okay, you ready?"

Hasim took a deep breath. "Yeah."

"Pud Galvin?"

Pud hissed.

"Good enough." I opened the door.

They weren't ready. Can anyone really be ready to meet a god? Hasim gasped and Pud shrieked. I couldn't blame them.

The temple of Shub-Internet had once been two floors, but the ceiling dividing the two had been torn down and fallen away, giving the central room that vaulted feel that all churches need. Alcoves along both sides were filled with robed priests tapping away at their devices—desktops, tablets, laptops, and even phones. Their faces were swallowed in shadow from the hoods of their filthy black robes. The only visible skin was their hands, gray from lack of exposure to the sun. Thirteen pointed stars, made from reclaimed circuit boards, glittered around their throats.

The god appeared to be bursting out of the far side of the room. Shub-Internet's eyes glowed ominously, an array of screens of all sizes, ranging from old televisions to modern plasma screens, each displaying a mesmerizing confusion of seemingly random images: from a GIF of Homer Simpson backing into a hedge, to a video of a woman giving a makeup tutorial, to a man eating shit on a skateboarding jump. Tentacles emerged from all around the eyes, writhing over the ceiling and squelching across the floor, growing more and more dense the closer to the screens they were, until the floor was nothing more than a squirming mass of bio-mechanical horror. The black rubber tentacles laced through with segmented metal were slimy with some kind of foul lubricant. Every one was tipped with some kind of tool—a plug, or calipers, or a drill, or something only Clive Barker would have a name for. Any number of things that would have no doubt thrilled a hentai fan, but filled me with a dread. As I stepped, a few reared up like cobras to watch me. Shub-Internet's attention was electric on my skin.

The god had grown since the last time I had been there. Tentacles breached the walls, the floor, and even the ceiling, probing for more data. The far wall wasn't even visible anymore beneath the mass of eldritch data god, and the constantly-wiggling tentacles gave the impression of something incomprehensibly vast, just out of sight. The stench of old garbage hung in the air and stuck to my tongue.

Under it all were the maddening sounds. First was the clatter of the printers, running behind everything with no clear source. The tentacles sliding over one another was a persistent hiss, with the occasional dip into something that sounded like a mouth. And, of course, the god spoke. Its constant, mad babble was behind everything as it collated everything. *Everything.*

"Lee Goldberg became enraged when Psych was more concerned with the Degas brothers. I too like scissoring. That's obviously why they were killed—they were freakishly multi-jointed devil spawn," the god whispered.

"What *is* that?" Hasim asked.

"Shub-Internet. God of the internet. Knows all, understands nothing."

"Why do I have to stand near it?"

"Adam? *Adam?*" The voice started at about an eight, and by the second "Adam" was at a shrill eleven. The speaker emerged from an alcove, stumbled over a tentacle, but kept coming, his watery eyes blazing with anger and insomnia. He was a bit shorter than I was, and he walked with a hunch which did him absolutely no favors. He looked like if Templeton the rat from *Charlotte's Web* turned into a human but didn't do a great job, and in the process lost the last grasp on personal hygiene. This was Fabian Strudwick, the High Priest of the Servants of Shub-Internet, and one of the most unpleasant people I knew.

"Who's Adam?" Hasim asked.

"Me." I raised my voice. "Hey, Fabian. How are you?"

"You got a lot of nerve coming in here after last time."

"My large adult sons have become trapped in the percolator again," Shub-Internet hissed. The watching tentacles swayed back and forth in a hypnotic dance.

"What happened last time?" Hasim asked.

"Mina decked him."

"Where is she?" Fabian demanded. "I vowed to show her the error of her mistake."

"She's not speaking to me anymore."

"Oh," he said, visibly deflating. I think he'd been rehearsing his righteous anger for so long and now everything was downhill. "Is *he* going to punch me?"

I looked at Hasim. "I don't think so."

"I don't really *punch* people," Hasim said. I don't think Fabian noticed the all-important emphasis.

"What are you doing here?" Fabian asked. "I saw a thing that you're some half-assed fixer or something? Then you disappeared."

"Oh, well. There's that. I actually wanted to talk to you about Shub-Internet."

"The second I cracked it, it started jizzing all over the sink," said Shub-Internet.

"You're looking to join up. Take your vows and truly join in faith the worship of our All-Consuming Formless Ebony Mother. Well, there's a lot to do. The digital apocalypse isn't going to bring about itself."

"It's not? That's a relief. No, I don't want to join up. I need to ask for a favor."

Fabian's smug expression curdled into an angry frown. "You know, when she hit me, I wasn't that hurt. I was pretending. For her benefit."

"That's big of you."

"I thought so. She's not welcome here. If you're hiding her or something."

"The Apes are up at the bootleg store, but the footprint is so small," Shub-Internet insinuated.

"How would I possibly hide her?" Mina had the kind of hourglass figure that launched bombing raids over Dresden. Hiding her was about as likely as Hasim spontaneously turning into a penguin.

Fabian looked me over, and no doubt put Mina's zaftig curves in his mind, and then nodded. "Okay, fair enough. What do you want?"

"Well, for starters, I was wondering if you'd had breakfast yet?" I handed him the wrapped parcel.

"Is this from Lucky Boy?" he gasped. I nodded. "Aw, ham," he whined. He still unwrapped it and shoved about half of it into his mouth. For a moment, the overwhelming stink of garbage was held at bay through an excellent combination of grease and starch. "If you'd brought sausage, I might be listening even closer," he said around a bolus.

I burped the remnants of the sausage burrito and hoped he didn't notice. "I wanted to ask you something about Shub-Internet."

He nodded, his method of eating putting to mind an anaconda going to town on a capybara. Behind him, the eldritch techgod continued to writhe.

"I was about to ask about progressive ska," Shub-Internet informed us.

"Shoot," Fabian said.

"When it eats something, is it gone forever?"

"It's not known as the Eater-of-Characters for nothing."

"Can it eat anything?"

"Not *anything*. I don't think it could eat, like…a battleship. Not yet, I mean. I'd need to give it more of a maw."

"*More* of a maw?" Hasim squeaked. Pud grunted, pressing himself into my leg. He was swaying along with the tentacles, his monster eyes locked onto them. Fabian scarcely seemed to notice the chupacabra or the tentacles.

"Please don't modify this avatar. I already have issues with you giving a Cthulhoid monstrosity a body. It doesn't need a more dangerous mouth."

"Careful," he said, wagging the burrito at me. "You're treading awful close to blasphemy."

"Can it eat an idea?"

"Like a meme? I believe so. Memes, the good ones anyway, reproduce so quickly that it would be difficult to eat the whole thing. It would be like a whale wiping out an entire school of krill."

"Possible, just difficult."

"Nothing is beyond the means of a god."

"Let it just be talking tigers," Shub-Internet said.

"Shub-Internet has devoured ideas in the past," Fabian said.

"Like what?" Hasim asked.

"If I knew, the idea wouldn't be eaten, would it?" Fabian sneered, then gave me a "get a load of this rube" eyeroll. I did my best to tamp down my intense loathing for the man.

"Could you get it to eat a *specific* idea?"

Fabian looked at me, suddenly keyed into what I was saying. "I think so. The right spells could encourage it along. Wrap any idea in porn, Shub-Internet would go for it."

"Great! So how do we get started?"

Fabian stared at his burrito and shifted uncomfortably. "Well, you would need Shub-Internet first."

I pointed at the Lovecraftian abomination at the other end of the room. "Check."

"Not exactly."

I rubbed at the sudden, sharp pain between my eyes. "Out with it."

"How much do you know about Shub-Internet?"

"Assume nothing," I said.

The thing about Fabian is, he always looks weird when you're not punching him. So any interaction with him is a constant struggle not to return him to his natural state of being punched. I was having a hard time with that at the moment. I didn't need delays or bullshit.

"Shub-Internet first gained consciousness—its version of consciousness—on ARPANET back in the early '70s. As the Internet became a thing, it escaped, and wormed around until the mid-'90s or so. A bunch of government sorcerers managed to wall it off and then imprison it in the Pentagon."

"Yeah, the five points. Perfect binding circle. They've got a ton of fun stuff locked up in there."

Fabian coughed. "Well, they *did*. I don't know if you remember, but not too long ago the Pentagon got broken. By a plane."

Hasim's eyes widened. "Was that their whole plan?"

"No, stupid." Fabian snapped. "That was an accident."

"Right. Shub-Internet got out," I said, and pointed once again to the squirming monstrosity currently whispering about how it discovered this amazing recipe for chickpea couscous while hiking on Mount Parnassus.

"They locked it up again," Fabian said.

"Then what the hell is that?"

"Spawn of Shub-Internet. We peeled off some lines of code, and wouldn't you know it, the code could grow on its own, so long as it was fed. This, and any other 'Shub-Internets' you might run into out in the world are just spawn. They can do some damage, but nothing like the real thing."

"I take it that this does not qualify as a memevore."

He shook his head. "No, you need the god itself for that. Government sorcerers caught it again, and this time they locked it up in a deep underground military base."

Hasim giggled. "A D.U.M.B.?"

I snorted. "I never thought about it."

"My god is in jail and you think it's funny?" Fabian screeched.

"I mean, a little."

"You know what, Adam? Fuck you. Fuck you and whoever this is, and fuck that weird dwarf who *should stop chewing on cables.*"

I turned around and Pud looked up guiltily. Guess he had made a decision about the dancing ones. "Stop it," I scolded.

"Is he human?"

"He's a tulpa," I told Fabian.

"Right."

"Tell me about this D.U.M.B."

"The *deep underground military base* is the one underneath Denver International Airport. You know it?"

I nodded. "I've been there."

"It's a detention facility for anything that the government deems is too dangerous to just be out and around. Like Shub-Internet, probably that weird dwarf of yours."

"Tulpa."

"I thought he was a chupacabra," Hasim said.

"It sounds to me like you want Shub-Internet sprung from the pokey. That about right?"

Fabian laughed. "Oh yeah. And while you're at it, how about a blowjob from Twilight Sparkle?"

"Well...I can't arrange *that*. But let's say I get your god out of the D.U.M.B., that'd be worth a favor or three," I said.

Fabian was still locked in the hilarity of me making headway on my quest. "Sure. If you release Shub-Internet into the world, I'll get it to eat whatever ideas you want. I'll destroy entire schools of thought at your whim. Fuck it, I'll destroy the entire idea of ponies."

"But then how will they blow you?"

"It was a joke! Now don't make me regret helping you."

"Are you helping me?"

Fabian sighed, taking another bite of his burrito. "The two of you chucklefucks wouldn't know an IP from an AP. You're going to need hex support."

"Road trip!" I wrapped my arm around Fabian's shoulder. "You get to pick the music every third hour. I like Boston, Hasim listens to this weird French hip hop..."

Fabian shook me off of him. "Not me. I'm not going anywhere with you two idiots. I'm going to send a subordinate, because that's what subordinates are for. Give me your phone."

I unlocked it and handed it over. Fabian opened up the notes app, wrote something and handed it over. It was an address in Toluca Lake, ironically not too far away from Hasim's residence. "This is one of your cultists?"

"She's good enough to help you out."

"And if she gets gunned down by government goons, you're not losing any sleep."

He shrugged. "She should have gone out with me. I don't even like Indian girls anyway."

"Fabian, I want you to know something. You're a terrible person. Just...the worst."

Fabian looked at me like some dogshit he'd just stepped in. "Big words from a bum. Now go do your stupid thing. If you fuck up, it'll be funny, and if you make it, I win."

"See you in the funny papers."

As we left the temple chamber and returned to the hallway, Hasim said quietly, "I didn't like him."

"No one likes him."

"Probably why he has to live in a basement with a monster."

For whatever reason, that got me. I was still laughing when we got to the car.

chapter
seven

WHEN BREAKING into a government installation to free an eldritch god, it behooves one to be completely supplied. Besides, Griffith Park was kind of on the way to Toluca Lake. When we pulled off into the park, Hasim frowned. When we left the paved road for dirt, he finally spoke up.

"We seeing another cult?"

"Oh, goodness no. The Servants of Shub-Internet are the only cult that could help us."

"That guy you were talking to didn't seem helpful."

"Well, he thinks he's using us. Which he sort of is, but I don't have a lot of options right now. If you want to kill an idea, it's basically Shub-Internet, or I go door to door with a hammer and delete it from every mind manually."

"That's terrible!"

"You committed murder for money."

"Well...yeah. But it wasn't random. I wasn't knocking little old ladies over the head with a hammer."

"No money in that."

Hasim shifted uncomfortably in his seat, staring out at the dun-colored hills. "I'd quit if I could. You know, turn over a new leaf."

"Is it a marijuana leaf?"

He laughed. "I got some back at my place. Alamut Black. If we're going to Colorado, I should pack a bag. I'll bring some! Probably do you a little bit of good."

"You're coming to Colorado with me?"

"Yeah, of course."

"Why?"

"You're going to break into a government installation. That's not something you let a friend do without backup."

"What happened to keeping your nose clean?"

"I'm not going to kill anybody."

"Hasim..."

"Stop trying to talk me out of this shit, Bobby. You came to my door for a reason, and it actually feels like you're trying to do something good."

I didn't have much to say to that. What do you do when someone you've always thought of as an acquaintance at best gives you a Samwise Gamgee pledge of friendship?

"I can't guarantee you won't have to kill anybody," I said finally.

His smile didn't have much warmth in it. "We all have skills, I guess. That's mine. Wouldn't expect it to get left out."

I nodded, retreating back into my mind where I could work the puzzle box of a plan rather than deal with all the big, messy feelings that were making me do it in the first place. I was already regretting returning to Griffith Park. Felt like the scene of a crime up here. I'd kidnapped myself and the ransom was this madness I'd set us on. I ran what I knew about the military base through my head while considering the giant question mark of whoever Fabian had referred us to. At least those problems had solutions, a binary path that would lead somewhere definite. The world had far too few of those.

I wound through the hills, going from a dirt road to the mere suggestion of one, and just when it seemed like we were wandering aimlessly into the past that the first European colonists found, we crested a hill and there was Mikhail's shack slouching against the flat blue sky. I stopped the car and got out amid the swirling dust.

"What is this place?" Hasim asked.

"Russian numbers station. Mikhail broadcasts codes."

"He's a spy?"

"I don't know. Maybe. It's possible he's a spy for a government that doesn't exist anymore."

"What are we doing here?"

Mikhail stepped out of the shack, holding onto the doorjamb. He regarded me with faint nervousness. "Bob? Did you kill that guy?"

"Change of plans," I said, filling up a pail of corn and refreshing my bottles of moonshine. One spritz for the bottle, one for me, one for the bottle. Sure, I smelled like a preserved corpse, but I was also severely impairing my fine motor skills. Win-win.

"Who's that?"

"A friend of mine."

"Hasim," Hasim said, getting out of the car and offering a wave. "Wait, am I still Lionel...Penny...feather...I forgot the name."

"This is a secret installation!" Mikhail screeched at me.

"This is a shack in Griffith Park," I said.

"It's a *secret* shack!"

"Don't worry about him. Hasim's cool."

I threw the corn in the backseat and Pud yowled like an alleycat. Mikhail screamed and retreated into the shack. "You still have that monster?"

"I can't get rid of my spirit guide. Not until whatever he's guiding me to has been done." I tried to be as patient as I could. It seemed like no one understood spirit guides these days.

"What are you doing, then?"

I grinned. "We're going to destroy QAnon."

"What do you mean?"

"The conspiracy theory, not the guy who stole it. We're going to go get a god out of cold storage and feed the whole goddamn conspiracy to it. And when it eats up every single trace of the idea, all these maniacs can find something else to do with their fascism."

"God? Cold storage? Fascism? Bob, you're not making any sense."

I crossed the short distance, a sunny grin on my face, and Mikhail recoiled in fear. I spoke to him slowly and clearly, so he would actually get it and understand that I was on a good and holy quest. "The US government has the god of the internet locked up in a secret military base beneath Denver International Airport. This god is a memevore. It can eat every trace of that conspiracy bullshit off every computer in the world, and then I'll no longer be the asshole who fucked the planet!"

"You can do that?"

"No one has yet, but no one has ever had what I have: a chupacabra and a can-do attitude."

Mikhail looked at me like I was crazy. Maybe I was; I wasn't in the best position to judge. I went past him and grabbed the rest of my things from beneath the rusted cot. I didn't have a whole lot. Most of what I owned were clothes that were in the process of disintegrating into filthy rags. But they were my filthy rags and I wouldn't be coming back here.

I dumped it into the trunk. "Hey, Mikhail? Thanks for letting me crash with you. And whatever you're doing...I hope it goes really well."

"Thanks? And you're welcome."

Hasim, who'd been contemplating the sagging pile of scrap that had been my home with an air of deep concern, returned to the car. I started it up, leaving Mikhail and the tiny shack in a haze of dust. That would be a series wrap on Mikhail. Hard to put a concrete value on what he gave me, but it was something. That mattered.

"So...you were *living* there?" Hasim asked.

"Yeah."

"How long?"

I shrugged. "I don't know. Time gets weird when you're 18th century longshoreman-drunk all the time."

"You could have called me."

"No, I couldn't have."

"I would have—"

"It wasn't about you, not really. See, there was a small list of people who could look at me, but the thing is, I couldn't stand them being able to look at me."

"Oh. That's rough. And now?"

"And now, I have a spirit guide-approved plan. Means everything."

Toluca Lake is a neighborhood just past the dividing line into the Valley. It's hilariously suburban, designed for the entertainment industry to commute over the hill into the studios. It didn't imply a ton of money, but it certainly indicated that whoever we were there to meet wasn't hurting. The house in question was a Craftsman covered in white shingles with green trim. It didn't look like the kind of place where you'd find a cultist who worshiped a doomsday deity. A substitute teacher maybe.

We pulled up right in front of the house and got out, all three of us. We weren't the most respectable bunch, that was for damn sure. I walked up to a low porch and found a healthy ficus sprouting out of a brass pot in the shape of a giant squid going nuts on a submarine.

"Does that feel like foreshadowing to you? That feels like foreshadowing."

Hasim squinted at it. "Because we're like a ficus?"

"Yeah, Hasim. I was concerned about our general ficusosity."

"That can't be a word."

I knocked on the door while Pud sniffed at the plant. He had stripped down to nothing but the hat back in the car. In that way, he was a lot like my Uncle Lou.

A shape passed in front of the windows in the door, distorted in the wavy glass. My overactive imagination started designing the perfect Shub-Internet cultist who would be opening the door. I started out pretty normal, like Fabian, but bigger. Then I threw in a little Wilbur Whateley to the equation, some tentacles with mouths on them, that kind of thing. Then I just dispensed with all subtlety and the cultist was a combination of Yog-Sothoth and a bottle of Mountain Dew Code Red.

That wasn't who opened the door. I had somehow forgotten Fabian's weird little incel dig at the end of his rant. "She wouldn't go out with me." While I had difficulties thinking of a woman who was *in* Fabian's league, this woman was so far out of it that any attempt to date her would have resulted in the utter destruction of the natural order. She was the kind of woman that abruptly made me remember I looked like I lived under a bridge and not an especially good one.

She wasn't made up, her shiny black hair up pinned up in an indifferent bun, and she was dressed in a pair of leggings, big socks, and a tank top and sweatshirt, with a chunky pair of hipster glasses. She was still a knockout, a stunning beauty who probably looked incredible no matter what she was wearing. She was small and slender, and could have been out of her mid-twenties, but apparently unafraid of answering the door to a pair of strange men. Her skin was a brownish-bronze, her almond-shaped eyes a darker shade of the same hue. She even had a hawkish nose, giving her general gorgeousness a sense of character and an illusion of attainability.

"Yeah?" she said, looking at me and Hasim. We were both momentarily stunned. And sure, I was dead below the waist, but I could still appreciate her the way I could still appreciate a sunset. In this one instance Fabian had shown excellent taste, and this young woman had shown even better judgment.

"Uh...hi. I'm Bob, this is Hasim. Fabian sent us." I made a Voorish Sign with my fingers. I felt like I was in high school and I was late for a test.

She wrinkled her nose at me. Probably caught a whiff of the industrial solvent on my breath, or else that was just a reaction to hearing Fabian's name. Both were equally likely. "What does he want?"

"He didn't call you."

She shrugged. "He might have. I don't answer his calls."

More evidence of her excellent judgment.

"Can we come in?"

She laughed. "No! How the fuck am I supposed to know who you are?"

I made the Voorish Sign again. "Like that?"

"Try again."

Pud loped into view, apparently finished with whatever deep discussion he was having with the ficus. "Glah!" he said to our contact. I winced, ready for the screaming.

The young woman threw the door open wide and dropped to her knees, absolute joy exploding over her face. "Oh my god! Who's the cutest buddy ever? Who's a buddy? Who's a buddy?"

Pud was apparently a buddy. Within seconds, our contact had Pud on his back and was scratching his tummy while he made happy chupacabra sounds.

She looked up, beaming. "What is he?"

"He's Pud Galvin, my spirit guide."

"A chupacabra," Hasim added.

"He's *adorable*. What does he eat?"

"Uh...goat blood and breakfast burritos?" I hazarded.

"Aw, I bet he's hungry. Who wants some goat blood? Who's a handsome buddy who wants some goat blood?" She got to her feet, heading back inside and Pud scrabbled after her like a happy puppy. "Well? Are you coming in or what?" she called from the other room.

Hasim and I looked at each other and shrugged. We went into the young woman's living room. It was nice in here. Very suburban, if one didn't notice the occult texts on the shelves or the framed print of The Dream of the Fisherman's Wife over the fireplace. A small Christmas tree, decorated with garlands that looked like octopus tentacles, stood in one corner. She leaned against the doorway separating the kitchen from the living room with Pud behind her, his face buried in a dish. Blood slopped onto the wide tiles of her floor.

"So, Bob and Hasim, huh? I'm Riley Yay!"

"Riley Yay?"

"No, there's an exclamation point on the end. It's a cheer. Riley Yay!"

"I've never met someone with punctuation in their name," Hasim said.

"It's a stage name," Riley explained. "So what did Fabian send you here for?"

I'd been hoping Fabian would do some of the heavy lifting, but it sounded like any word he put in would have done more harm than good. "Before we get any further, I want to emphasize how well I do not know Fabian, and how I like him even less. He's my point of contact with the Servants of Shub-Internet, and that's it."

"And I just met him like two hours ago," Hasim said. "He's a dick."

"Okay, good. Still doesn't answer my question."

"This is gonna sound a little crazy. We want to break into the deep underground military base—"

"The D.U.M.B.," Hasim said, snickering.

"—under Denver International where we plan to free Shub-Internet."

"You two are Servants? I feel like I'd know you if you were."

"I'm an Assassin," Hasim said.

"And I'm unaffiliated," I finished. Pud loped out of the kitchen, blood all over his cheeks. He wandered over to Riley and flopped on his back. She sat down and rubbed his chest. "I guess he's with the Little Green Men."

"Huh," she said, concentration clouding her features. Her attention went from me, to Pud, to Hasim. I could see her measuring the three of us, and the only place we weren't found wanting was with Pud. "Yeah, okay," she decided. "I need to grab some stuff."

She turned on her heel and went down a hallway, past two doors, and disappearing into the one at the end of the hall.

"This is a nice place," Hasim said.

"It really is."

Pud hopped off the sofa and loped into the kitchen, hunting around for more goat blood. "You mind if I use the bathroom?" I called.

"Be my guest," Riley yelled back. "How long do you think this trip will take?"

"That's an excellent question," I said slowly. "I think we're best served if we go in ASAP. Use Christmas as cover."

"We're staying in a hotel for a night?"

"Holy shit, I guess we are." I was coming to the rapid realization that I didn't have the cash to finance any of this. Not a flight into Denver, not even a stay overnight. "You think hotels in Colorado accept corn as legal tender?"

"What?"

"Nothing, just thinking out loud."

I opened the first door in the hallway and I found...I don't quite know what I found. It looked like a muppet's boudoir. The floor was covered in multicolored fur, everything in deep shades of blue, green, and black. A bed, shaped like a clamshell, took up the center of the room. Facing it was an impressive computer setup, including what had to be one of the most expensive cameras I'd ever seen. Overhead, the light fixture looked to be the bottom of a submarine. A giant plush squid took up a great deal of the bed, and maybe it was The Dream of the Fisherman's Wife out in the living room, or maybe it was the collection of lubricants on the shelves behind the bed, or what the tentacles were tipped with, but I put together what was going on. I shut the door.

"Not the bathroom," I said to Hasim.

Riley's bathroom was clean and pleasant, and other than more nautically themed decor, entirely unremarkable. Although after everything, I couldn't really ignore how many tentacles were in this place. I suppose it made a certain amount of sense for a Shub-Internet cultist. Then again, I'd been living in the hills and drinking myself to death, so I shouldn't be judging.

As I left the bathroom, the door at the end of the hall opened. Riley leaned out, and behind looked like a normal, if decidedly pelagic bedroom. "It's cold in Colorado in December, isn't it?"

"Yeah, probably." I looked down at my own outfit that was more rip than cloth, and thought about the sorry state of the rest of my clothes.

Riley stared at me. "You haven't really thought this through, have you?"

"No ma'am."

"Well, at least you're honest, I guess," she said, ducking back into her room. I rejoined Hasim in the living room, my mind weighing options and not being thrilled with any of them.

"I like her more than the other guy," Hasim said.

"Low bar, but yeah. I hear what you mean."

"Why isn't she in charge?"

"Why isn't the twenty-something nice young woman in charge of an overwhelmingly male conspiracy when there's a forty-something arrogant asshole guy available?"

"Okay, when you put it like that." He looked down the hall. "You think she's what we need?"

I shrugged. "I hope so. Fabian wants Shub-Internet out of the clink as much as we do, so he'd send us with someone with the technical knowhow to get it done."

"You think that's all we need her for?"

"How well do you know computers? Electronic security systems?"

Hasim waggled his hand. "If I want to get in someplace I'm not supposed to be, I sneak my way in as like, a waiter or something. I try not to put an electronic lock between me and a target."

"I'm the same way. Only problem is, there's going to be more than one electronic lock in a deep under—"

"A D.U.M.B."

"Dude."

"It's funny."

I sighed. "Well, we'll be dealing with electronic locks and computer security whether we like it or not. In theory, Riley should know what she's doing. Supposedly, there's no such thing as a Shub-Internet cultist who can't make a computer sit up and bark like a dog."

"You think we can trust her?"

"You're asking if we can trust a gorgeous woman on a dangerous heist with religious overtones?"

Hasim thought about it. "I guess it depends on which Indiana Jones movie this is."

I touched my nose. Riley emerged from the hall carrying a backpack and two bags. She had thrown a jacket and some shoes on. "Okay. I'm ready to go."

Hasim looked at me, narrowing his eyes like he'd just worked out a clue. "Hey, Riley. What's your favorite Indiana Jones movie? *Raiders* or *Last Crusade*?"

"I've never seen an Indiana Jones movie," she said blithely.

"Nice try," I monotoned. "And sorry for taking you away for Christmas."

"This is more important," she said. "It's not every day you get a chance to help your god."

"You knew the thing downtown wasn't it?"

"Fabian tries to keep it secret, but he can't help bragging when he thinks he's done something impressive. It's pretty much common knowledge with the Servants."

Riley locked up as we left, and I led her out to the Belle. "This is your car?"

"Yep."

"You have some taste," she allowed.

"Shotgun," Hasim said.

"Seriously?"

"You should have called it."

I opened up the trunk, and Riley only hesitated a second before throwing her stuff into the collection of detritus that made up my entire worldly possessions. Then we all piled into the car, and I tried to work up the courage to do what had to happen next. I had no money to finance this thing, but I knew someone who might. She was one of those I dreaded to face more than any other. One of the ones I'd betrayed.

"Hey, Bob? What's with the corn back here?" Riley asked.

"Help yourself," I said. "It's the one thing I have a ton of."

chapter
eight

LOS ANGELES IS COVERED in tiny streets that you can live within a mile of and never even know they're there. These avenues are capillaries on the hilly terrain, hiding houses that were built in the early studio days by set carpenters with too much time and creativity on their hands. I parked in front of a small home partially hidden by birds of paradise and banana trees, halfway between a Spanish bungalow and a fairy tale castle. Dense greenery shielded every house on the street from every other.

I felt like my heart had been replaced by a jackhammer operated by Tor Johnson.

The thing about hitting bottom is that you keep a mental ranking of your friends. At the bottom are the acquaintances who aren't close enough to consider helping you. In the middle are those you'd consider asking for help. Right at the top are the ones you can't bear to see you in your present state. And at the very top are the ones whose disappointment hits like a gunshot. Disappointment that comes from betrayal is the worst kind.

"You okay, Bobby?" Hasim asked.

"Oh, I'm dandy." I slapped the steering wheel a couple times like that would help and practically launched myself out of the car. The others followed. I think Pud was picking up on my mood, because he loped over to my side and made a whining sound deep in his throat.

I tried to run my hands through my hair, but they just came away greasy. I touched my matted beard and thought about how I must look... Yeah, best not to peek under that rock. I'd showered at Hasim's, but it wasn't enough. I'd need more than that before I'd banish what neglect had done to me. No time to do much of anything about it now, and the truth was I probably needed a power washer and some industrial delousing. My steps were heavier than the stones of the walkway. I kept thinking that there had to be another solution here. A little money meant I could avoid this conversation. *Goddamn it.*

I knocked on the door, stomach churning like I was about to tell the principal that I was the one responsible for a terrorist attack on the school. My old friend Lara Hernandez answered.

Lara is tall, and if you take into account her big bottle-blonde hair, she's taller than me. Her features are bold, with probing brown eyes, full lips, and a square chin. Her skin is light brown, and her cheeks are dusted with some acne scars that she usually covers with foundation. She was made up, though not quite elaborately as she usually was. She wore a white wrap dress and a pair of flats.

Lara was a friend from way back. She was a gofer around the same time I was, only she kept her loyalties welded to one group: the Hermetic Order of the Golden Dawn. She stuck with them, and became a minorly important part of the city's function. Back in the day, she trusted me with what was, at the time, a secret, and I had handled it well. So we were the kind of friends with history. History that I was about to throw a bomb at.

"Can I help— Bob, is that you?" The recognition was tinged with more than a little horror. It's always nice to know that as bad as you think you look, the truth is even worse.

"Hi."

"What are you..." she noticed the two people behind me. "Hi."

"Can we come in?"

"Uh...yeah." She waved us in. Lara likes everything bright and clean, something about the clean flow of energy from here to there. I'd call it New Age nonsense, but it seemed to work for her. Much like her outfit, she decorated almost entirely in white, with a few gold accents—that was more lightness and energy talk. She explained it one time, but it's not like I listened. "Whoa!" she blurted.

"It's okay, he doesn't bite," Riley said.

"And who are you?" Lara asked Riley.

"Oh, sorry," I said. "Hasim, Riley, Pud Galvin, this is Lara Hernandez."

"Hasim Khoury," Hasim said, shaking Lara's hand. "It's nice to meet you."

"I'm sorry, the monster's name is Pud Galvin?"

"He's a chupacabra," Hasim explained.

"He's a buddy!" Riley said.

"He's my spirit guide," I said.

Lara's head snapped to each one of us and her eyes narrowed. "Are you serious?"

"As Walter Cronkite reporting on a kitten fire."

"So you vanish for a year, don't call me, on some kind of ascetic hermitage where you incarnate a fucking *spirit guide*? And then you just show up to my house acting like this isn't a big goddamn deal?"

"I'm sorry?"

"Goddamn right you are. What did that girlfriend of yours have to say? I can't imagine she was happy about you living in what I can only assume was the outhouse of a junkyard."

"Uh...that's kind of the whole story. Can we sit down?"

Lara was confused, which she habitually hid by being annoyed and officious. I knew her well enough to recognize it, and it was preferable to what I knew would be honest anger and hurt once she understood what was really going on here. She looked us over, and nodded to herself. "They can. You...you're coming with me." She pulled me down the hall.

Along with some lovely artwork, Lara had a picture of a tiny woman posing in front of a pink building against a backdrop of vibrant green. It was her mom back in Honduras, the one person in her family still speaking to her. I almost asked about the old lady, but guilt tossed a big bucket of ice water on that plan.

Lara didn't notice my hesitation, instead throwing open the door to her obsessively clean bathroom. "Get in there. Take yourself the longest shower of your life. You'll find scissors and clippers in the medicine cabinet. I want you to cut the tangles out of your hair and tame that Manson shit you've got going on." She opened up the mirrored door to show me the shaving implements. Wouldn't be my first time with a pink razor. "When you strip down, you put those rags outside the door. I'll stick them in the wash and pray they don't come apart. You can use my robe."

A murmur of conversation bubbled in from the other room. Nerves gripped me, so I turned on the shower, partially just to drown them out. Then I peeled off my clothes and dropped them outside the door like Lara asked.

I couldn't remember the last time I'd felt warm water like this shower's. Hasim's shower had been lukewarm at best, and truth be told that was heaven at the time. Lara's shower was a few more steps up from a sink in a Burger King bathroom. This time I attacked the body parts I'd just sort of rinsed before. I scrubbed myself raw and still felt dirty when the water started to sting.

When I judged there was nothing more that could be taken off me, I turned the shower off and wrapped a small white towel around my waist. My bones looked like they were trying to break through my skin from the other side.

I wiped the mirror and looked at the half-mad face staring back at me. My hair was past my shoulders and my beard reached the middle of my chest. Both stuck out at crazy angles, following the natural contours of my cowlicks exaggerated by caked-in filth. The scissors started the process, cutting the hair down to a manageable length, and the clippers were next, bringing hair and beard down to a uniform fuzz.

I rinsed myself off once more, then gathered as much of the cut hair as I could off the floor and dumped it into the trash. There was no way to get it all. Lara would probably find little strands of dark hair stuck in the tile grout forever. I pulled on a fluffy white robe, and it was the softest thing that had touched me in memory.

My bare feet expected a thorn or a sharp rock as I walked into the living room, but found only smooth hardwood floor. The four of them had settled down in the front room, Lara on a chair, Hasim and Riley on the sofa, and Pud wandering around, babbling to himself. Lara kept her eyes on the chupacabra, halfway between distrust and confusion.

The humans all had a mug in front of them, the rich scent of coffee hanging in the air. I hadn't had coffee in a long time. It had never been my favorite, but at that moment I craved it almost more than moonshine.

"I knew you were in there somewhere," Lara said.

I touched my face. "Not for lack of trying, I guess."

"This one," she said, indicating Hasim, "said that you should explain what you're doing here. So we've been making small talk, waiting for you to wash off that hermit look. In the meantime, I learned that you brought an Assassin and a Servant of Shub-Internet into my house. I also learned that you're possibly dating his mom?"

I shook my head and glared at Hasim. "I'm not dating his mom."

"I said you *wanted* to date my mom."

"I'm not going to keep doing this."

"Out with it. Why are you here with this menagerie?"

I swallowed. The coward in me had hoped that one of them might have broken the news. No such luck there. It had to be me. So, wrapped in that silly bathrobe, the belt pulled as tight as I could around my bony hips, I tried to figure out where to begin. I started with the poison envelope, the one with the job inside. "Make a conspiracy," it said, and along with it, the bribe from the devil himself, if I was feeling especially Protestant about it. The money was long gone, but the devastation it prodded me to commit lingered on.

When I started talking, it got easier, as though the truth had been dammed up and just needed a single stone removed to get flowing. Or maybe I wanted Lara to absolve me. Sure, I had hurt Hasim and Riley with my actions, but they didn't matter to me in the way Lara did and always would. So I told her. Told her the job, told her what I did. I started with the anonymous job, the laziest conspiracy ever, then right into Paul Mallon seizing the whole thing from me in a digital coup. Then the whole thing got eaten up, and now it was just political orthodoxy.

The entire time I got to watch Lara's face. Got to watch exactly what my actions bought. At first she merely frowned, until she got the gist of where I was going. Then her face went slack with wide-mouthed horror. Oh, but that was too vulnerable, and vulnerability was something one only shows to a friend. She snapped her mouth closed, her eyes narrowed, and the muscles in her jaw twitched, the only motion in a face of stone. A fire sprang up behind her eyes and her lip curled, and when I finally went silent, she whispered with the finality of the Grim Reaper, "Motherfucker. You know what my fucking life has been the last couple years?"

I flinched. "I can make a few guesses."

"And now I have to hear that you of all people were the engine on a good chunk of it."

"Wait," Riley said. "*You're* QAnon? How is that even possible?"

"I'm Q, not QAnon. They'd tell you there's Q and there's anons, but...it's not important. I don't even think they bother with that shibboleth anymore. And I *was* Q. Then it was Paul and now I guess it's no one, but that doesn't really matter."

"I don't get how it got so big," Hasim said.

"This motherfucker knows how the mind works," Lara said. "He knows where evolution built in all the shortcuts so that a clever ape could get his greedy hands on some berries without getting eaten by a sabretooth tiger. It's all pattern recognition."

Riley nodded. "That makes sense."

"It does?" Hasim asked.

"It's like this," Lara said. "Learning is all about recognizing a pattern and extrapolating. Since learning is pretty much the only advantage our ancestors had, we got real good at it. Problem is, sometimes there isn't a pattern—it's just a coincidence. But what this motherfucker knows is that the human mind won't necessarily know the difference. Put a pattern, even a fake one, in front of enough people and some will take it as meaningful. So he basically did a cold reading of a message board, fed them back what they wanted, let them work out the patterns that weren't even there, and surfed that wave. That about right?"

"Yeah," I said. "That's about right."

"And now you got people calling me a pedophile because I want to piss in the ladies' room like the fucking lady that I am."

"I'm sorry."

"Fuck you. We're not at sorry yet. Did you even think about what you were doing?"

"Not even a little. It was a job. A job I half-assed."

"You know how much excuse the motherfuckers need to go after somebody like me?"

"Less than nothing, last I checked."

"You're goddamn right. Now tell me one more thing," she said, voice quavering. "Why am I not throwing you out into the street?"

I shrugged. "I threw me out into the street. Well, *Mina* threw me out. She was right, though. So that's where I stayed. I thought I should just keep out of the way of the world. But the other night I had an epiphany. I called on...I don't know. The universe maybe? I called on something to help me make sense of what had happened, and I turn the corner, and I see a chupacabra just going nuts on this goat. I watched those things tear the greatest Assassin alive into pieces..." I turned to Hasim. "That's what happened to Tariq Suliman."

Hasim's eyes got as big as flying saucers. "Glah!" Pud said. Hasim flinched.

"I didn't know if I was drunk or what. Well, I was drunk. I didn't know how drunk. Didn't know if I was seeing things. So I sat down and talked to him. He could have killed me any time, but he didn't. Later I realized it's because he's a tulpa."

"You learned that word from *Supernatural*," Lara said.

"It's what he is."

Lara frowned at the chupacabra. Then she shook her head and said, "Go on."

"Pud Galvin listened, and that's when I came to my epiphany. I can kill it."

"Kill what? The conspiracy?" Lara asked.

I nodded, pathetically eager to get Lara to understand what I believed I did. I went over the plan. I explained that if anything out there could eat an actual idea, it was Shub-Internet. I told her about the deal with Fabian, and that Riley was our resident expert. The four of us were going to break into the facility—

"The D.U.M.B.," Hasim said.

"Not now maybe?"

Riley furrowed her brow, the wheels turning behind her eyes.

"What brought you to my door?" Lara asked.

In some ways, this was the hardest part to say. The culture at large had conditioned me into believing that this was shameful. That it was somehow worse than the whole fascism thing. "Money," I said. "We need to fly into Denver International, and we need a night in a hotel to plan. The one thing we don't have is financing."

Lara was silent for what felt like forever. She stared at me—into me, really. The anger still blazed, but she was keeping hold of it. Finally, she spared a look for each of my companions, experiencing Hasim's guileless smile, Riley's eager mien, and Pud's...whatever it was chupacabras did.

"You think that the three of you have a snowball's chance of getting this done?"

"I don't know. All I know is that I have to try."

She got up. "I'm going with you."

"You don't have to."

"The hell I don't. You want this thing to work, you need me. You're talking about containing a god, and right now all you have is one of that same god's cultists who you just met this morning. No offense."

"Oh, none taken," Riley said.

"I'm not letting you anywhere near an actual god without a white witch."

"A white witch?" Riley sneered.

Lara pointed at her. "I haven't decided if I like you yet, so you best pipe down." Riley, like anyone confronted with Lara, quailed. "This thing is important enough that I want someone I can trust out there, and right now, of the peop...entities in this room, I'm the only one I completely trust."

"Lara—"

"Did I say this was a conversation? You fucked me over and now you want my money. These are *conditions*. I'll finance this thing, but I'm part of the team."

Something about having Lara along made me feel a little better. Nothing against Hasim, but I didn't respect him the way I did Lara. And she was right on the money about Riley. I didn't know her. I wanted to trust her, but she was a question mark at this point.

"Done," I said.

She nodded. "I'm going to get packed and put your things in the dryer. Do you have other clothes?"

"Of course!"

"Do they look like those?"

"Oh, you bet."

"Well, we're not flying like that."

"Got any clothes here?" I asked her.

She put hands on her hips. "I'm not in the habit of letting gentleman callers leave their shit here."

"I have to swing by my place to get a bag," Hasim volunteered. "He can borrow some clothes from me."

"That's done. Now excuse me." Lara disappeared down the hall. Hasim's gaze followed her the whole way.

"How do you know her?" he asked.

"We're old Army buddies."

"You were in the Army?" Riley asked.

"No. Why, what have you heard?"

Lara took her time packing. In the meantime, I drank her coffee, luxuriating in the warmth, but not expecting the buzz that seeped into my limbs. I couldn't get Lara's expression out of my mind. To know that I hadn't just made her mad, but that I'd betrayed her, *disappointed* her, was enough to make me want to find a hole. First things first, I supposed.

"So...I don't get it," Hasim said. "These QAnons..."

"There are no..."

He waved that off. "Whatever. They think the government is controlled by this group of Satanic child molesters. What's supposed to happen?"

"The Storm," I said. "They think there are a bunch of sealed indictments that will be acted upon at some point. Basically, the military will round all these people up, try them in military courts, and execute them."

"That doesn't sound like a trial."

"Now you're getting it."

"Hold on, they *have* the government," Riley said.

"And they're using all that pent-up rage, all the excuses to go after all the people they hate. They want to hurt, that's it. They have the perfect exuse."

When Lara returned, she was carrying two large bags. "I booked our tickets. We're flying to Denver tonight out of LAX. Let's go get what we need."

"What about him?" I asked, pointing at Pud.

"We'll need a pet carrier. A *covered* pet carrier."

Pud made a sad noise. We made our way out to the car, and Lara paused when she saw it.

"Still got it," I said.

"Yeah," she said sadly.

"Shotgun!" Hasim called out.

As Lara climbed into the back, she stopped. "Why is there corn all over the floor?"

"You want some?"

She picked up a cob and squinted at it. "You haven't been *eating* this, have you?"

"Almost exclusively."

"Okay, concerns about nutrition aside, you see this?" She pointed to some rusty deposits on the kernels. "This is ergot. If you've been eating this, you've got ergot poisoning."

"Oh," I said. Everyone stared at me. "Well, that explains all the witch burnings."

chapter
nine

IN THE MIDDLE of LAX stands a structure that looks like the headquarters for the Legion of Doom. It's an easy leap to think it was actually designed by a conspiracy of that name, but sadly, it was just a misguided architect in the '60s looking to add a bit of zeerust to a location no sane person would ever go happily. Now it just sits there, waiting for a Karl Stromberg who would never return.

We parked the Belle in long term parking and grabbed our bags. When Lara saw the state of my luggage and what I considered to be necessities, she flat out refused to bring them. "We have to pick up clothes for the job anyway," she said. I grabbed the bottle with the dregs of shine sloshing around the bottom. She snatched that from me and hucked it over the fence at the edge of the lot. It came to rest at the base of a small bald hillock of dirt next to one of the runways. Reminded me of me. I sadly bade goodbye to the glorious memory-eraser.

Coaxing Pud into the carrier was a bit more of a chore. He went in only after extensive cajoling, burrowing among the blankets we filled it with, cuddling up with a stuffed owl Riley had insisted on buying him at the pet store when we grabbed the crate. Checking Pud like that made me twitchy. Didn't feel right with him so far away. My mouth watered, and I looked over at the bottle lying in the dirt. There was only a single string of barbed wire at the top of that fence. I could hop it, catch a few last moments of bliss there right next to the bottle. Then it was time to go, and I had to leave the beloved shine behind.

I was relatively clean and dressed in Hasim's clothes, and I could almost pretend to be a person like everyone else. But I didn't belong there, and eventually the other airport denizens were going to work that simple fact out. The last-minute holiday travelers would point at me like Donald Sutherland at the end of *Body Snatchers* and I'd be exiled back to the hills where I could eat more ergot-flavored corn.

Of course, when we hit security, my companions, who were all broadly-speaking brown, were the ones put through the wringer. As for the twitchy white guy with no luggage and a fake ID, I was clearly not a security threat. Joaquin, my ID guy, did good work, but I didn't for a moment think that was why I got the wave. Hasim got it worst of all. By the time he was through, Lara had had time to hit the convenience store for snacks. She shoved a paperback into my hands. "There. Read that."

"Thanks?"

"If you spend the whole flight drumming your hands I'm going to lose my shit."

The flight was relatively short. I sat next to Riley, who spent most of it staring out the window, while I stuck my nose in the book Lara bought me. I had hoped that it would be some kind of parallel story to mine. That's what it should be, according to the laws of meaning. That way, I could read it, get some perspective on my present situation, and then maybe at the climax, I could bust out some lesson that would really turn things around.

Sorry, no. It was a book about a spy who didn't want to be a spy anymore and had to do one last spy job. It was passively right wing in the way those sorts of things are, making tons of assumptions that never quite pan out, but then, they're not supposed to. Of course, it kept me relatively quiet, which was the real point. I barely drummed my hands at all.

When the drink cart arrived, I was about to order booze, but Lara snapped, "He'll have a ginger ale."

So I drank my ginger ale, I read my terrible paperback, and I wondered what the hell I was doing. It's one thing to have a drunken epiphany on a hilltop and it's another thing entirely to be on a plane on Christmas Eve with every intention of committing sedition to free an eldritch god. I pulled my phone from my pocket and stared at the blank screen. The pictures inside, the last good ones, called to me to wallow in my lost past for a while. Instead, with great difficulty, I looked over at Riley, who watched the puffy white clouds below us.

"Can I ask you something?"

"Sure," Riley said.

"You weren't raised...Shub-Internet, were you?"

"I've heard that's a thing. Like, there are some second-generation Servants out there."

"We have to be coming up on a third generation, right?"

"Law of averages. I've never met any. To be honest, I'm not really welcome at the temple."

I thought back to what Fabian said. "I'd say I was sorry to hear that, but I've met Fabian."

She chuckled. "Right. Well, to answer your question, I was raised Catholic."

"Kind of a big jump. Catholic to techno-Cthulhu."

"Less than you'd think. Why do you ask? I mean, no offense, but you strike me as one of those atheists who's real angry about the whole religion thing, while just kind of ignoring the fact that you've been creepily insisting you have a spirit guide since the moment I met you."

I coughed. "Okay, that...uh...that hit."

She shrugged. "A lot of Servants start as those kind of atheists. You go from not believing there's any universal truth to actively wanting it destroyed."

"I have a hard time believing in universal truth when lies get far more traction."

"Point," she said. "But you never answered why you asked."

"I asked because I don't know you. I know that Fabian doesn't like you, which is a good sign. Take the others. Hasim was raised Muslim and along the way he joined a sect. Lara, I think she was Catholic way back, but she's a Gnostic Christian now. I get the evolution there."

"So you wanted to have a deep convo about religion with someone you just met."

"Yeah, pretty much. I'm about to trust you with a lot, and getting to you know you seemed like a good idea."

"I can accept that. Are you asking me what a good Catholic girl is doing writing digital prayers to the idiot god of the internet?"

"Pretty much."

"You're assuming a lot. How well do you know the Servants?"

"Technically I was a Servant at one time." The look she gave me could have stripped the paint off a speedboat. "Right, okay. Back in the day I used to work for every conspiracy, cult, and secret society there was. That used to mean membership, or the next best thing. I was a member of the Servants in that whenever Fabian needed something done that he didn't want to do, he'd call me, I'd do it, and like a week later I'd find that the number in a tiny offshore bank account was a little bit higher." I sighed. "I hated that thing too. I dealt in cash back then, but you know Fabian. Say the word 'cash' and strap in for a lecture about how exchanging colorful tree bark is what monkeys do."

"You do not strike me as the kind of guy who has an offshore bank account."

"Well, I don't anymore. So in answer to your question: I know the Servants well enough to fake my way through an interaction with Fabian Strudwick, a man who has never listened to another human being in his entire life."

"Why listen to someone else when he can hear himself talk? Okay, so from like, the outside, the Servants look like a big mass, but the truth is there's a range of beliefs. It'd be like thinking every Christian was one of those ones who speak in tongues, right? On one end, you have the hardcore apocalypticists who believe that Shub-Internet's ultimate destiny is to destroy the internet. Eat it all up till there's nothing left."

"And they think that's a good thing?"

"Enh..." she waggled her hand. "They think more that it's inevitable, so you might as well get onboard."

"Kind of a weird set of beliefs for a bunch of programmers to have."

"Not really. When you know how rickety the whole thing is, absolute destruction becomes terrifyingly probable. There's huge sections of digital infrastructure that's maintained by like one bored dude in Minnesota or someplace."

"That's awesome." She shot me an ironic thumbs up. "I'm guessing you're not one of these, then."

"Nope. I like the internet. I make a good living thanks to it."

"And yet you worship a god that could destroy it."

"Wouldn't you want to placate the one thing that can eat a big chunk of your life? Look, a digital priestess like me can work around a lot of stuff, but I need it to *be* there."

"And sometimes destruction is a good thing."

"Exactly. Some shit out there should be eaten. Destroyed and forgotten. Shub-Internet is the one being out there that can do that. Doesn't it make the most sense to be the one feeding it?"

I had to digest that. Riley made a disturbing amount of sense. "Huh," was all I managed to say, though.

"So, do you trust me yet?"

"No," I said, "but I like you."

"Join the club."

I had to laugh. "There's a club of people that like you but don't trust you? Which one is Fabian?"

"Oh, neither. He doesn't believe, not in the way that I do, or the apocalypticist weirdos do. He's in it for the money."

"Not the power?"

"There's a difference?"

I raised my cup of flat ginger ale to her. Riley had given me a ton to think about, and though I stared at the paperback for the rest of the flight, my mind ruminated on her words. That's what this whole thing was, when you washed off the glitter. It was a small group of people making money by feeding hate. My first two lives—as a gofer, then a fixer—had been feeding that same hate. I was that one bored programmer in Duluth, but the infrastructure I was maintaining was a siphon made of hatred and fear, sucking out the money of the people too full of both to see it for what it was.

We were quiet until we landed at Denver International a couple hours after dark. It had been a long while since I was there. This was back in the fixer days, a simple prisoner transfer. Sure, a terrifying prisoner who could break bones with his bare hands and probably wouldn't mind giving me some payback. But I wasn't going to see him on this thing. He'd never know I was here.

As airports go, there's no single one at the center of more conspiracy theories than DIA. This might be because of the giant demonic statue of the horse outside. Look, sometimes a giant demon horse is just a statue. It has as much occult significance and artistic value as the old Scary Lucy statue in New York. And sure, when you look at it, thirty-two feet of blue fiberglass with blazing red eyes, you wonder who in their right mind ordered it built if not to signal some kind of occult allegiance. But here's the thing, this idea that secret societies are obsessed with signaling each other with symbology that the normies can't work out is pure fiction. It's what a large part of QAnon is built on, and like everything else in that arena, it's bullshit. It's that pattern recognition firing off in the brain, drawing connections between happenstance and coincidence. Occult groups use symbols for the same reason as any other group does. It's a marker of membership, of status, of in-grouping. And occasionally, to keep cryptids on the side of the fence you want them on.

I do realize that I was knocking symbols while in the presence of a skilled hermeticist and a computer programmer/possible witch, but go with me.

Anyway, Blucifer, as the horse is known, is just a terrible statue. I think it was a misguided attempt to reference Colorado's obsession with horses. Nothing says obsession like a four-story version of a beast with devil eyes. Which is not to say that the conspiracy nuts were entirely off base with this one. After all, we were going to free a god that had been confined to the Pentagon.

As we walked to baggage claim, I clocked what I could. Cameras were everywhere, not unusual considering we were in an airport. We pushed past large crowds, crowds so big that at times it was tough to see where the cameras even were. More people than should be there on Christmas Eve, and in point of fact, didn't seem to be moving very much. After picking up our bags, we waited for the last member of our group.

A wide-eyed porter pushed the crate up on a cart, Pud growling and muttering on the inside. "You should probably take your dog to the vet," the porter said, noticeably shivering.

"He's not a dog," I said.

"Thank you," Lara said.

The guy scurried off before Lara could even hand him a tip. I knelt in front of the crate. Pud made keening noises, lurching to the front and gripping the cage with his claws. I patted his weird talon. "It's okay, buddy. We'll let you out at the hotel." He retreated again, a baleful shadow, his eyes glowing like coals.

The area outside the climate-controlled airport was a winter-blasted wasteland. Or, at least to the eyes of a Southern Californian who had been living outdoors and hadn't even known it was Christmas it sure looked like it. Sure, someone used to the cold might have seen a lovely brisk evening, but to me, I was Steve Buscemi in *Fargo*, freezing my ass off in unspeakable pain and looking for a place to bury a little ill-gotten loot.

We piled into Lara's rented minivan, shivering as the meager heat brought our core temperatures back to something south of popsicle. I don't know why she picked a minivan. It felt pointed. Like she was a soccer mom taking a crew of unruly kids on our weekend activities. Thing was, she wasn't exactly wrong about any of that, if that was indeed what she was thinking. Hell, a minivan might well have been the cheapest way to transport the five of us and I was looking for patterns where there weren't any.

The motel she picked, not too close to the airport but not far either, couldn't have been more generic had it been painted white with blue trim and in even black letters had read "MOTEL" along the side. It could have been one of half a dozen different chains, the kind of place people go to do things they don't want remembered. Hell, if I'd had the scratch, it would have been the perfect place for me. Just lock me up in a room that looks like every other room and eventually I could fade into the overwhelming beige of the decor.

Lara parked by a side entrance. Looked like the way into a clinic. "We're down at the end over here. Guy at the desk said there's a decent pizza place down the road too that's open. Otherwise, there's vending machines around the corner." She turned off the car and handed out the card keys. "Bobby and Hasim, you're in 147 with the spirit guide. Miss Shub-Internet and me are next door in 148. We should be right through the side entrance here. Let's settle in and get something to eat in about a half hour."

Hasim and I hauled Pud's crate out into the Denver night, and I never thought I'd be cold enough to consider self-immolation, but here we are. Our rooms weren't too far from the entrance, and though I'm sure the hall was heated to Colorado standards, we were still shivering when we piled into our rooms. Hasim cranked the heater while I opened up Pud's cage. Pud hobbled out, wrapped in the woolen plaid blankets, clutching his owl, and watching me reproachfully. He looked like a grandma. "Glah," he said.

Hasim tossed his bags in a corner and clicked on the TV. The newscasters were warning of a big storm coming in over the next couple days. "Looks like we're in for a white Christmas," the smug asshole behind the newsdesk said.

"This might sound silly, but when I cooked this plan up I didn't remember, you know, winter. Does that make me Napoleon? I'm feeling like Napoleon."

Hasim turned away from the window in defeated wonder. "Dude, if you start thinking you're Napoleon we're in bigger trouble than I thought."

"I didn't say I *was* Napoleon. Just that I managed to fuck up in a similar way."

"Yeah, you gotta mind your Ps and Qs at Raging Waters," Hasim said, and I didn't ask him to elaborate. He went to the thermostat to see if he could coax another degree or two from it. "You're good sleeping with the heat on?"

"Oh hell yeah. We're not turning it off for as long as we're here."

I stretched out on the bed. That was right around the time I realized I hadn't slept on a bed in a long time, and more recently, I hadn't slept in over twenty-four hours, so there was that. But even before the night of my epiphany, I'd been sleeping on the wire frame of a rusty cot with only a few ragged blankets. The motel bed was almost too soft. I felt like I was going to fall through it, and if I did, there was no way I'd ever stop falling. I sat up, my head spinning.

Hasim settled down on the other bed. "Hey, can I ask you something?"

"Yeah," I said, moving to the floor between the beds. It was more solid down here. I immediately felt better. Pud loped over and settled down next to me. I petted his head. The silver spines that ran from his forehead down his back laid flat and he made a sound that was almost like a purr.

Hasim shifted to his side, leaning over the bed to look at me. "What's Lara's deal?"

"Her deal? She's Golden Dawn, big into hermeticism...she's Gnostic."

Hasim squirmed in embarrassment like a schoolboy. "Is she single?"

"I have no earthly idea. I haven't talked to her in forever."

"Oh. Damn. You think she'd be into going out with me?"

"I don't know. I mean..." I tried to think back to any of Lara's boyfriends I'd met. None of them had been Assassins, but I couldn't decide of that was a point in Hasim's favor or not. I did think he needed to be warned, though. Lara had baggage. "Look, if you want to date her, there's something about her you need to know."

"What's that?"

I took a deep breath, wrestling with the awkward truth that could instantly turn Hasim against Lara and might even submarine our current team up. He had to know. It wasn't fair for him to go in blind. "She likes Nickelback."

Hasim laughed. "That's it?"

"Like, a lot."

"Don't be a snob. The important thing is, does she like Phish?"

"Does anybody?"

Hasim rolled onto his back and out of sight. "You're such an asshole."

He wasn't wrong. Sure, I'd done a bad thing. A *very* bad thing if I'm being honest, but I couldn't shake the fact that the speed with which I'd been edited out of my social circle's lives pointed to a deficiency in my character. I should probably work on being nicer, which apparently included no unprovoked shots at jam bands while Hasim was around.

"Can you do me a favor?" I asked. "If you plan to ask her out, can you wait until this job is over?"

"Yeah, of course. I should get to know her a little bit too. What does she like?"

"Let's see… Coffee, Valentinus, long foreign movies. She loves *Doctor Zhivago*. Don't get excited, though. Not a single cannibal in that one."

"I didn't think there were cannibals in that movie."

"Why am I the only person who thought that?"

"What else?"

"She's loyal as hell. The thing about Lara is that once she's decided you're her friend, she'll move Heaven and Earth to help you. She might complain while she's doing it, might call you a few names, but she'll be there. If actions are more important than words, then you're on her wavelength."

"Yeah, I got that impression. What with her hating you and still flying us all out to Denver to commit treason. So you have a high opinion of her."

"In my first life, I didn't really have any friends. Mostly because I was lying to everyone I knew."

"Including me."

"Yeah. I mean, you and I were friendly and all, but Lara was a friend. Lara was the first person I actually didn't lie to, but that was only because she didn't lie to me. She started it. And it's a hell of a thing to have someone offer trust and friendship when that's the one thing you don't have a single bit of."

"Damn. That's deep."

"It's all in the past now, but yeah. At the time, that mattered."

He was silent for a bit. "One other thing. What's she got going on, you know, down there?"

"How the hell should I know? I don't make a habit of asking about my friends' genitals."

"I know, and it's always kind of hurt my feelings."

I stared at the ceiling, wondering if I was really going to do this. "Hasim? How's your penis?"

"Real good, man," he said with genuine gratitude. "Thanks for asking."

About a half hour later, we went to Lara and Riley's room, shivering in the muted cold of the hallway. When Riley opened up, Pud gave her a resentful grunt and shuffled inside. I wondered if, before he came here from whatever spirit guide waiting room he'd been cooling his wing membranes in, he'd hoped for a warmer assignment. It's December, and it's his turn, and fortune of fortunes, the poor schmuck who needs guidance is in the City of Angels. Then I had to stab him in the back like this.

"Aw, poor little guy is shivering," Riley cooed, following Pud to scratch behind his ear bumps.

"Close the door, you're letting the damn heat out," Lara scolded us from where she reclined on the bed farthest from the door. After what Hasim told me, it was hard to miss the way his gaze lingered on her.

Sitting on the floor by the other bed, Riley scratched Pud's head while he purred happily. "Who's the best buddy?" she demanded. "Who?"

"We're planning," Lara said to me, sitting up. I nodded in confirmation. "I'm calling for pizza. Who likes what?"

The group of us engaged in a bit of spirited back and forth. Lara liked the fancy stuff—you know, artichoke hearts and the like—and I think Hasim would have gone for anything Lara said. Riley was fine with pepperoni, but asked for mushrooms as a condition. Pud didn't have a vote, but we got him chicken wings anyway. When a group of people ask you what chupacabras can eat, sometimes you blurt out the first thing that comes to mind. During the order, Lara squinted at the little monster and said, "Mild," and that might have been the first time anyone gauged a chupacabra's preferred spice level. Hasim went out for drinks and came back with a few cans of soda. Apparently they had to keep the machines inside or the cans would explode.

"Okay, so tell us what you got," Lara said, propping up some pillows on the headboard to sit more comfortably.

"First, I think we need some basics, because there's stuff I'm not clear on. What *is* Shub-Internet exactly?" I asked, parking myself by the window, keeping an eye on the parking lot through the small space in the curtains.

"That's not a good sign."

"The God of the Internet," Riley said.

I waved that away. "I don't mean the metaphysical explanation. Let's say Egon Spengler saw Shub-Internet. What would he think it was?"

"Egon Spengler believed in ghosts," Hasim pointed out, taking the other chair, but moving it away from the window before settling.

"Ugh. Fine. Someone who doesn't believe in anything even remotely supernatural."

"Penn and Teller?"

"They believe in libertarian economics," Lara said.

"I didn't want to get hung up on this," I said.

"No, I know what you mean," Riley said, continuing to pet the chupacabra. "If you want to get sacrilegious, Shub-Internet would look like a worm. But like, a *giant* worm."

"Oh shit, Shai-Hulud?" Hasim said. Riley stared at him in confusion.

"A worm like a computer virus," I said. "Not a sandworm."

"Oh yeah, totally. Wait, is it called Shub-Internet because it's a reference?"

"To what? I don't know what's going on," Riley said.

"They're talking about *Dune*. It's not important," Lara said.

"You take that back," I hissed.

Lara rolled her eyes and gestured to Riley. "You were in the middle of making sense."

"Right, yeah. So Shub-Internet is a big worm. Bigger than anything a programmer would've ever seen, and probably their first question would be what a worm needs with that much code. If that muggle kept checking back, they might notice that the code itself changes when they're not looking at it. But yeah, baseline, snap judgment, a worm."

"Perfect, okay. And a worm can be put on a device and moved place to place?" I asked.

"Kind of," she said. "Shub-Internet grows and moves of its own accord. It will take data and destroy it, but it will also consume it, turning that code into *its* code. Sometimes it will cease to exist where it used to be, but..." She shrugged. "I think I know where you're going with this. You want to know what it would take to move Shub-Internet."

I touched my nose. "Bingo."

"Shub-Internet can move through any open network connection. Hardline, wireless, doesn't matter. To reliably keep it trapped you'd need it to be physically disconnected from any network, and of course any Wi-Fi. To be safe, you'd stick the prison machine inside a faraday cage and then surround it with the proper runes."

"That's reliable?"

"As reliable as these things get. To get it out, you wouldn't be getting it *out,* technically. You'd need to plug a device directly into the prison machine and get Shub-Internet to infect that. It *spreads,* as opposed to moves. Kind of."

"But that can be done?" Lara asked.

"Oh yeah. Your standard laptop should be able to hold it pretty well. It'll be bricked when Shub-Internet's done, but it'll hold. One thing... there's no guarantee that Shub-Internet will infect a new device. I mean, I think it's probable, but it's not a sure thing."

"So...fill it up with bait," Hasim said. "Same way you catch a fish."

"Phishing for Shub-Internet." Riley smirked. "I like it."

Then the pizza got there. I ate in silence, mulling the plan over. Simple was probably better. It had been a long time since I tried to do anything like this. I couldn't help but wonder if I still had "it." Whatever it was. That magic that had once made me bulletproof.

Right about then, the food hit. I'd spent a long time not eating any sugar at all, and sugar is basically a drug for our primate brains. When the Dr. Pepper invaded my frontal lobes on a blitzkrieg of sucrose tanks, my doubt collapsed. I had the plan, and it would work. I saw it, clear as day, every piece functioning like a Busby Berkeley dance number.

I hopped up from my chair to work off some of the energy and called out our must-have list. "We're gonna need two dark suits, two business casual outfits, a pet cage, a badge, a dolly, a clipboard, a sheet, a laptop with a hard drive full of bait, some cables, and a hacksaw. We go in, we get enough of Shub-Internet onto the laptop, we carry the whole thing out, hook up to Denver International's Wi-Fi, and we've just released a digital apocalypse god into the wild."

Four faces stared at me with a mixture of awe and confusion. I took a breath. Turned out I needed one.

"I'm going to gloss over the fact that you want a hacksaw," Lara said, recovering from her momentary astonishment, "and go right to the part where I think we have a pretty big problem. Do you know where, in the facility we've never been to, they're keeping the digital god-monster?"

"I've been there," I said. "Not recently, but it's a detention facility. They lock up cryptids like that."

"Who does?" Lara asked.

"The government," Hasim said.

"Yeah, *the* government is a fun lie we tell ourselves. Our government is a maze of bureaucracies that kind of work together and kind of hate each other, all headed up by a bunch of empty suits that do whatever they can to stay comfortable. And that's before you throw in the various secret societies."

"I shouldn't vote, then," Hasim said.

"You should vote for the suits that say the less sociopathic stuff."

"A smart woman told me that's the first step in getting the less socio-pathic stuff to happen," I said.

Lara's face softened for a moment, but the anger returned swiftly. "It's a first step and a damn inadequate one, but that's it. And keep your lips off my ass."

"I figure it has to piss someone off when I vote," Riley said. "So I do it out of spite."

"Come on, Bobby. Who runs this place?" Hasim asked.

"I don't know if there is an actual organization behind the whole thing. That whole maze of bureaucracies and conspiracies and suits, they all want to keep the money flowing. The stuff they lock up tends to be the stuff that would hurt that flow."

"Then who are the men with guns? There are always men with guns at a place like that."

I took a deep breath. "Quackenbush Security."

"Fuck," Lara said, setting an unfinished slice aside.

"Those assholes?" Riley said, trying to dab hot wing sauce off Pud's face. "They were all over the place where I grew up."

"Where did you grow up?" I asked. I couldn't think of a single place—

"Cabazon."

—other than that one.

"Oh shit, the place with the big dinosaurs?" Hasim said, checking from box to box for a slice we'd missed. He finally found one and returned to his seat, happily eating. The Cabazon Dinosaurs were probably most famous from their appearance in *Pee-Wee's Big Adventure*. They're a sixty-five-foot T-rex and a 150-foot brontosaurus that used to stand beside a lonely desert road in Coachella. Things had been built up since, but they remained as kitschy roadside attractions.

"Yeah. There's a reservation right there. We have a casino now and everything."

"Put a pin in that," I said. The Cabazon res was at the center of a sordid conspiracy around faulty intelligence software sold to other governments, complete with your standard suite of obvious murders the authorities called suicides. Quackenbush Security was up to its eyeballs in it. That whole thing was far from the worst thing Quackenbush ever got up to, but it was the closest to home. The government sometimes used reservations to get around local laws, and someone had to secure the facilities they used. Enter Quackenbush Security, a bunch of over-paid psychopaths who only answered to the Prince of Darkness at the head of the corporation, its founder Irving Quackenbush.

"Who's Quackenbush Security?" Hasim asked.

"Private military organization," Lara said, disgust drizzled over every word. "Far right wing. If there's a government installation, chances are Quackenbush is guarding it. They have deep pockets and important friends in Washington. Overseas, they get up to just about every war crime there is, and they charge the taxpayers a mint to do it."

"They're just cocky assholes with guns," I said. "They'll never see us coming."

"Do they guard Area 51?" Hasim asked.

"Bet your ass."

"Okay, not crazy about this, but I still need to know if you know where our target is," Lara said.

"Not the foggiest clue. I'm going to let them take us to it."

"I'm all ears."

"Okay, we split into two teams, Team Crichton and Team Chiana—"

"No! None of your silly shit. We're doing this right. Team Swords and Team Pentacles."

I sighed. "Fine." Then I told them the plan.

We dialed in on the details amidst the grease-stained pizza boxes and empty soda cans. I could see that my enthusiasm wasn't mine alone. Hasim and Riley believed in me, and Lara, she did the best she could at finding weak points and was irritated when she couldn't. I was beginning to think this mad plan really was possible. Of course, that's always when things turn to shit.

chapter
ten

AS I EXPECTED, the bed was too soft to sleep on, so I curled up on the floor in a nest of blankets. At a certain point in the night, Pud cuddled close. Best night of sleep I'd had in a long time, and the dreams that usually howled through my subconscious were a tiny bit quieter. The next morning we went out and got everything on the shopping list. Finding stores open on Christmas Day was a pain in the ass, but thanks to Sweet Lady Capitalism, not impossible.

Lara and Hasim both donned suits that made them look like Mulder and Scully. Well, if Scully was six feet and blonde, and Mulder was Lebanese. Riley and I could pass for office workers in our button-up shirts and slacks. With her thick glasses and hair pulled up into a bun, she really did look like IT. As for me, it felt strange to wear clothes that smelled fine and only had holes where they were supposed to be. For the first time in a long time, I was comfortable. It wouldn't last, but the duration of the car ride was pleasant at least.

Pud went into his pet carrier, again with protest. We sawed most of the way through a few bars and I did my best to communicate to him not to break out until Lara gave him the signal. I think he understood. If not, well, the plan would be going about as well as I suspected it would. I had to trust in whatever link we had as a spirit guide and a spirit guide...guidee.

We returned to the airport. My blood jumped like grease in a fryer.

The boundless confidence of planning had curdled into the doom and gloom of action. I played out the perfect version in my head knowing that the whole thing would go pear-shaped at some point. As much as I could diminish Quackenbush Security to the others, they were an army of brutal killers. They would have absolutely no compunction about putting a bullet in our heads and that's if we were lucky. School of the Americas grads think Quackenbush Security mercs should chill out a bit.

We pulled the van into short-term parking. Showtime.

Team Swords—that was Lara, Hasim, and Pud—went ahead, just far enough so that we weren't arriving together. Hasim pushed the dolly with the gimmicked pet carrier on top with Pud crouched in the cage, the sheet over the top. Hasim was armed. Watching the Assassin hiding knives on his body was a pretty sobering experience. Hasim presented as a genial stoner—because he was—but that disguised the fact that he had made a living killing people. I briefly wondered if he needed that many knives. His suit was like a cutlery store, but here's the thing: you don't last as long as I did by questioning men with that many blades in easy reach.

Next was Team Pentacles, which was Riley and me. Riley held the clipboard, one of those thick metal medical numbers, under one arm. Riley was the nicest doomsday cultist I'd ever met, but it's amazing how much I could dwell on the "doomsday cultist" part of that without properly appreciating the "nicest." Especially while walking into a proverbial lion's den armed with nothing but a laptop filled to the brim with porn, tucked away inside that clipboard.

The thing is, if you want to belong in a place, the trick is looking and acting like it. Fake it 'til you make it, as someone said. Good news is, everybody is. Oh sure, there are always one or two psychopaths in any given location who actually believe with all their hearts that they truly belong, but 99% of the human herd is pretending at every moment of every day. We all think we somehow sneaked into this adult world and we better play it cool or somebody will notice we were just three kids in a trenchcoat.

Team Pentacles *looked* the part, and that was the important bit. Anyone who saw us would think we were IT, and might entertain fantasies about Riley taking off her glasses and shaking out her hair, if they were into that sort of thing.

Riley was jittery. Didn't take a body language expert to see her quivering like she'd just pounded a pitcher of espressos. Perfectly natural to have some nerves on a heist, but for this thing to work, we had to be irritated, bored, and distracted. It was Christmas, and our bosses had cruelly violated the Christocapitalist social contract that regarded December 25th as a day set aside to be annoyed by family and to sell who we were. To make our reasons for being at the D.U.M.B. real, we had to keep that in our brains. My heart was ticking like the nuke at the end of *Goldfinger,* but I had to look like I was mentally steeling myself to explain to Uncle Phil why we don't use *that* word anymore.

Team Swords, on the other hand, were the picture of confidence. Lara once told me that she'd spent so much of her life pretending to belong that it was just second nature. All that practice was paying off now. She moved in that brusque, quick manner that told everyone around her that she had a job to do and it was going to get done, so getting out of her way was the wisest course of action. Hasim pushed the dolly with a resigned slouch to his shoulders. He was an expert at getting places he wasn't wanted, all while carrying Mafione Custom's entire catalogue on his person. And he usually did it while baked out of his mind. *Should we have made him smoke out first?* I wondered. *Would he be better if he actually had a blunt hanging from his lips like a cartoon gangster who was also really mellow and kind of wanted to house a whole box of graham crackers?*

Riley let out a quavering breath, fogging in the winter cold. I don't know what it was, but her being nervous made me calmer. "Just like whatever the programmer equivalent of riding a bike is," I said to her.

She nodded. "Piece of cake."

The doors to the airport slid open for us. The crowd was packed shoulder-to-shoulder. As a rule, airports are crowded *before* the holidays and *after*. Not *on*. Generally, on the day itself, you're at wherever you intended to be. These people didn't seem to be going anywhere. It felt like they'd arrived where they intended to be, which was bizarre, because there is no place on the planet Earth where "I had *such* a lovely time at the airport" is anything but the ravings of a madman. They were packed in like sardines on a Tokyo subway, so that any movement meant slinking through nonexistent gaps while muttering "Excuse me" on repeat.

Maybe I'm the paranoid sort, but I started clocking some similarities between the airport people. Their faces were overwhelmingly white, with only a bit of color sprinkled in just to head off the most obvious take. I spotted more than a few red baseball caps, and that's the wrong color for Colorado fans. The American flag fluttered on shirts and jackets, sometimes with eagles, guns, and the Constitution. It's unfortunate when symbols of your country's flag put you on edge, but I suppose that's what happened when you had an infestation of fascists.

The first Q didn't shock me. Emblazoned in the stars and stripes on a t-shirt, the goddamn thing *taunted* me. I turned away, only to nearly run into another stretched over a broad back and reeking of Old Spice. And another. Another. Fucking Qs everywhere. They loomed out of the shouldering mob, surrounding me, their creator. Dr. Frankenstein never had to contend with an entire airport filled with his abominations, and unlike old Victor, I couldn't just burn the place down and consign my creation to ashes.

For so many reasons.

"You okay?" Riley hissed.

I was clammy all over, and my heart had grown spider legs and was attempting to crawl out of my throat. "Never been better."

"You looked like you just bombed at open mic night."

"I'm okay. It's just...these people..."

"Try doing this looking like me."

"Right. Yeah, I know." I had camouflage. Riley, Lara, and Hasim didn't. I hadn't painted that target on them, but I *had* served up the excuse. I gulped in air, put one foot in front of the other, and tried to ignore the feeling that I was being slowly strangled by the entire crowd.

Riley's hand closed on mine, small but warm and strong. "It's okay," she said. "Piece of cake, remember?"

"Yep, piece of cake." Or, you know, it would have been, to this man I'd become in my second life. The man I was in my first probably could manage it. This shell, whatever I was now, who knows? I had been living on a hill, among garbage for at least a year, with all my skills rotting away in the hot sun, and here I was, attempting something that may never have been done, that may not be *possible*. I was walking into the great wyrm's den naked, no Sicarius Draconum, no shield of dragon scale. I was packing a panic attack and a few outdated pop culture references. My anchor was Riley's hand, and I held on. She wasn't scared. She *believed*. Okay, so she believed in an eldritch god—who was real, so points there, but still—but she believed in what we were doing. Maybe she even believed in me a little. The Qs looming up like fever dreams faded and I concentrated on the solidity of her hand.

Up ahead, Team Swords disappeared through the unmarked door that led into the D.U.M.B. No way back now. We were locked in. Riley squeezed my hand once and let me go. "Let's do this," I said. I don't think I stuttered too much.

Over my two lives, I had walked into places where entire cults wanted me dead. And okay, it didn't always turn out great, but I did it and lived to tell the tale. Riley might not have known that, but her squeeze reminded me that I didn't need to be that guy. I could just pretend to be him for the next hour or so. And besides, it wasn't like I had to pretend about much of anything once I was done. So I sucked in a deep breath, squared my shoulders and marched into the dragon's lair.

The door opened to a hallway, as institutional blue-gray as the rest of the airport, the kind of color that makes it easy to forget you can paint walls things like purple or pink. At the end, an elevator waited like an executioner. My heart was still working on the tick-tick-boom, and I did my best to focus on the hour later when all of this was someone else's problem.

We hit the button for the elevator. I flexed my hands once, but no more than that. I didn't need anyone looking at them too much. I always had good hands. After my exile, they were out of practice. I hadn't done a real lift in a while. The stuff I was doing wouldn't be overly complicated, but a secret military base surrounded by black ops mercenaries is never the ideal place for card tricks.

The elevator opened up, empty. That meant that Team Swords was at the guard station. So now I was on the hook for three more lives, which was good. That would keep the pressure off.

The elevator dropped a few floors and the door slid open. Men with guns were waiting. Two of them, dressed like they should be shooting up some small desert town halfway across the world, stood between the entryway and a corridor that led deeper into the facility. One of them—his nametag said TUCKER—was directly obstructing Team Swords, while the other tapped at a computer terminal. Tucker wore a look on that tightrope between exasperation and fear that said he regretted trying to obstruct Lara from a place she wanted to go. I might not have a ton of sympathy for military contractors in general, but I had a bit for him then. Hasim, for his part, stayed quiet, ready to push the cage containing my spirit guide as soon as he got the word.

"—Hermetic Secret Service and if you think I'm keeping this monster in my car you need to have your head checked!" Lara barked, waving a badge around. The badge was mine, and it was legit, or it had been. It didn't have even a fraction of the authority we were pretending it had, but that's hardly the point. Shove a tiny copper shield in someone's face and watch how quickly instinct takes over. Hell, that's why fascism worked so readily.

"Hey," I called over to the guards. "We're from hex support."

"One second," said Tucker. He faced her wearily. "We don't have any record of a prisoner transfer."

"Does this look like a prisoner to you?" she demanded. "This little bastard was out around Boulder turning the local livestock into a Luby's. We already have more sightings than HQ can clean up!"

"I'm sorry, I don't want to interrupt, but we're already late, and we really need to go over these new standards," I broke in.

Of course, I wasn't sorry. This was the whole idea. Hasim would tell you that the human body has weaknesses. It's the reason you kill people by wrapping piano wire around their necks as opposed to their self-esteem. Although, I suppose if you wrapped enough around the latter, eventually depression would do the work for you, not to belabor the metaphor. Hasim's skillset involved making the human body fail, usually by hitting one of those weak points with something hard and sharp. Mine—and Lara's—were more organizational than that.

Groups of people, whether they were cults, secret societies, or supernatural prisons under large airports have weak spots too. And just like the weak spot of the human body being the mewling thing we use to interact with the world—you know, the head and neck—the weak spot is wherever that organization interfaces with the rest of the world. This is the spot that needs to be the most secure and is the least able to deal with something as simple as too many things at once.

"What's your name?"

I waved some old credentials at him. I was glad I hung onto all my old IDs then, let me tell you. "Colin Reznick. Like I said, hex support."

"Excuse me, sir?" Lara said, turning to me. "Until you got a monster in a damn cage that these two jokers won't take, can you sit back?"

"Hey, I'm late too, lady. I got a job. Excuse me, guard? Call your on-site guy."

"On-site guy?"

"Yeah, whoever's in charge of your hexes. Your warding! You have a guy, right? I didn't just fly to goddamn Denver to find out you don't have a guy?" I gave Riley a frustrated shrug. She returned it, obviously fighting a smile.

"I don't care about hexes. You think hexes can do a single thing against this?" Lara demanded. "You know what it did? It ate every chicken, sheep, goat, and cow in a hundred mile radius. When we found it, it was in the middle of trying to eat up an old Bob's Big Boy statue."

"I *hope* it was eating it," Hasim mumbled.

"Well, any way you slice it, that Bob isn't the same man he used to be."

"Miss, I don't have any recor—"

"Fantastic," I broke in. "Look, just call the guy on staff. He got the email. Reznick. R-E-Z-N-"

"There isn't a *record* because we just caught the damn thing!" Lara shouted. She jostled Pud's cage, and Riley sucked in a breath. What we knew and what they didn't was that we'd sawed through a good chunk of the back bars. One good hit, and the cage was a convertible. Thankfully, the cage held. Pud played the part, though, snarling and yowling like an alley cat in a tilt-a-whirl.

"Beau, call the freak, would you?" The guard still in the booth— that was Beau, I guess—picked up a phone wired to his console.

"That's an HR complaint waiting to happen, my dude," Riley called.

"She should know," I said. "Because of her, we all had to sit through sensiti—"

"Excuse me," Lara said. "Do *you* have a monster in a cage? No? Well, everybody who doesn't have a monster in a cage needs to shut the hell up."

Beau hung up. "Freak's on his way. Donnie, why don't we just...I mean, we got a whole pen of the little bastards in back there. Brass don't give a shit if we throw one more in."

"Listen to Beau," Lara said. "Beau knows where the Pope shits in the buckwheat."

"In the *woods*," I corrected. "Popes shit in the woods."

"I always pictured them going in those big hats," Riley said.

A figure grumpily turned the corner of one of the side passages, walking at us with the agitated quickness of a man angry about someone telling him how to do his job. He had a bowlegged stance, and kept his arms cocked at the same angle. By the looks of him, he was skinny as a collection of reeds. He was dressed a lot like us, in a checked shirt and a pair of chinos, but as he got close enough to make out his features, I saw why they might have called him the name. He wasn't especially funny looking—he had a kind of round Ozarks face and a pleasant smoothness to his features. No, it was because every inch of exposed skin was tattooed with magical runes. Made the smiling headshot on the ID card clipped to his shirt pocket pretty distinctive.

"What's so important you needed to call me right now?"

"Ah, Fred, these two say they're from HQ and—"

"You know, the monster didn't suddenly vanish," Lara snapped.

"What's that?" Fred asked, pointing at the cage.

Lara flipped up the sheet, showing Pud. "The terror of the high plains."

Fred snorted. "Escort them back to the holding pens. Put this one in with the others." He shook his head, muttering, "I swear, it's like I have to think of everything."

"Hi," I said, stepping forward and thrusting my hand out. "Colin Reznick. HQ sent us over with new protocols for..." I dropped to a mutter, leaning in, "Shub-Internet." What Fred didn't catch was me lifting his ID. Pulled it right off his shirt and slipped it into a hip pocket.

"Why?" he snapped. "It's contained fine."

"Don't ask me," I said. "I do what they tell me."

"Fine, fine. Come this way." He started down the hall, and Riley and I fell in behind him. We were in. I couldn't quite believe it. There was still a ton of space for this thing to go hilariously wrong, but for the time being, it was cream cheese.

Fred led us past multiple patrols, all men in camo, toting assault rifles and generally looking bored. Soon the hallway had heavy doors on either wall, each one with an armored window. I didn't look, mostly because I had to pretend I was as jaded as the government sorcerer leading us.

"Do you mind my asking what you were up to when they called?"

"I was cataloguing the contents of...how familiar are you with the Holliday Vanishing?"

"A little. Whole town in Wyoming just disappeared, right?"

"We have a dollhouse recovered from the town before cleansing, and periodically, the pieces move around on their own."

"Move around?" Riley asked.

"Exactly what it sounds like," Fred said. "So you tell me, what are these new security measures? Because I am fully qualified, you know. I might not have a degree in computer science, but I have experience. Relevant experience. I've been locking that thing up since we got it. And you want to talk runes?"

"I can see you're very into runes," I said.

"You work with as many anomalies as I do, warding yourself starts to seem like a bare minimum, believe me."

"I do," I said, holding my hand up in supplication, "and we're not trying to step on your toes here. We're just coming in to make sure everything is up to the new standards."

"Like we need *new* standards. Either one of you ever work with Shub-Internet?"

"I've encountered and successfully bound several of its spawn," Riley said.

"Spawn," he snorted. "How?" Riley tipped up her clipboard, showing off the top sheet. It was scrawled with lines of code, alternating with a series of occult symbols. I didn't have the foggiest clue as to what it meant, but it looked good. Fred's eyes widened. "Oh. Oh, well then. Why didn't you say so?" He started walking faster.

I looked at Riley. She shrugged, then wiggled her fingers like she was casting a spell.

"You weren't one of those that caught the damned thing to begin with then?" Fred asked.

"Nope. How did that even happen?"

"It managed to get into the main server of a porn company out in the San Fernando Valley. They only noticed because half of their movies were gone and the other half were...changed. Still don't know how the hell it did that. The thing stayed in there, just feasting, apparently. Like a pig that gets caught in a fence, but eats so much it can't get back out. The wet boys who caught it brought the whole server wrapped in police tape covered in every ward you can imagine. Looked like gang tags from Rivendell."

"Sounds like you got lucky," Riley said.

"When it comes to an entity like that, there's only getting lucky. Otherwise, it slips away."

"How do you feed it?" I asked.

"Feed it? It doesn't need to eat. It's not alive."

The look of horror on Riley's face could have frozen magma. "It *needs* to eat."

"So what you're telling me is that Shub-Internet has been rotting in an oubliette for years and it's starving. That's *awesome*," I said. See, I said things could still go wrong.

"Security risk in feeding it. Besides, what does the sentient internet even eat?" Fred snorted.

"Porn!" Riley squeaked.

"Yeah," I said. "Why do you think there's so much of it?"

"Because we're disgusting apes who will use any excuse to paw ourselves?"

"Okay, so there's that."

"Y'know, if you get rid of porn, people start eroticizing weird shit," Riley said.

"I don't know a damn thing about that," Fred said in a tone that suggested he knew intimately what she meant. "Anyway, here we are."

We stopped in front of a door, but this one had a large window next to it, showing off an antechamber with two more armed guards. The lights inside were dimmed and red-tinged, either because that was somehow helpful in containing the idiot god, or just because they wanted it to look more ominous. Riley and I exchanged a look. We hadn't been expecting another layer of security.

"And Shub-Internet is..."

Fred gestured to the antechamber. "The server is behind that door. Here, I'll let you in and show you what we..." That was right about when I noticed I was going to have to plant his ID on him. I was working out the logistics, but the universe had other ideas. A klaxon hacked the air right in two. Swirling red lights gave everything that festive air of a police riot.

Fred's face fell in confusion, looking at the lights like they were the ones breaking in. "The hell is that?" He ran two steps down the hallway, stopped and turned. "Wait here!" He jogged around a corner and out of sight.

"Did you signal the others?" I asked.

Riley shook her head. We'd expected *something* when Pud broke out of his cage and started his rampage. The klaxons felt like overkill. "No. Maybe Pud got out early?"

I peeked through the window. The two guards were engaged in intense conversation, most likely over whether they should leave their posts. When two men with assault rifles are in a debate, I generally like to keep out of it, but I knew I would have to get past them eventually, and siccing them on whatever caused the commotion seemed like a good bit of serendipity.

Right as I went to the mechanical lock, a figure turned the corner.

There's something about seeing a completely unexpected thing that roots you to the spot. Your brain reboots as it tries to contextualize something that, rationally, has no context. I have a clear memory of the figure walking in slo-mo, but that had to have been edited in after the fact. My mind was deciding that this bullshit had to be a movie, because if this was reality then there wasn't much we could do about staying sane.

The figure was probably a man, which I admit was guesswork

thanks to the concealing nature of the outfit, but I had to believe no woman possessed the complete lack of self-awareness to be dressed like that. He wore jungle camouflage fatigues, which stood out nicely in the institutional surroundings, under body armor emblazoned with a Punisher skull. His face was entirely covered with a skull bandanna pulled over his nose to fit snugly below his iridescent mirrored shades. He topped it off with a helmet mounted with a GoPro. The helmet even had #DeathsHeadPatriot scrawled in white along the front and sides; I'm guessing to follow his massacres on social media. He raised an AR-15 at Riley and me, and barked something, but I couldn't hear him over the blood pounding in my ears. About five minutes ago, he'd been milling around with like-minded fascists upstairs and now he was about to commit a double murder.

This was far from the first time I had a gun pointed at me. Not great for my mental health, but it did give me an advantage over regular people who spent their lives never wondering if an armed maniac was going to cut this particular Arby's trip short. Riley was entirely frozen next to me. She'd stand rooted to the spot while this Punisher-cosplaying fuckface put a bunch of holes through her, and the world would be poorer for it.

I grabbed Riley and ran for the door across the hall. Maybe my brain had managed to register the lack of keycard security, because that's what saved us. The gun barked, sending hot pinpoints of wind streaking past us. We slammed through the door, falling onto floor of the room beyond. A breakroom, as it turned out, complete with vending machines, tables and chairs, a fridge, and a corkboard advertising paintball weekends and someone's ska-jazz fusion band.

"Riley, are you hit?" I got to my knees. She was partly under me, but thank Shub-Internet, she was moving. She flopped over, and for a heart-stopping moment, I imagined a sucking hole in her chest. Another corpse we could add to my butcher's bill.

My breath came back when I didn't see any blood, not even one of those wounds that waits until you think everything is okay to start bleeding.

"I don't think...I don't think he got me." She was trembling all over, but her eyes were clear. She was dealing with what happened, or more likely, filing it away so she could deal with it later. The first time I'd been shot at, I got the hell out of that Brotherhood of the Magic Bullet meeting and spent the evening shivering under a scalding hot showerhead thinking I'd never be warm again.

I moved back, letting her sit up. "Oh shit," she said.

"Where are you hit?"

"I'm not," she said. Then she held up the clipboard. Two holes had been neatly punched in the back.

"Oh shit," I agreed.

She opened it up, revealing that the laptop we'd brought entirely for the purpose of smuggling Shub-Internet out, now had two mashed up copper slugs in it. We were so fucked.

WE DIDN'T HAVE a lot of time to dwell on our precise level of fuckedness, though it was somewhere between trapped-in-a-clown-college-at-night-while-wearing-cotton-candy-underpants and the-Predator-unexpectedly-coming-home-early-from-work-while-we-were-making-sweet-love-to-his-wife-of-twenty-years. The maniac coming up the hall hadn't stopped, and the approaching rat-a-tat-tats told us he planned to put holes in more than just Best Buy's cheapest laptop.

I hugged the Jurassic-aged coffee vending machine slouching next to the doorway. The damn thing was as solid as a roadblock. I gripped both sides and threw my entire weight into it, rocking it back and forth like we were at a Christian middle school dance and any second the vice principal was going to cruise by to remind us to leave room for the Holy Ghost. Riley scrambled to her feet and joined me; she cottoned to what I was up to pretty damn quick.

Every time G.I. Faux let loose another burst of fire, I fought the urge to flinch. Look, just because I've been shot at a truly distressing amount of times didn't mean I liked it. Plus, I didn't want to be killed by that asshole out there. That would have been truly humiliating.

The machine rocked higher and higher, poised on its point of balance, but not quite ready to topple. Outside, the pop-pop-pop of the assault rifle closed in. Then the coffee machine went up on one side and hung there for a moment like LeBron James soaring in for a dunk before crashing to the floor. The front glass sprouted lightning bolt cracks. We had slain the beast and barricaded the door.

A second later, the handle rattled, followed by the insistent thump of a shoulder being thrown into the door. I stepped behind the wall and a moment later pulled a frozen Riley over to me. Bullets punched through the breakroom door.

"Come on," I said. I dropped to the floor and she did the same, and we army crawled for the exit on the far side of the room.

Behind us, the shooter rattled and raged, but the coffee machine effectively stymied him. I reached up and opened the door on the other side as silently as I could, and peeked out. This looked to be an office area, complete with a cube farm, desks, filing cabinets, and even a water cooler. No shooters. We closed the door behind us, muffling the frantic rage of the gunman.

An agonized moan drifted out somewhere from the cubicles. I followed it to one of the main aisles, staying low. A streak of gore ran from the other side, forming a perfect snail trail leading right into one of the cubes. You didn't need to be Kraven the Hunter to track that. I crept to it and peeked in. The source was a man, dressed not too differently than I was, except for the bullethole in his shoulder. When our eyes met he nearly screamed. I put a finger to my lips. We compromised when he merely squeaked.

"It's okay," I said, slipping into the cube with him. "We're friends. Well, maybe that's pushing it. We're not going to hurt you."

"Terrorists," he gasped. "Terrorists in the building."

"Sure looks that way." I pulled off the dress shirt, leaving only my undershirt between me and the air conditioned atmosphere. I found a letter opener on the desk and cut along the stitching of the sleeve, took the mass of it, wadded it up and put it to the wound. "Hold there, as hard as you can take."

"Aren't you going to pull the bullet out?"

"God no. If I started rummaging around in your arm, I'd probably kill you and I'd definitely give you more nerve damage than you've already got. The bullet's fine where it is. You've sprung a leak and we just need to plug that until you can get to a doctor."

"Oh God, I'm gonna die," he moaned.

"In a philosophical, 'we're all just decaying meat on this crazy marble' way, sure. But if you shut the fuck up and do what I say, you should be fine. What we need to do is stop the bleeding and then stash you in a cubicle that doesn't have a giant streak advertising where you've been. Sound good?" He nodded. "So, like I said, hold onto this as tight as you can stand."

He grimaced. "Hurts."

"I hope so. There's a bullet in there." He laughed, then winced. I wrapped the sleeve around his shoulder, then moved his hand, and tied the whole thing in place. He groaned in pain. "Okay, now for step two."

I slunk under one shoulder and braced myself. With difficulty, and significant help from Riley steadying him, we got to our feet and moved to another cubicle. I set him gently on the floor where he crawled beneath the desk. "If I can, I'll send help," I said. "In the meantime, sit tight and think small thoughts."

"Thank you. Who *are* you guys?"

"Hex support," Riley said.

We left him there, staying low, and headed for the door at the other end of the room. Shouting and gunfire echoed up the hallways. I couldn't make out individual words, but the tone sounded disbelieving and celebratory. I wasn't a fan of that combo.

"Okay, how do we unfuck this?" I asked. "We need a new laptop?"

"What? Oh, right. Yes, that would do it."

"We both have phones. Is that enough space to hold Shub-Internet?"

She shook her head. "We'd need more phones. Or a tablet. Something like that. We could upload it onto those, then when we're out of here, I can combine the pieces into what we need."

"There we go."

"Give me your phone," she said. "I need to wipe it. Was there anything on here you needed?"

I hesitated, my hand quivering. The last picture I had of Mina would be gone. I'd have lost her for real and forever. This job was more important than my sentimentality. I could keep her in my memory. I forced my hand into my pocket to withdraw the phone, unlock it, and held it out to Riley. "Nope," I said with what I hoped was a light enough tone. She tapped at the phone, handed it back, and did the same to hers. The device felt brittle in my hand. The screen said it was reverting to factory settings. When it had those pictures on it, it had still mattered. It had been more than a mere object. Now it was a brick of nothing.

"We need to put some porn on it," she said. "Shouldn't need much, after what Fred said. I think I overprepared the laptop to be honest."

"Porn? How? We can't get to the internet from here."

She looked at me like she'd caught me trying to eat soup with a fork. Then, deliberately, she put her phone down the front of her pants and I heard the fake camera shutter sound.

"Well, how was I supposed to think of that?"

"Haven't you ever sent a dick pic?"

"Of course not!"

"You're about to send your first one."

"What about you? You can…"

"It's your phone. Plus, this offends me as a professional. You're lucky I took one."

"Fine." I stuck the phone down my pants and got a snap of my junk. "I've always wanted to send a dick pic to Cthulhu."

We still needed one more device. Riley and I hit the desks, ransacking every cube in hopes of finding a random phone, a tablet, anything. Our wounded friend didn't have his phone on him, but in between gasps pointed us over to Processing, which was the office across the hall. I told him to sit tight, even though he didn't really have a say in the matter.

We crept to the far doorway and I cracked it. Voices and scattered gunshots came louder, but I didn't see any of their sources. I kicked off my shoes and pulled off my socks.

"What are you doing?" Riley asked.

"Floors outside. When we're off the carpets, I want to be quiet."

"I'm keeping them on," she said dubiously.

I poked my head out. "It's clear." We flitted across the hallway to the door on the other side. A Quackenbush Security man lay in a pool of blood against the wall. He wasn't getting up. I went to his body and pulled the walkie talkie off his belt. He didn't have his phone either.

"Where the fuck is it?" came a voice from the hall somewhere behind us, too loud and too close. I shouldered my way into Processing and was relieved to find no one in there. A desk sat dead center. I slid over that, just catching myself before landing on the dead woman behind it. She'd been in her fifties or so, a substitute teacher who happened to be wearing a vest made of raw hamburger. Whoever shot her had used the whole clip. Gore splashed the desk in front of her, the tables and filing cabinets behind. A pool of crimson spread around her.

I let myself down just out of range of the blood. "Careful," I warned Riley. She slithered across the desk and gasped when she saw the ruin of poor Mrs. Carruthers the algebra teacher. She took a deep breath and dropped down behind the desk next to me, shrinking from the spreading stain of blood. We waited in silence for the inevitable sound of the door opening.

The voices outside got closer and closer, the words muddy with the wall between us, or maybe that was just the roar of blood in my ears. The door banged open, and I could *feel* them in the room. "Nope. Another damn office."

"You sure?"

"Yeah, I know the difference."

The door closed, and both Riley and I learned to breathe again. I crept to a small alcove between a filing cabinet and a supply closet and clicked on the walkie. As quietly as I could: "Swords, come in, Swords, over." I repeated it a few more times, before,

"Pentacles, is that you?" Lara's voice.

"You're alive."

"So far. When did this place turn into a country club turkey shoot?"

"Looks like that's what the assholes upstairs were here to do," I said. "Do you have Hasim and Pud?"

"Yeah, they're fine. Couple of those militia guys aren't, if you get my meaning."

"Can you get out?"

"The hell you say."

"Your job is done."

"Is yours?"

"Minor setback. Turns out laptops aren't bulletproof. We're working on a solution."

"We'll meet up with you. Help out."

"No, just get out of here. We'll rendezvous upstairs."

"Bob, this job is tits up. You need to get that girl out of there before one of these Nazis does something to her."

"Bullshit. We can still do this thing."

"Put the techwitch on."

I handed the walkie to Riley. "Hi?" Riley said.

"You on board with this?"

She took a deep breath. "Yeah. I'm okay. We're on it."

"Fuckin' fine. If you two get your dumb asses killed, don't expect me to cry at the funeral."

"Ten-four," Riley said, then shrugged, mouthing to me *I don't know what to say.*

"One more thing. Did that asshole strip down to his undershirt at the first available opportunity?"

"How could you possibly know that?"

"And is he wearing shoes?"

"Seriously, do you have a camera in here?"

"Bob, you complete fucking moron."

I grabbed the walkie, I couldn't help myself. "I'm in *Die Hard*!" I squeaked. Riley stared at me in disbelief.

"This is real life," Lara said with elaborate patience.

"It's even Christmas!"

"*Die Hard* was on Christmas Eve."

"Technically you're in an airport so this is *Die Hard 2*," Hasim's voice came over the line.

"It's close enough!" I snapped.

"Oh shut the fuck up," Lara said. "I need to know you're taking this seriously. You're in an underground military base surrounded by armed terrorists who'd be only too happy to kill you."

"Yippie ki yay, chupacabra."

"Oh, Jesus."

The door thundered inward. "Reach for the sky, pedos!" came a shout from the front of the room. I clicked off the walkie talkie, and in the quiet after the command, that click echoed. "Who's there? Braxton, you hear something?"

I peeked up over the table and got my first glimpse of the two of them. They looked somewhat like the Punisher cosplayer who blew holes in our laptop. One wore black coveralls, the other desert camo, and neither looked like they fit particularly well. Their body armor was good quality too, and I was perhaps strangely relieved not to see a camera on either one. Only one wore a helmet, the other a backwards MAGA cap. One covered the lower half of his face with a skull bandana, the other an American flag. Of the most concern was the favorite gun of any mass shooter, the AR-15s they packed with all the attention to gun safety of Vincent Vega ready to shoot Marvin in the face.

"Use my codename. What's wrong with you?"

"Shit, sorry. Rodrick Gland, did you hear something?"

"We're in a deep state rat maze, and you're using real names. Fuck, Jayden, what's wrong with you?"

"You just used my name!"

"Whatever, Patriot Gunner Jesus is Lord Hashtag WW1WGA is too long to say every time."

"You could just say Patriot."

"I say that, everyone in here that's not one of these globalist pedos will turn around. It's not good for opsec. But seriously. I heard something in there."

"Anybody in here?" called Jayden. "Come out, we won't hurt you." It was one of the least convincing promises I've ever received, and I once heard three senators sing "Never Gonna Give You Up" at a DC karaoke night. Anybody who leaves the house carrying a long gun is waiting for the flimsiest excuse to use it.

Riley was completely frozen, deer-in-the-headlights, coed-in-the-hockey-mask. It dawned on me that it was not an unreasonable assumption that a bunch of white guys with guns might be the kind of terror she'd lived with since she was very small and heard about what happened to her ancestors. I put my hand on hers and gave it a soft squeeze. Maybe I could return some of that strength she'd given me on the way in. She started up like a stalled motor, her big eyes flicking to mine. I gave her a slow nod and hoped my face showed confidence I hadn't felt in years.

"Could be you imagined it," Braxton said. These two had accents, subtle ones that only sprung up in the wealthier suburbs. The internet had largely flattened American dialects, but the well-off always affect something, just so they can signal to the plebes and to each other that they're better. It's a laziness to the vowels that suggests you should do half the work of finishing their thought for them.

"I'm telling you, I didn't."

"Could you imagine if we found the entrance?"

"We'd be heroes. Bet we could get on Sander Siegel's show."

Braxton snorted. "Sander Siegel's a closet globalist. He doesn't believe in Q."

"Yeah he does! He calls us patriots!"

"What else is he supposed to call us?" Braxton wondered. I had a few thoughts.

I thought about explaining to them how easy it is to get on Sander's show, but I didn't think they'd appreciate that little revelation. Plus, whether Sander believed in Q was immaterial: it was horning in on his grift, but enough of his audience believed, so he couldn't kick too much. The two fascists poked around the front desk, edging closer to the side that lifted up and allowed entry into this back area.

Jayden lifted up the counter. He called out into the darkness where Riley and I huddled like terrified forest animals. "Anybody back there? Last chance now."

We didn't take him up on the opportunity. The center of the room was a collection of tables, desks and filing cabinets—an effective barrier, if a small one. Jayden and Braxton crept down the front way. "Got a body over here."

"Globalist pedo?"

"Must be."

The gunshots were like a thunderstorm in the room. Riley jumped, clamping a hand over her mouth to push back the scream. The crack from the gun reverberated, pounding painfully at my eardrums. When the sound reluctantly faded, it left a whine in its place.

"What the fuck, dude?"

"She was a pedo!"

"She was also dead."

"Yeah, well now she's super-dead."

"You fucking idiot. I can't hear a fucking thing anymore!" Jayden whined. I could barely hear him. I shook my head, trying to clear it, but the whine stuck around. *Thanks, Braxton, you trigger-happy idiot.*

The two fascists made their way down one side, and Riley and I kept the central island between us and them. Riley was in as bad shape as I was, wincing and fiddling with her ears whenever we weren't moving on all fours. At least the pain gave us a chance to focus on anything besides the two armed men hunting us. We stayed low, crawling, trying to keep pace with footsteps we could barely hear. I peeked up over the side, and there they were, creeping along like death, their rifles out like they'd seen done in the movies.

"What if they already found it?" Braxton nearly shouted.

"If somebody found it, we'd hear them," Jayden said. "Imagine you're a sex slave, right?"

"Done."

Jayden paused, straightened, and stared at Braxton. For the first time, I was disappointed that I couldn't read their faces. "Okay, you escape your slave pens, what are you gonna do? It's like the end of *Temple of Doom.* You're gonna sprint out of there, screaming the whole time, and you're not stopping until you're in the arms of your parents."

"It won't be exactly like *Temple of Doom.*"

"Why not?"

"Those kids were...I don't know...Indians?"

"We have Indians here."

"No, convenience stores, not scalping."

"Right, yeah. These would be white kids. I heard the Cabal likes blond kids best. I mean, you can get an Indian kid for like a buck, a buck fifty maybe. I'm guessing."

"Yeah," Braxton agreed. "It's the white kids they really want."

I didn't have time to really unpack the layers there, but hoo boy. There was a lot going on, and it wasn't getting solved anytime soon.

We reached the entryway, where a section of desk could be lifted and poor Mrs. Carruthers could go to the breakroom. I slunk underneath it, then turned. Riley followed. And, of course, that's when things got bad.

"Hey!" I couldn't tell if it was Braxton or Jayden over the budding tinnitus, but one of them had spotted us. Riley skittered over the last bit of floor and the world exploded again. The specific impacts of the bullets were impossible to track beyond the unhelpful blanket of "every- where." I'd been shot at enough to keep my wits about me, and they said one thing: if we moved, we might get hit. If we froze, we were 100% dead. I could see Riley tombing up, wanting to take the easy way, so I grabbed her hand and hauled. She followed, and so did the bullets, desk and floor popping all around us.

But the fun thing about firing fully automatic is that there aren't as many bullets as you think there are. It's not like the movies where Bruce Willis can just sort of spray the area for solid minutes. It was a few seconds—which can feel a lot longer when it's coming your way—and then the weapon clicked dry. Braxton and Jayden didn't know that, judging by the panicked sounds of reloading. It gave Riley and me the time to slip out the door.

The hallway was empty. I bolted for the door of the other office, but that cracked open from someone using it on the other side. I skidded and turned, sprinting down the hall with Riley following. We turned a corner, just in time to hear Braxton shout, "He's over—" Whatever he said next was erased with a cascade of gunfire. There was a lesson some- where in all of that about proper gun safety, but now wasn't the time to talk about it.

Riley and I hit a T-intersection. I turned left and around the corner a booming voice bellowed, *"Be not afraid!"*

"Oh fuck," I said, turning around and collecting Riley.

"What?" she said.

"Not that way. *Really* not that way."

We went right. A door—a welcoming door with a keycard lock— waited. I shoved Fred's card in the reader, the light went from red to green and the lock clicked. I pulled the heavy door open, and Riley and I slipped inside. Fluorescent lights flickered on, revealing rows of metal shelves, filled with cardboard boxes and plastic bags. It looked like an evidence room.

Riley had her back to the wall, sucking breath, still clutching her perforated clipboard. She either hadn't thought to drop it, or it had become some kind of security blanket. Hell, it had saved her once. Maybe hanging onto it was the smart move.

"You're bleeding," I said, indicating a laceration on her arm.

"You should talk," she said, nodding to my head. I touched my forehead and found blood gumming up my hairline. Another wound ran over my left foot. As though acknowledging the wounds made them real, they suddenly stung. I thought about the bullets turning things like desks and linoleum into shrapnel.

"You okay otherwise?"

She looked away. "Never been shot at before."

"It's not fun. You handled yourself well. First time it happened to me, I filled my pants up with piss. You could have sailed out of my jeans."

"I...I peed a little."

"No shame in that."

"You been shot at a lot?"

"I've been hunted for sport."

"You *what*?"

"Most dangerous game. I used to have a reputation. It was mostly lies, but I used it so that all the psychos would think twice about tangling with me, even if I've never won a fight in my life. So this rich guy—Bavarian Illuminati, so the real deal, got his money when a distant ancestor hit a bunch of people with a mace or something—he decides he wants to hunt this fixer he's heard keeps Lady Luck in his pocket. He has his goons kidnap me, drive me out to this ritzy estate up in Big Bear, and he hunts me, with rifles and dogs and shit."

"You're joking."

"I wish. Not my favorite night, but you want to know the worst part?"

"This wasn't the worst part?"

"After I get out of there, maybe like six months later, I'm doing another job—this black bag thing for Malta—and guess who I run into?"

"The rich asshole?"

"You've never had an awkward moment until you've run into the guy who hunted you in a social setting."

In spite of the seething terror we'd been living with, she giggled. "What'd you do?"

"I made a lot of passive aggressive hunting comments, and I planted a fake hoodoo bag on him. Hopefully he lost a night or two of sleep." She laughed again, and I could see some of the tension uncoiling from her body. "We're almost done here. Only two more things and we can go."

"Thanks, B," she said.

"Don't mention it. What do you say we ransack this place?"

"This where they confiscate stuff from prisoners?"

"That'd be my guess."

We commenced ransacking, pausing only when the commotion outside got closer than we would have liked. We froze solid, cocking our heads, hunting for the sound that would indicate that one of the maniacs outside had zeroed in on this place.

"Hey, B? Those two fratboys, they thought this place was some kind of human trafficking operation?"

"That's about right, yeah. Apparently they got it into their heads that this was where the bad guys keep pens of kidnapped children to await their eventual fate of being molested and eaten."

"They can't *really* believe that."

"It's hard to say what anyone actually believes. But it does seem awful convenient that the stuff they say they believe just gives them the exact right excuse to do what they always wanted to do. 'Oh, you always hated this one specific group? Pretty cool that they're such monsters you can shoot them and still sleep soundly in the knowledge that you're a good Christian.' The fact that they never seem to believe that the people who agree with them politically are up to the same stuff kind of says it all."

"The human mind is capable of some amazing gymnastics."

"You're not kidding." I opened up one of the boxes and came face to face with an anime body pillow and more Bazooka bubble gum than anyone could consume in a lifetime. "Tell me you're having some luck."

"No...wait." Rustling came from her side of the room. "Come on come on be what I think you are," she murmured. "Fucking jackpot!" Riley emerged waggling a tablet. She hooked it to her portable charger and had broken in and wiped it in nothing flat. She then hooked it to her phone. "Copying my shitty porn onto it," she said by way of explanation.

I went to the door and listened. Sounds ebbed and flowed like racist tides. When the hallway was as quiet as it was likely to get, I turned to Riley. "Ready?"

She gave me a grim-faced nod. I shouldered open the door.

The hall was a lot like how we'd left it, but someone had written WE THE PEOPLE in feces along one wall. I tried to imagine the dedication it would take to do that and came up short. In any case, the person who did needed to get more fiber in their diet.

We backtracked our way to Shub-Internet's cell, first making our way through the institutional hallways that were now strewn with the detritus of the invasion. A couple bodies, blood and sundry fluids, some spent bullet casings, and a lot of food wrappers. If we remembered one thing about the sacking of the Denver International D.U.M.B. it would be that a great deal of snacking was had. And the poop declaration. So, two things. The dead would be forgotten, because that's the way this world works.

We paused at corners, peeking around them, avoiding the few disorganized patrols we happened across. Whatever had happened looked to be winding down, and not because heavily-armed mercs were making an example of them. It felt like a party that had mostly run its course and everyone was slipping out before the clean-up.

When we went to the hallway between the first office we'd cut through and Processing, we found three dead fascists, cut down by gunfire. It looked like the aftermath of a Tarantino movie, one on the office side, and on the other, Braxton and Jayden. All three of them were dressed in the same ersatz uniform, though the one guy I didn't know had a cartoon frog emblazoned on his body armor.

We went around the long way and found the entrance to Shub-Internet's prison room. "Let's get this thing done," I said.

Fred's card got us into the first chamber, and then the second. The men who'd been guarding it were long gone. The first thing that hit me was the sound. I hadn't been expecting the room to be so goddamn loud, worse than the gunshots that still whined in my ears. The howl of the servers, amplified by the acoustics of the room, pounded me with a physical force. It was like the entity wanted us to know we weren't welcome.

Riley nudged me, handing over a pair of earplugs. She'd known, bless her. Those went into my ear canals and the cacophony got to a manageable level, but I swear I could now hear whispers at the edge of the wailing.

The second thing to hit me was the cold. There wasn't much I could do about that. Not after I'd stripped off my shirt and shoes. It was a freezer. I could survive that for a few minutes.

The server holding Shub-Internet towered in the center of the room. Racks and racks of circuit boards hung from the ceiling. Maybe it was functional, but I couldn't escape the idea that these idiots had caught a literal God and had displayed it like a prize marlin. Even if Shub-Internet wasn't really aware the way we understand it, I had to imagine it would want vengeance for that disrespect. Each board looked like a city in miniature where a hive mind forming the idiot God of the Internet could populate. And hunger.

The room was built around this prize, perhaps the most dangerous thing the government had ever caught. The walls were night black, etched with glowing runes, focusing the arcane power inward. The air was alive with something—maybe magical energy, maybe plain old electricity—but it made me feel like a bug who just realized that the ground he was walking on was flesh, and the owner of that flesh knew I was there.

Fred, assuming he was the one who had put these runes in place, came from an eclectic tradition. Examples from every magical tradition under the sun, and more than a few I couldn't ID, decorated the walls. If not for the computer hanging martyred in the middle of the room, this place would have been a wonderful set for an occult-themed serial killer.

Riley got to work. She hooked a cable up to the tablet and from there to one of the boards. She spent some time staring at the screen. How long? It's relative. When you're in a freezing room with a god while an army of white supremacists ran rampant outside, even a couple seconds can seem like geologic time. All I know is that sometime between five seconds and a thousand years later she broke into a grin, locked eyes with me, and shot a thumbs up. A few moments later, she unplugged the tablet, handed it to me, and motioned. I handed her my phone. She repeated the process for it, and this one was faster, and then the process again for her phone.

"*Got it,*" she mouthed.

I couldn't believe this had worked. I'd come up with a crazy plan to steal a god and it had somehow *worked*. For a second, I felt like a man worthy of being hunted for sport again.

We took out the earplugs, dropping them on the floor as we left the server room. The whole place had become a trashcan. No reason not to fit in.

"Now let's get the fuck out of here," Riley said.

"Couldn't have said it better myself," I said, opening up the door into the hallway.

And this was my fault. I'd let my guard down. I'd let myself feel good, like I wasn't the piece of shit who'd spent a year drinking his soul away. I'd thought I was someone.

"Hey, you! Freeze!"

Two of the militia guys looked like Braxton and Jayden and the others. There were more, average looking men and women, decked out in Q shirts and MAGA hats. All of them were filming or snapping pictures with their phones, or else they had cameras on their helmets. That's what this was for some of them, the pursuit of *content*, a digital grifter's lifeblood. They'd found it in a secret prison housing just about everything except what they were looking for.

"Riley, you need to run. Fast as you can," I murmured.

"They have guns! They'll shoot us."

"Don't worry about me. I can bluff them. I'll meet up with you topside. Now, please. *Run.*" I raised my voice, affecting an easy grin and waving. "Hey there, fellow patriots," I said. "Sack any good Deep State fortresses?" Riley, bless her, made a break for it.

"Hey! She's getting away!"

"Don't worry about her," I said, stepping between the barrel of one gun and Riley's back.

One of the militia guys demanded, "Why are you dressed like that?" and I could hear the confused frown in his voice.

"Because I'm in *Die Hard*," I said truthfully.

"It *is* Christmas," said one fascist.

"But we're in an airport," protested the other. "It's more *Die Hard 2*."

"Plus, *Die Hard* is on Christmas Eve, not Christmas Day," said a third.

"I like the one in Russia," decided a heavyset man in a shirt depicting an eagle grasping a Q in one hand and a gun in the other.

"No one likes that one," assured the first guy.

A finger pointed in my direction, and the voice carried queasy recognition. "Wait a minute! I know him! I saw him on PatriotNet! He's one of them! He's with the deep state!"

The guns came up. They didn't need much of an excuse, and had been hunting for one as soon as they slapped eyes on me. They were too late, though. It wasn't the militia guys that got me, it was the regular folks. The mob surged forward, and in a split second, a meat shield stood between me and the guns. Didn't help much, because that meat shield wanted my blood too. One of them planted a fist in my belly, and I folded up. Then came the hits and kicks, and pretty soon I found some darkness to hide in while they beat me.

chapter
twelve

CONSIDERING the amount of times I'd woken up beaten, bloody, and tied to a chair, you'd think I would have gotten used to it. Hell, I could break it down into quantifiable stages. First, I would surface from the kind of nightmare that's black and sticky like tar. Whatever torments had been wracking me—little devils that looked like Nixon prodding me with shrimp forks, say—would retreat into the murky depths of my memory, but the pain, the individual pinpricks from their utensils, those would keep right on stinging. My head would be thundering in its cracked case, and I'd get to wonder if my time unconscious hadn't cost me the ability to calculate tip on a bar tab. This step proceeded without any significant adjustment. I was momentarily grateful for the reassuring sameness of it all.

Second, I would open my eyes. That would touch off an avalanche of ache just beyond my orbital ridges, and whatever light was present would stick me harder than those Nixon devils. My vision would be blurry, mostly colors at first, until my eyes figured out how to focus again and the gum cleared away. The colors this time around were khaki and crimson. The strain in my back was thanks to my being slumped over. I was staring at my lap, now splotched with congealed blood. Breathing hurt too, like a screwdriver was sticking out of me, wiggling whenever I inhaled.

Step three was the worst. This was where I had to pull myself upright and have a look around, and hope I wasn't concussed so badly I'd vomit all over the place. This was right about the time I noticed I was cold, but not freezing. My ears still whined shrilly from the gunshots, but over that I could hear the banshee wail of wind through trees.

Okay, step three, for real this time. I lifted my head up, and my gorge climbed right up my throat. I swallowed, trying to adjust to the pitch and roll of this stormy sea I'd found myself on while my head thudded in time with my heartbeat. The whole thing felt like it would crack open if I didn't move gingerly enough. Ghostly fingers brushed my face, tickling me from the source of the stinging, leaving warm paths that quickly turned icy.

I blinked a few times, each one dropping a blurry veil from my eyes. I was in a utility closet. I was almost disappointed in its crushing mundanity. A secret lab, or maybe a bunker, that was more my speed. That's what you want, with an alien or an immortal German gearing up to interrogate you. I was in the suburbs, and not even particularly interesting suburbs. A broom and mop leaned against the wall next to me and a hot water heater filled up the rest. That at least was pleasant, a warmth over my skin that I was far from used to.

I wiggled my arms experimentally. They were behind my back, and, I found, handcuffed to a chair. Fun fact about handcuffs: they all use the same key. In the old days, I'd kept one hidden on my person for just such an occasion. In a pinch, I could open one up with a paperclip.

Of course, that was the old me. I didn't have a key, and I didn't have a paperclip. Hell, I didn't have a chance. Just to hammer that home, my legs were tied to the chair legs, making movement impossible.

Maybe a foot or two in front of me was a white door. I stared at it, trying to make sense of where the hell I was. I didn't remember all of the beating; I was pretty sure of that. They'd worked me over good. It would have been easier to identify a point on my body that *didn't* hurt. Every time I shifted a new pain point flared up. The screwdriver in my side noodled around and I hunted for a way to not breathe. My nose sluggishly leaked blood into my beard. A couple of my teeth were loose like old boards in a condemned house. Never get on the wrong side of an angry mob is my point, I guess.

As I was cataloguing my frankly depressing array of injuries, the door opened to reveal a good-looking blonde woman in her forties. She was dressed in a workout fleece and running pants, and though I never once doubted she got her steps in, I got the impression this was more about uniform than practicality. Her hair was pulled back into a bun so tight it was probably in the process of making diamonds. The way this woman looked—far too perky and put-together—I was suspicious instantly. She had the aura of someone who could go from cheerful to rattlesnake mean if the service wasn't to her exacting standards. Granted, that I was bound and beaten in what I assumed to be her utility closet might have had something to do with my overall negative impression.

Behind her, I caught a glimpse of a gleaming and spotless kitchen. Everything was white and pale wood with unobtrusive track lighting. Her good taste annoyed me.

"Oh good, you're awake," she said. The tone was right to convey concern, but the substance was entirely absent. It was an uncanny valley for voices—just close enough to reality to be disturbing. "You took some nasty hits on the head."

"Who are you?" I was somewhat relieved when the words came out more or less as I intended them to.

"Oh, don't hurt my feelings," she said, striking a pose. She was very attractive in an "I'm going to call the HOA on you if you don't get that grass down to a quarter inch" kind of way. I tried to place her. She clearly thought I *should* know her, and maybe if I managed to play her game I'd win a little goodwill. Had she been in a commercial? Was she a Real Housewife?

"The female lead in the last Neil Breen movie," I hazarded.

She laughed. "I don't even know who that is."

"Your loss. You're into QAnon."

Her laugh molted into a condescending smile. "There is no QAnon. There is Q and there are Anons." That was one of the cult shibboleths, and though I wasn't happy to hear it, at least it was expected. "You don't look like you're into lifestyle, are you?"

"That's putting it mildly."

"I'm Eagle Mama!" She said it like she was certain I was either winding her up or else I was just being silly.

"I'm really sorry, miss."

"It's Mrs."

"Still sorry."

She put her hands on her hips in a sitcom "What am I going to do with you?" way. I hoped it involved a bathroom and some water. I wouldn't say no to a blanket. "Well, if someone like you had been following me, I wouldn't be doing my job very well, would I?" She pulled her phone out of the pocket of her fleece, tapped it and held it in front of my face.

She was showing me an Instagram account. The picture was of an orange candle that looked like it should have other candles sacrificed to its elephantine corpulence. *Love the new apricot love from #Candlelight!* I stared at it in mute incomprehension. I felt like I was trying to solve the riddle of the Sphinx, but she'd asked me why the chicken crossed the road.

Eagle Mama scrolled down once. Now it was a selfie of her holding up some face cream. *My skin has never been smoother! Thanks, #BlushingBride!*

The truth hit me with a brutal right cross as the last vestiges of any belief in the inherent goodness of the universe was forcibly expelled from my soul in a single blow. It was the exact feeling a Russian mobster gets when he finds out the dog he ran over belonged to Keanu Reeves. "You're an influencer."

"I provide valuable insights on a number of wellness, fitness, and cosmetic properties," she said, pocketing her phone.

"Why couldn't you have been a CIA torturer?"

"Oh, I'd never let a representative of the deep state in here."

"That's probably smart."

She watched me with an unblinking stare that made me feel like an overpriced candle whose scent wasn't quite as advertised. "You're probably hungry," she decided.

"Thirsty more than hungry, but yes, please."

"Wait here," she said, and then laughed, like she'd caught herself by surprise with her little joke. I smiled at her and entertained fantasies of strangulation. She returned to the kitchen, shutting the door of the oubliette. Outside, the wind continued to howl.

When you're tied to a chair, there's a temptation to really take stock of the series of events that brought you to the situation. The human mind is always on the search for reason, for causality. "If I hadn't done X, Y, or Z, I wouldn't be in this situation." It's the same pattern recognition that drove a significant chunk of the world mad, a hunt for reason where emphatically there was none.

Didn't stop me from going through the steps, if only to find a way where this was all my fault. "If I hadn't tried to clean up my own mess, I wouldn't be in this situation" wasn't the kind of lesson I wanted to take away. I could have been back in Griffith Park, listening to Mikhail monotone his way through a string of unconnected nouns, poisoning myself with mash whiskey, ergot, and self-loathing. No, this was better. I had the ghost of a chance to fix things here. I just needed to figure out where the three devices containing Shub-Internet were. When the mob attacked me, I'd had two—the phone in my pocket and the tablet in my hand. Not to mention where exactly I was, and what this perky maniac wanted with me.

I cursed inwardly. Why hadn't I given the tablet to Riley? Because I was feeling my old self. I thought I could talk my way through an angry mob. I thought I could tap into the old magic that had let me walk between the raindrops. I'd put on a mask and thought it was my face. I'd ignored that I wasn't that guy anymore. I was a shed skin that hadn't figured out there wasn't a snake inside.

Eagle Mama returned holding a tray. My eyes went to the glass of water, tracking it all the way until she set it down in front of me. The water was fizzy with slices of cucumber floating in it. I didn't usually feel this homicidal, but a man can only be pushed so far. Still, my mouth was dry enough that I would have given motor oil a shot had she brought it.

"Undo my hands so I can eat?" I said.

She clucked her tongue. "I don't think so. I wasn't born yesterday."

"Could have fooled me. You look so young."

"Oh, I'm gonna have to watch out for you!"

I gave her what I hoped was my least creepy smile. "Can't blame a guy for trying."

The meal she brought me didn't look tasty, but it would photograph well. I think it was a sandwich whose bread had been replaced with kale. She'd posed it on the plate and napkin at such an artful angle, I'd be willing to bet that it was presently farming likes on her Instagram. *Got this keto-friendly wrap for the man I kidnapped! #Blessed.*

She held up the sandwich, and though it tasted like bitter dirt and my own blood, I ate it. The water was as refreshing as sparkling water ever is, which is not much. I didn't know if sparkling water was lying about being soda, or lying about being water, but it was one of those.

Through a bite, I asked her, "Can I have my stuff back?"

"What stuff?"

"My phone, for one."

She laughed and shook her head. "Oh, come on now. So you could call your pals in the deep state?"

"I wouldn't call them pals." *But I* would *call them.*

"No."

"There was a tablet."

"A tablet? I didn't see one of those."

"You found me..."

"...in that deep state prison under the airport, yes. Well, my husband found you."

"Did Mr. Mama happen to see a tablet?"

"Mr. Mama? Oh, he would not like that. He would not like that at all. Maybe you follow him! Patriot Bond?"

"I am one hundred percent certain that I don't."

"If you had, maybe you wouldn't be in the situation you are now."

"Yeah, I've been thinking about that. What *is* my situation exactly?"

She smiled at me. "My husband will talk to you when he finishes at work."

"It's Christmas."

"When you're a patriot, every day is a work day. Besides, patriots need encouragement on a day like today more than any other."

"Wait, it *is* Christmas, right?"

"For a few more hours. He'll be here when he can. Sit tight." She replaced the empty glass and plate on the tray and picked it up.

"Listen, it's pretty cold in here. Any chance you could bring me a blanket?"

Her smile never wavered. "You deserve a lot more than a little cold." The door shut with the finality of a black site prison cell.

I have spent a lot of long nights in my tenure, first as the Information Underground's gofer, then as its fixer. This was the longest. Whoever had flypapered me to this chair had done a damn good job, and I was out of my usual tricks. I'd let the skills rot. I was stuck in this damn closet and the cavalry wasn't coming.

The cold was the worst part. I could really only sit helplessly and shiver. Try to bunch up to squeeze some warmth out of my own body, only every time I did that, something in my chest ground together, and a bright lance of agony pushed me into a slightly less uncomfortable and colder position. I regretted leaving my footwear and my shirt, but the fact was, they wouldn't have done much.

The humiliation wasn't fun either. At a certain point in the night I gave up and pissed myself. The momentary relief helped alleviate some pain, and the warmth of my urine was almost a blanket for all of five minutes. But then it cooled off and I was left even colder than before.

The hammering in my head receded and I was seeing okay. I stopped feeling the sluggish track of blood down my face. I waited, miserable and afraid, in the dark.

The thing about living away from modern distractions, as I had for a year, is that it's boring. Our brains have gotten used to the constant stimulation of the internet. In fact, social media algorithms specifically farm our rage to make money. I'd gotten used to a lot of long, dark nights of the soul. Granted, not ones where I was freezing, beaten raw, and sitting in my piss, but it was the same ballpark. I started the night by running through old episodes of *Farscape* in my head. Then I moved into a catalogue of every rotten thing I'd done. I finished it off with an elaborate revenge fantasy. By the time white light seeped in from the under the door, I had lived for six lifetimes.

The closet door opened not long after. I was certain it didn't mean anything good for me, but at least it was a change. Eagle Mama was dressed in the same outfit as the previous night, albeit in different colors. The man with her, who I could only assume was Patriot Bond, was dressed like an investment banker. He looked like his favorite joke was a homophobic slur shouted at top volume. And, horror of horrors, he had Ronald Reagan's haircut. That son of a bitch. That used to be *my* thing. Although, these days it was an entirely different terrible haircut that could short circuit conservative brains.

"So, what do we have here?" he asked, smiling in the way he'd once heard it described in passing by a sociopath.

"I was just asking myself the same question." My voice was wobbly from, well, everything, but I'd be damned if I let these two see me sweat.

Eagle Mama wrinkled her nose. "Somebody had an accident."

"Yeah, the facilities here aren't great."

Patriot Bond walked over to me and squatted down on his haunches to look me in the eyes. "Who are you, really?"

"You wouldn't believe me if I told you."

"Try me. I've been researching the crimes of the deep state for years now. There's very little that could shock me."

"I'm Q."

Patriot Bond gaped at me, then burst into laughter. It was the first genuine thing I'd seen him do. "That's funny. Isn't that funny, hon?"

Eagle Mama tittered. "So funny."

"Help me out here," I said. "Who do *you* think I am?"

"Not Q!" Eagle Mama said.

"Common misconception anyway," Patriot Bond said. "Q isn't one man. He's several members of military intelligence. Are you a member of military intelligence?"

"More of an asset. At one time." I frowned. "If you don't know who I am, what am I doing in your closet? Hold on, are you two serial killers?"

They laughed again, enunciating each individual "ha" like dummies worked by an untalented ventriloquist. "No, we're not serial killers," Patriot Bond said.

"Imagine!" Eagle Mama agreed.

"I'm a day trader. Wifey here is an influencer."

"You can be those things and still have a crawlspace filled with dead Boy Scouts. It's called multitasking."

"You see," Patriot Bond said. "Notice how quickly he goes to child murder. Got a lot of experience with that, do you?"

"Can I make a guess here? You," I nodded at Patriot Bond,

"watched one of those YouTube 'documentaries' that's been floating around. Something spoke to your...I'll be generous and say your soul. So you started reading Q drops. Not on the actual site where Q posts, but on an aggregator, so you won't have to wade through the cesspool that is the chans. I bet you have it on your phone even. You showed them to the missus here and now the two of you are digital soldiers, posting memes and raiding the odd government building. And now you're both making a living on the grift."

"We're patriots," Patriot Bond said, confirming my story.

"Actually I—" Eagle Mama started, but Patriot Bond cut her off with a gesture. I suppose that amended things a bit. *She* had been patient zero—not him.

"How did you wind up at the base under the airport?" I asked. "Q didn't mention it."

"Q hasn't posted for months. The movement is beyond Q now," Patriot Bond said.

"Someone posted the call to action on this Facebook group we're in," Eagle Mama explained. "He said that one of the places they keep the kids for trafficking was under the Denver airport. See, they can get the kids in and out secretly on planes and there's all that weird stuff underground. Plus, the horse."

"Yeah, the horse was a dumb move," I said.

"What do you know about the horse?" Patriot Bond asked, narrowing his eyes.

"It's a bizarre statue. Attracts attention."

He was smug. "They can't resist signaling to each other. It's not enough that they kill children and drink their blood, but the Cabal has to do it in plain sight."

"Rub our noses in it," Eagle Mama said.

"Which is what I should do to you for making a mess on our floor," Patriot Bond said. He broke into that reptilian smile again, and I didn't doubt for a second he'd do whatever sick thing popped into his head. "Hon? Why don't you get the computer? About time to go live, isn't it?"

"You got it!"

She went back into the house as he pulled my phone from his

pocket, and held it up in front of me. "She told me you wanted this. I'm wondering why." He moved around behind me, and I felt him press my thumb against the screen. "What's on here that you need so...what the fuck is this?"

He held up the phone, displaying a picture of my junk. "That's my favorite picture of myself," I said. "It captures my poetic melancholy."

He pointed at me. "You're a freak." He poked at my phone. "This thing is broken."

"Yeah, I think I gave it a venereal disease when I took that pic."

He grimaced, turning the phone off, and slipped it gingerly into his pocket as though it was going to infect him. I tracked which pocket, just in case. "Fuckin' pervert," he hissed.

Eagle Mama came into the room before he could get really salty with me, carrying a laptop under one arm. "So, what's a pair of fascist kidnappers want with little old me?"

"Fascists," Patriot Bond snorted. "Call anyone you don't agree with a fascist."

"No, I call fascists fascists. There's a pretty clear definition, and if you were part of that raid on the airport, I'm comfortable lumping you in that box."

"We voted for Obama," Eagle Mama blurted. Then, with a guilty glance at Patriot Bond. "Well, *I* did. Before I found out about the Cabal and what he was up to, of course."

"That's not the slam dunk you think it is."

Patriot Bond broke in. "We just want freedom, like all Americans do. We want a strong military, a strong border, and we want to remove corruption from government."

"...and you're hunting a secret society of evildoers who practice blood libel and who coincidentally all line up with your political enemies. Yeah, I'm not seeing any historical parallels here at all. I'm convinced. Where do I sign up?"

"Nice try."

"I recognized you," Eagle Mama said.

"How?" I asked. I was genuinely confused. I spent the bulk of my life not being recognized, especially not by the likes of these two.

"Sander Siegel talked about you on his show. That you're some far left Antifa BLM terrorist."

"Fantastic. You beat that guy up one time…"

Patriot Bond shook his head. "I never trusted Siegel before. Always seemed like a closet globalist to me. But he was on the money with you, wasn't he? We get the message to liberate the kids under the airport, and who do we run into, but you."

Hell of a revenge for Sander, when you got right down to it. Sic a mob of these maniacs on me, and give them my location. "Out of curiosity, how many kids did you rescue?"

"What?"

"From the prison under the airport that was supposed to be full of them. How many kids did you save?"

They both shifted uncomfortably. "They must have moved them before we got there," Eagle Mama said.

"It's the only explanation," Patriot Bond said.

"I might be able to think of one more." I sighed. "For what it's worth, I've been described by people who know me as sociopathically apolitical."

"You're not talking your way out of this."

"Wouldn't dream of it. What is this? I'm still unclear."

"Hey there, patriot family! It's Eagle Mama with a special offer!" She was in the process of giving the laptop an evening news-ready smile. "During our heroic occupation of the deep state installation under the airport, we managed to capture this notorious deep state operative!" She turned the computer around so the webcam could see me in all my sorry glory. "And we're offering him to you! That's right, make us an offer and this deep state pedo is all yours. Do with him whatever you want. We don't want to know! Anything goes, no holds barred! The bidding starts at a thousand dollars. Be generous! All proceeds will go to raising aware- ness! We're all patriots here!"

I stared at the two of them, stomach twisting until I thought I might make a bigger mess in their closet. I couldn't help it—tears choked me when I said, "You're auctioning me off to be murdered."

"It's always a good idea to diversify your investments," Patriot Bond said.

"Have you ever seen the *Purge* movies? Because I'm starting to get flashbacks."

"Oh goodness no," Eagle Mama said. "Way too violent."

"Of course."

The thing was, for as soul-wrenching as it had been to be kidnapped with no way out here, the caliber of "patriots" who'd literally purchase me to torture me could be so, so much worse. Every dark fantasy they had about punishing their enemies, visited on me. And the worst part is they'd already absolved themselves of it, because in their minds, I was the evil one.

"This is exciting!" Eagle Mama exclaimed. "Come on, let's all watch." She turned around and knelt by me, her husband on the other side. From the looks of it, she was on some kind of off-brand bidding site. The major ones had rules against selling people, or so I assumed. The design was chunky, the lettering mostly in Cyrillic script, but that didn't tell me a whole lot. I thought, *I'll have to ask Riley.* But squeezed my eyes shut when I realized I'd probably never see her or anyone I knew again.

The centerpiece of this auction was the video Eagle Mama had just taken, the freeze frame showing my face, streaked with blood, purple and swollen down one side. I didn't look great, if I'm being honest. I looked like, well, like I had been worked over by a mob of fascists. Next to the video, the money ticked upward in $5 increments. There was, apparently, some interest in killing me. Hard not to take that kind of thing personally.

The bidding only went on for about two hours, and after the boredom of the previous night, it was a quick two hours. Even these dark web sites or whatever they were probably didn't want to press their luck. It's not often that you can find out the real, monetary value of your life. Mine was worth $5235. Neat.

"Huh. I was hoping for more," Eagle Mama said.

"Next time we take a deep state pedo on one of these things, let's make sure we get someone people know. Could you imagine if we got Hillary or Brandon?"

"We could put in that pool you've been wanting!"

"I thought the money was for raising awareness?" I said.

"Helping us helps the movement," Patriot Bond said.

"I'm going to contact the buyer," Eagle Mama said, taking the computer over to the workbench lining the garage. She tapped at the keys and a moment later uttered an excited squeak. "Oh my god! You're never going to guess who it is." She turned, beaming at me. "We get to meet Sander Siegel!"

chapter
thirteen

WHEN THE GARAGE OPENED, the winter air hit me with the force of a bodyslam. My lungs instantly ached, and pulling air past my busted ribs made it more unpleasant. Snow piled high along the sides of the road and the wind raked us with claws of pure ice. A black Escalade and a silver Mercedes waited in the spacious driveway, both under a layer of frost. Eagle Mama pulled the Escalade into the garage with Patriot Bond directing her in like an air traffic controller. I don't think she needed the help, but he needed to give it to her.

They closed the rattling garage. Eagle Mama fetched a towel after Patriot Bond told her to. She spread it over the backseat while he did the work of getting me out of the chair. Then he frogmarched me over and loaded me into the back of his car. My phone was still in his pocket, and I couldn't do a lift with my arms behind my back. Maybe once, but not anymore.

When we finally got moving, the heat in the car was a relief, kneading some feeling back into my toes. I stared out the window into the frozen Colorado landscape as the SUV made its way through unfamiliar neighborhoods. I was lost in a strange land, with no way to signal to Team Swords or the other half of Team Pentacles.

The two in the front seat were quivering masses of nerves. They kept talking in jagged sentences about how exciting this all was, and I got the distinct impression that as soon as I was handed over to my eventual murderer, they'd start trying for that first kid.

We started out in the heart of suburbia, but they were headed for the towers at the center of the city. The radio was turned to a top forty station, so I got my walk to the gallows scored by Taylor Swift. Sidney Carton, eat your heart out. Their GPS dispassionately broke in periodically to let them know they were going to have to make a left at the next stop sign.

We passed a single pedestrian in the cold, a white-haired man in black. I thought it had to be the same guy I'd seen outside Hasim's, but that was impossible. The momentary feeling of recognition was colder than the air outside, and I choked on my breath. Then he was gone. Another person I'd never see again.

"Okay, it should be up here on the left," Eagle Mama said.

The street looked to be an old industrial section of town, but it was hard to tell. Swirling white obscured nearly everything, giving the city a frightening and ethereal feel. For me, it might as well have been an alien planet.

Patriot Bond pulled over and hauled me out of the car. The brutal cold made me try to fold my body up like a doomed insect, but Patriot Bond wasn't having that. He held me by the back of my neck, shoving me along. The ground felt like broken glass. Every step shredded my bare feet further.

Patriot Bond hammered the metal door of the brick building before us. What with the cold and my extensive injuries, I felt like I should be sharing one last drink with Keith David while we patiently waited for the other one to sprout tentacles. A swig of whiskey sure sounded good right then. I'd maybe worry about that little spark of addiction if I thought I was going to survive the next hour or so. Knowing you're going to die is quite freeing, as it turns out.

The door opened to a slab of beef that looked more like Ice Age megafauna than a human man. He was so big, he was only partially visible in the doorway. I'd only seen a few people his size, and they were all either Russian mobsters or displaced Atlantean nobles. From the looks of him, he'd been created by a mad doctor who now profoundly regretted meddling in God's domain.

"Special delivery!" Eagle Mama chirped.

Siegel's Monster waved us in. I'd say he stepped aside, but it was more like a tectonic shift. He lumbered down the hallway, his jacket making zipping sounds as it touched either wall. I peeked through the few doorways we passed, finding rooms that had been abandoned a long time ago. There wasn't even fresh garbage from homeless residents taking shelter. Whatever this place had been, it had been forgotten for years.

A doorway at the end of the hall opened up into a large room with a vaulted ceiling. It was a room that could only have been designed with the intention of making snuff. An industrial sink stood against one wall, and at the other side, made out of Home Depot plywood, was something that looked like a seesaw.

"Hello there, Bob." Sander Siegel stood up from his desk. He had his whole home office recreated against the wall opposite the gallows. The L-shaped desk, the computer, the psycho wall, the logos that were almost, but not quite Nazi symbols. With the exception of a few more wires snaking out of the room, it was like he'd transported that section of his Burbank home two states over. His little anime girl, Tiger J, gazed coquettishly from her place of honor next to the computer.

"Five thousand to kill me? That's a little desperate, don't you think?"

Sander gave me his baby-toothed smile. "I can't wait to see how cocky you are in a minute."

"Our money?" Patriot Bond said.

"Of course." Sander picked up a fat envelope from his desk and carried it over. After meeting Siegel's Monster, anyone would look small, but Sander was positively tiny. He made a motion to grab my arm, but Patriot Bond stopped him.

"Just a second." He opened the envelope and counted. "It's all here."

"Of course it is. I want his phone too."

Patriot Bond smirked, and glanced at me like we had an inside joke. "It's all yours."

"Unlock it."

Patriot Bond turned the phone on, then mashed my thumb onto

the screen and handed it over. Sander took it and yelped. "What the heck?"

"It's all that was on it."

"What's wrong with you?"

I shrugged. "Ergot poisoning?"

Sander set the phone on his desk with obvious disgust, not wanting to touch it more than absolutely necessary. "Pleasure doing business with you," he said to the two influencers.

"Where we go one, we go all," Eagle Mama said.

A tiny furrow of disgust passed over Sander's face, but he nodded. "And also with you."

"You're shorter than you look on TV," Patriot Bond said.

The rage that flashed over Sander's features could have sparked a forest fire. When he spoke, it was a little too fast. "You watch my show? So nice to meet a fan. You can see yourselves out."

Patriot Bond and Eagle Mama retreated, leaving me in the custody of a man I'd beaten up at the start of this whole thing. What I wouldn't give for a little moonshine and ergot. I'd take him and Siegel's Monster on. Sure, I wouldn't last long, but it would have been something. As it was, I couldn't do much more than impotently huddle and shiver.

"True believers," Sander said as the door shut like a tomb.

"Tough to tell. The line between grifter and mark has gotten awful blurry lately."

"*Grifter*," Sander sneered. "You liberals always spit that out at anyone making a living."

"Not a liberal."

"It's capitalism, Bob. The goal is to make money. No one is forcing anyone to watch my show."

"Well, with social media algorithms being what they are...people are kind of being forced."

"You're breaking my heart." He gestured to the DIY home improvements on the other side of the room. "You're probably wondering what those are for."

"Actually, I was wondering how ships in bottles got that way. They're so small."

"I think the most fun in this will be fixing that smart aleck attitude of yours." He appraised me, stepping forward and wrinkling his nose. "You smell like piss and you look like shit. I think this will play better... Gaius, his shirt, and his pants."

Siegel's Monster put one hamhock on my undershirt and pulled it away like it was made of cotton candy. My pants offered about the same resistance. Now I was shivering in my underpants. I got the first real look at my body. My ribs were a mass of black and blue, my skin a cross-hatching of cuts. I looked like I'd bailed out of a car going at highway speeds.

"This is getting weird," I said.

"Get your mind out of the gutter. That outfit of yours won't play for the cameras. This is better. It will make the audience think about prisoners of war, which you are. Congratulations."

"I should congratulate you. This is pretty elaborate for a hit. Set up a raid on the base under the airport, get your paws on me, and then an execution for the cameras. For as much as you say you hate ISIS, you sure are cribbing from their playbook."

"Muslims didn't invent propaganda. And besides, I'm not going to execute you. At least, not yet."

"Then what are you going to do?"

Sander gestured, and Siegel's Monster grabbed me. I felt a key at the lock of the handcuffs and those fell from my wrists. I didn't have time to cradle the freezing hurts at my wrists, though. He hauled me over to the seesaw, and that's when I realized what it was. The goon shoved me down on the plank so that my feet were up and my head was down. Sander tossed him some rope, and he trussed me up like the guest at an Ewok feast. I gave an experimental struggle, but I couldn't move. I had the uncomfortable sensation of knowing exactly what a moth caught in a spider web feels like.

Sander strolled over to me. "You're going to admit, on a livestream, that you're Q. That you made the whole thing up."

"Wait, what?"

"I got started in this business years ago, before Q was even a twinkle in your eye."

"Not to be that guy, but there's nothing new about Q. I literally just took old conspiracy theories, slapped a new coat of paint on them, and hauled them out to the market. After that, it was just listening to the boards and feeding them back exactly what they wanted. The easiest cold reading in the world. You know, before Paul Mallon stole the thing from me."

"Paul Mallon," Sander sneered. The thing about Sander is that he could sneer without meaning to. I think it was his default way of relating to the world. "That guy is a poser. What has he ever done but peddled smut? And now he's some conservative hero?"

"It's a damn shame. I mean, you've been doing the work."

"Thank you. But he has Q, doesn't he?"

"That wasn't my fault. He stole the account. And his posts are garbage, just from the standpoint of someone who takes a little pride in their work. Sure, the theory itself was lazy bullshit, but I put more effort into it than Paul ever did. That guy literally just posted a picture of an American flag one time. What the fuck even is that?"

"The only thing Paul Mallon ever put effort into was being a creep."

"See, Sander, you and me can get along."

He smiled at me, and suddenly I saw the kid he had been. The kid who wore ties and talked too formally. The kid who followed the rules, because that's what they were for. The kid who was small for his age and had a squeaky voice that never really changed. The kid who had been beaten up every day of his life. Didn't excuse what he had become, but I got it. "You're not getting out of this," he said.

"Sander, I'm sor—"

"Before Q, things were wide open. An independent like me could make a good living in broadcasting. Then Q comes along and that's all anybody wants. You have to nod to that garbage before you can get to the meat of your argument. A *real* argument for *real* conservative values."

It clicked into place. "You're mad because Q contradicted the continuity you established."

"You need continuity! You need canon! Without it, stories are just chaos. If they're going to speak to your audience, they need internal logic! You can't just make things up and pretend they all fit when they obviously don't!"

"The more people believe Q, the less people believe you."

"It's *fewer*," Sander snapped. "Not less. *Fewer*."

"You're mad because Q fucked up your grift, and you're going to torture me until I admit it."

"It's not a grift!" he shrieked. He took a deep breath, centering himself. "It's not a grift. There are legitimate problems in this country and I'm pointing them out."

"All the brown people, for one."

"I'm not a racist. I want a strong border because I think we should take care of Americans first."

"But taking care of Americans is socialism."

"*Opportunity* is the key. What's to stop an immigrant from starting their own channel, like mine? Doing what I do?"

"Like...other than everything?"

"I'm performing a service. The problem in this world is that you can't get any attention with unadorned facts, can you? You need an element of sensationalism."

"Which is why you pretend that grieving families whose children were murdered at school are crisis actors."

"The Second Amendment is our only bulwark against tyranny, against the hordes of immigrants who want to take what we have, against Islamic extremists who crash planes into our buildings."

"Yeah, none of that sounds racist at all."

"Islam is a faith, not a race."

"Would you prefer I used the more general term *bigot*?"

"The point is, our Second Amendment protects us. But it's not, in the modern parlance, sexy. So I dress it up a little to get citizens to defend it. That's all."

"Is this where I point out that the Second Amendment isn't in any danger and never actually defended us from any of those things, or are we not worrying about that?"

"You know, it's going to be so fun to wipe that smug look off your face."

"Once you start torturing me, you know I'll say anything to make it stop, right?"

"Sure," Sander said, "but my viewers don't know or don't care, doesn't matter either way. Let's get started."

He sat down at his computer and put headphones over his perfectly coiffed black hair. He smiled at Tiger J, kissing his finger and touching her face. "Good evening patriots, the Sander Siegel show is back on the air, bringing truth to you on this dark night of American liberty. I have a special guest for everyone today, but first I want to talk about the importance of keeping our elections secure from voter fraud."

chapter
fourteen

I DON'T KNOW what was worse, being waterboarded or sitting through Sander's show. I hoped to never do either one again.

Sander started his show with his customary fascist rant cloaked in good manners and bad logic. He said a lot of things "for the sake of argument," which meant he was making things up that would agree with the point he wanted to get to. After he made a point he was particularly proud of, his sneer would curl up into something that could almost be a smirk, and he'd readjust Tiger J. She would be invisible to the camera, but Sander knew she was there.

And then came the waterboarding. He filled up an old plastic milk carton with water from a sink in the corner of the room, then returned and set it down right next to me. He tipped the seesaw. Blood rushed into my throbbing skull. I could watch the jug out of the corner of my eye, translucent and milky.

It was pointless to talk to him, but I tried it anyway, my voice gone ragged with terror. He threw a towel over my face filling my nose with the smell of dryer sheets. Can't smell those anymore without having a panic attack. Then he asked me who Q was. I told him it was me. He didn't care. Torture is never about the information. It's about the one doing it, and what dark and sticky thing inside they need to feed. Then the water came.

They say it's like drowning. I believe them, and I hope to never drown. The world goes dark and heavy, and your body fights to breathe, but it can't. The screwdriver in my ribs twisted and bucked, fighting my body's natural desire to live. The water was lead in my sinuses, strangling me from every part. Then there was relief, just long enough for him to cross the room and fill the jug again. And then it happened again. And again. And again.

I have no idea how long Sander tortured me. He'd keep going until he had wiped the slate clean, made up for how I'd made him feel. But the problem was, Sander had felt small his entire life. He'd started to believe it, and all the wrongs visited onto him got wrapped up into how he felt inside. Scared, alone, mocked. I was here. I was helpless. So it would be taken out on me. He'd balance a ledger on my pain, only it never would even out. He'd always feel the way he did.

The water stopped. I spat and gasped at air turned gummy by desperation. My ribs had been replaced with broken glass. I wanted to cry, but that would only hurt more. "So why did you do it? Why did you make up Q?"

The real answer was for the same reason he had his little show: money. He didn't want to hear that. He needed an answer that would get the pain to stop. Maybe encourage him to put a bullet in my head. That's where this was going, and we might as well move things along. I had places to be. "I wanted to make conservatives look stupid," I said.

"You see, patriots?" he said to the camera. "The liberals are laughing at you. *Laughing*. They want you to believe this nonsense, because it means you take your eye off the ball. You ignore the real issues. What are you doing while you're worrying about Q's nonsensical and everchanging plan? While immigrants are replacing you, replacing you at your job, at your school, at the ballot box."

The old sink in the corner had a rattle in the pipes. By now, that sound made my entire body tense up like a bowstring. I couldn't see anything through the towel over my face, but I could hear Sander filling up the carton en route to another drowning.

I couldn't take much more. My sanity was hanging over the side of a cliff, its grip loosening. Pretty soon we'd hit the point where I'd have to give up and find a place to hide inside myself until this was over. One way or the other.

"All right, everyone. Let's get another answer out of the—urk."

The carton hit the side of my face, and though it hurt like hell, what with that half of my mug a mass of purple, the fact that it wasn't the water was a relief. I heard the carton fall to the concrete floor, vomiting out the water in pulses. The wet towel came away from my face, and though it was freezing in that room I almost wept with relief.

I blinked, the world a jittery blur. A shape loomed above me, a shadow. A shadow that smelled a little bit like good weed. It knelt down, and through my numbness I felt the ropes lashing me to the board loosening.

"Dude, you okay?"

Good weed, as in Alamut Black, the best weed, grown on a secret mountain by a sect of killers for a thousand years. I'd never been so happy to see Hasim Khoury in my life. I don't know if anyone had. He was dressed in black, a ski mask over his face, but I knew that voice, and I knew that smell. I reached for him, and he wrapped me up in a hug, pulling me off the board. "Don't worry, bro. I'm here. I gotcha."

I rested there, safe, and too weak to stand. My lungs weren't inflating all the way, and whenever they tried, my ribs convinced me that wasn't a good idea. I was still in that dark place, trying to claw my way out, but a memory sparked for my attention.

"Cameras," I croaked. "We're being broadcast."

"Oh shit."

Hasim let me go, and I collapsed to my knees, fruitlessly hugging myself. The water was icy on my skin. Hasim hurled first one webcam and then the other into the cement wall, where they shattered. Then for good measure, he returned, picked up the half empty carton and upended it over the computer, where it popped and sparked.

Sander lay on the concrete floor, halfway between me and the sink. His eyes stared glassily at the ceiling. Tiny, panicked breaths forced their way in and out of him, in time with a sound like bubbles being blown through pudding. A pool spread beneath him, and I thought of Mrs. Carruthers back at the Denver Airport D.U.M.B, as he stared terrified into the coming void. I suppose it was inevitable that he'd die in terror. He'd spent his life sharing that fear, nurturing it, making it grow. Now it was bleeding out of him all over this filthy floor.

I forced myself to stand. I wobbled a bit, and my rib sank its teeth into me. I shuffled over to the computer with difficulty. Hasim watched me, confused. I picked up Tiger J from her place of honor and returned to Sander. Kneeling took some effort. Hell, *breathing* took some effort. I set Tiger J on his chest, but his face didn't change. He was too far away from himself to move. Maybe too far away to know he wasn't quite alone.

I had to wait with him. Balancing the ledger myself maybe. Or maybe I just didn't want him to die alone. I had to sit there until he was all the way gone. Until his eyes slipped off of me and stared at something else. I wasn't mad at him. I got no pleasure from it. I just couldn't leave until he was dead. And then he was. Only then did I stand up. It was a bit easier this time, though I still felt like a balloon filled with used syringes.

"You good to go?" Hasim asked.

I pointed at the phone on Sander's desk. "Grab that. One third of Shub-Internet. Or maybe a quarter. I don't know how the math works."

Hasim pocketed the phone. "Are you okay?" He'd taken the mask off, holding it in the same hand he held a long and slender knife.

"Yeah." I took a step, stumbled and nearly fell. Hasim reached for me, but I held a hand out to stop him. "Like fifty-fifty."

"Sorry we took so long. Riley was tracking your phone, but it kept getting turned off." Hasim put my arm over his shoulder. "Lean on me, dude. You're good."

A thought occurred to me, and I just started laughing. It came out as a rasp, what with all the gasping and screaming I'd recently done. "Holy shit."

"What? What the fuck?"

"Sander Siegel spent his whole life convinced a Muslim was gonna kill him."

"Yeah, but I only killed him because he was hurting a white dude."

"Which makes it like a hundred times funnier."

"Yeah, you're not okay."

I kept making that ghastly non-laughter as he helped me up the front hall. Siegel's Monster lay in a motionless hillock of muscle and meat, Pud Galvin gnawing at his thick neck. The gargantuan body-guard's flesh was ghostly white. "Glah!" the chupacabra said when he saw me, taking a step and catching air, gore dripping from his maw.

"Wait, wait, wait!" Hasim managed.

Pud didn't listen. He soared into us, wrapped his bristly arms around my neck, and made little growling noises in his throat. I hugged him as best I could while Hasim held the both of us upright. "It's okay, pal," I told Pud. "I'm back."

We stepped around Siegel's Monster. Cold radiated from the metal door.

Hasim leaned me against the wall. Pud clambered down me reluc-tantly, but continued to hold my hand. "It's colder than a witch's tit out there," Hasim said, taking off his jacket.

"Which one? We got two witches, for a total of four tits."

"Put it on."

I did it, and for the first time since I woke up in that fucking garage, I felt a little warmth. It didn't last. When Hasim opened the door onto the street, all the hurts in my body exploded once again in the frigid night air. The icy ground might have cut my feet. The water still clinging to me froze. I shivered in the jacket as Hasim practically carried me to the van and hauled the door open, Pud loping along behind us. Riley was sitting in the middle seat, her laptop casting a soft glow over her face. The instant I saw her expression, I knew exactly how bad I looked. Lara, in the driver's seat, muttered a "Holy fuck," under her breath.

"The piece of shit waterboarded him," Hasim said.

I shoved Hasim off me and climbed in, stumbling before making it into the backseat. Pud followed, climbing into my lap and wrapping his arms around me. I hugged him, stroking his bristly fur. Hasim shut the sliding door and climbed in the front. The van wasn't warm, but after the outside, and even Sander's torture chamber, it felt like a hot bath.

Riley turned, the frames of her glasses throwing angry shadows from her eyes. "Are you okay?"

"I wish people would stop fucking asking me that," I said. Riley's expression fell.

"He needs a hospital," Hasim said.

"I'm fine," I lied. "We need to find the tablet. I need to know all of this wasn't for nothing." Sitting up straight was painful, so I partly reclined and tried to keep Pud from crawling over anything that was too broken. I kept thinking that eventually I'd find a part of me that didn't hurt. My head pounded, and I kind of wanted to throw up, but fortunately I hadn't eaten anything since that kale wrap thing. "Anybody have something to drink?"

"What do you want, dude?" Hasim asked. "We'll get whatever."

"Moonshine. But I should probably have something with electrolytes."

"No problem. Just sit back. Try to relax."

The van started to wind its way through the streets. Riley remained half-turned in her seat. Her glasses were mostly mirrors, one reflecting her computer screen, the other the streetlights outside. I was grateful I couldn't see her eyes; pity would have been bad, but genuine concern would have been so much worse. "I'm sorry it took us so long."

"You have your phone, right?" I asked. She nodded. "Hasim has mine. Now please tell me you can track the tablet."

"I grabbed the MAC address when we first picked it up," she said, like this meant something to me. "I can more or less figure out where it is."

"Thank Shub-Internet."

Lara pulled into a gas station, and she and Hasim went into the minimart.

"What happened?" I asked, before realizing that Riley couldn't read my mind and she would need a bit more to go on. "After the mob got me?"

"I ran, like you said. The place had more or less emptied out by then. I met the others upstairs, told them what happened and Lara started cursing. Said you were trying to be a hero but were just an asshole."

"Sounds right."

"She didn't mean it. She was scared, I think."

I snorted, regretting it as it meant the screwdriver gave me a poke. "She meant it."

"Well, once we figured out you weren't coming back, she was serious about finding you. Put me to work, but like I said, it was hard as hell. I found the auction finally and tracked that to the..."

"...torture chamber."

"Yeah. I'm sorry, B. I swear I went as fast as I could."

"I know you did," I said. I wasn't away from the drowning. I could still feel it. The towel wrapping me up like an octopus, the water wringing the life out of me.

Lara and Hasim came out a short while later. "Dude, you didn't say what flavor you liked, so I got you green," Hasim said, handing back a plastic bag of food. "I figured green means nutrition."

"Sound reasoning." I pulled out the bottle of sports drink and cracked it open. Putting it to my lips, I momentarily panicked, but I could swallow this. It wouldn't just flood into my sinuses. This liquid was going to go where it was supposed to. I took a few swallows, softening the dry rasp of my mouth, and investigated further. I found beef jerky, a bag of salt and vinegar chips, a crappy gas station sandwich, and peanut M&Ms. It was the last that arrested me. I turned the yellow and brown bag over in my hands, listening to the rattle of the candy inside. I used to eat them on jobs with Lara. They were my go-to candy. Hers were Mike & Ikes because there's something deeply wrong with that woman. She had remembered.

"We're gonna get you to a doctor, dude," Hasim said.

"Fuck you. I'm seeing this thing through."

"You've done en—" Lara started.

The words twisted that screwdriver, and the flare of rage and pain pulled the shout from me: "Don't you *dare* say that to me." The van went silent, everyone tensed like piano wire. I couldn't backtrack, so I leaned in. "I started this. I'm going to finish it. Just find that fucking tablet. I can rest in the car."

"Uh..." Riley glanced at Lara for confirmation. She shrugged. "Okay. Well, this whole thing works like hotter and colder. Pick a direction and drive, and I'll tell you if we're getting hotter or colder."

"You should just track the thing," Hasim said. "Pinpoint its location."

"That's not how this works. We're looking for it based on which AP it's using to connect... You know what? Just trust me."

Lara started the van. I gazed out the window at the lights and tried not to feel the hurts quite so clearly. Huddling in Hasim's jacket, with a chupacabra cuddled up to me, I was actually almost warm. In the seat in front of me, Riley would say "hotter" or "colder" and Lara would adjust the route to compensate. I started to eat. The jerky and the chips, sure, they were my flavor, but my throat felt like shredded meat. The smooth and near flavorless sandwich, lubricated with bland mayo was exactly what I needed. Before long, it was clear we were heading to the glittering skyscrapers downtown. Lara moved through these until Riley said. "Here."

"The Ritz Carlton," Lara said. "Of course it is. Let me figure out where to park this shitbox." She finally settled on the hotel's own underground structure, getting gouged for not being a guest.

"Let's see what we can see," I said getting up.

"Hang on, Bob." Lara got out and went around the back. She opened the small cargo area, and handed me my clothes, stinking and in terrible shape, but there. "If you're gonna be a stubborn asshole, you're at least not going to be a naked one."

She'd even left my IDs, my little collection of fake people from my first life. It had been over a hundred at one time, now down to barely a dozen. Another reminder that I was a shadow of who I had been. I struggled to get everything on. Bending over to get the shoes on my feet especially were agony, but no force on earth could compel me to ask for help. I handed the jacket to Hasim. "Naw, man. It's all yours," he said.

I nodded. "Okay. Let's figure this thing out."

"Wait," Riley said. She rummaged in her bag and handed me a phone. "Replace the one that's carrying the god piece. Our numbers are all in there." The five of us got out of the van. I could almost stand up straight, and I was calling that a victory.

"Maybe we should leave him here," Lara said, pointing at Pud.

The chupacabra hissed at her, and Hasim yawned, which soon

spread to the rest of us. It hurt like hell. "I don't think he's letting me out of his sight for now," I said.

"Goddamn it. Incarnate a familiar and that's what you fucking pick."

"I didn't pick anything."

"Could have had a nice cat. Maybe a raven. Shit, a coyote would be your style, and we could at least pretend it was a dog."

"My sister has a coydog," Riley said. "You know, half coyote, half dog? He's seven and not even housebroken, and this isn't even remotely relevant so I'll be quiet now."

Lara stared at Riley for several more beats. "Okay, everybody stick close. You're sure about the location?"

"It's using the hotel's Wi-Fi," Riley said.

"Let's hope it's not in one of the rooms," Lara said.

I tried to lead, but long, thudding steps hurt my ribs, so I shuffled along behind Lara and Hasim. We made our way to the elevator, and gathered around Pud to shield him from cameras. Hiding him from everyone would be impossible, so this would end up being the weirdest cryptid sighting for someone. When we were still, Pud pressed his side up against my leg, damn near sitting on my feet. I realize this is a short list, but as chupacabras went, Pud Galvin was far and away my favorite.

The elevator dinged open on the lobby. It was pretty empty, with only the staff behind the desks at the far end of the room. "Follow me," Lara set off with purpose to the hallway leading to the various ballrooms and meeting spaces off the lobby. Lara knew that if you walked briskly in any direction with a sense of purpose and an expression of annoyance, you could pretty much go where you wanted to. Project an aura that no one wanted to puncture, and they wouldn't.

Lara's instincts were good. The susurrus of many conversations and the clink of glasses drew us along. A man in a suit, the kind that said money without saying much of anything about taste, emerged from the ballroom and headed in the direction of the restroom. We opened the door and peeked in, not quite in a stacked heads Scooby-Doo way, but it was close.

I nearly busted out laughing. The pain stopped me, as did the fact that attracting that kind of attention would have probably gotten me killed. "This is it," I said, closing the door and beginning to move away, back to the van.

"How can you be sure? It looked like a rich dude Christmas party," Hasim said.

He was right. The ballroom had been decked out in green and red, lots of holly leaves and poinsettias. There was even a Santa, Mrs. Claus, and collection of elves by one wall, and what looked like a closed tent on the other. Tables ringed a central clear area, where men and a few women all in expensive formal wear. The styles ranged from *American Psycho* to Batman villain.

"For starters, I saw half a dozen right wing fixers, two QAnon grifters, a couple tech broligarchs, and one former employer. The idea of our tablet vanishing thanks to a fascist attack and it winds up at a hotel holding a fascist Christmas party? Too much of a coincidence."

"Let's go in," Lara said. "I mean, I'm the only one dressed for it and we can't take the monster, but it should be oka—"

"Are you out of your mind? We can't go in there without disguises."

"What are you talking about?"

I was getting heated. The screwdriver turned in my side, but I could take it. "That's a room full of some of the most powerful and extreme conservatives in this country. We're their worst nightmare!"

"I don't know about—"

I pointed to each of them in turn. "A Muslim professional killer, a trans Honduran witch, an Indigenous demon-worshipping sex worker, *and a literal illegal alien!*"

They stared at me. Finally: "Yeah, okay."

"What's the plan?" Hasim asked.

"Go to the front desk and tell them that a red van with a reindeer on the side is getting towed."

"Dude, there's no way that's a real car."

"It's parked four spaces from ours," I said.

"Oh. Damn." Hasim scampered off to the front desk.

"I see what you're planning," Lara said. "Not bad."

"Keep me from getting recognized."

We moved down the hall a short way and a moment later, one of the concierges nearly jogged into the ballroom. A short time after that,

Santa Claus emerged, grumbling and heading for the elevator. Lara stopped him. "Excuse me, sir?"

"Sorry miss, I don't got time to talk. The van's being towed."

"I apologize, but that was a little fib. We're actually from corporate, and we need to replace your crew."

"Replace?"

"You'll still be paid, but you get the night off. We just need your outfits, and you're free to go."

"Seriously?"

Lara nodded, completely sincere. "All the money, none of the hassle."

Santa snorted. "These guys don't even tip. They just want to sit in my lap and tell me they want a lower marginal tax rate on inheritances over fifty million."

"Enjoy your night off."

"I'll go tell the others," he said, looking seriously jolly.

The group of us returned to the parking garage and before long, Santa, Mrs. Claus, two elves, and a small man dressed as Rudolf the Red-Nosed Reindeer came out of the elevator. They stripped down in record time, each revealing some spare street clothes underneath. Santa sported some impressive prison ink up and down both arms.

"Enjoy yourself," he said, climbing into the van. The others laughed, proving that we would not, in fact, enjoy ourselves. The vanload of now defrocked North Pole residents drove off, leaving us with the collection of costumes.

I reached for the Santa outfit, but Hasim pulled it away. "Dude, I want to be Santa."

"Why do you want to be Santa?"

"I never got to be Santa before. Just, y'know, don't tell my mom."

"Why would he tell your mom?" Riley asked.

"Oh, he wants to date her."

"I don't want to date your mom, Hasim," I said.

"I think that's sweet," Riley said.

"Look, we're about to go into a room full of racists. They might accept a Lebanese elf, but they will lose their everloving minds if Santa's not white."

"As much as I hate to agree with him, he's right," Lara said, pulling on Mrs. Claus's red dress.

"Fine," Hasim sighed. "I get to be Santa next Christmas though, okay?"

"Sure," I said.

Wrestling Pud into the reindeer outfit took some doing. He growled and spat a lot, but pretty soon he was in his costume and he even looked kind of cute. That was Riley's opinion anyway, who wouldn't stop fawning over him. No pun intended.

I patted my simulated belly. "Let's find this tablet." Moving around in the Santa suit was never going to be easy, and my mounting list of injuries didn't make it any easier. Still, after being beaten on and near frozen, being in a padded furry suit was a nice change. Even if it did smell like the seat of a Harley Davidson.

Hasim slipped a couple blades up his sleeves. Lara squared her shoulders. Riley tapped at her phone. Pud farted. The five of us walked up to the ballroom. I like to think we did it in slo-mo, looking badass as possible in our yuletide cheer.

"Everybody keep your eyes open," I said. "Recognize anybody from the raid on the D.U.M.B., that's our likely culprit."

"I don't know how many faces I recognize."

"That's okay," Riley said. "A lot of people who were there posted their content all over social media. I've gotten a shit-ton of good images. I'll send them to your phones now."

"They just...posted their crime?" Hasim asked.

"Power of whiteness," Lara said, patting Hasim on the shoulder. "Just keep your eyes open and if anyone looks familiar, let us know."

He smiled sheepishly. "Yeah, no problem. I don't have the best memory is all."

"Who needs one when you're that good with a knife?"

Hasim straightened up, his cheeks a warm red. I didn't roll my eyes but I kind of wanted to.

My new phone buzzed. I opened it up and found a bunch of shots of the raid on the D.U.M.B. The expressions weren't what you'd think, considering. These people allegedly thought they were breaking into a slave pen of children who were being abused so their blood would taste better. You know, Pennywise's whole motivation. So you'd assume their expressions would be nervous, or steeled against the inevitable and bottomless horror they were about to confront. Instead I saw exultant triumph in their expressions. They looked like they were at a Fourth of July party during a particularly spectacular fireworks show.

"See? Don't have to remember a thing," Riley said with a grin.

I opened the door, boomed a "Ho! Ho! Ho!" and immediately regretted it. I put my hand over my busted rib, like that would help. One old bastard toasted me. "Let's mingle," I said, doing my best not to wheeze. Couldn't let the others know how fucked up I was. If we managed to pull this thing off, soon I'd get all the rest I'd ever need.

"Santa, Santa, over here!" I obligingly made my way over to a trio of young conservatives wearing identical charcoal gray suits, red ties, and flag pins. I searched their faces, but none of them looked like anyone I remembered from the D.U.M.B. or Riley's pictures—more like Brooks Brothers Riot kind of guys, but they were too young for that.

"And what do you want for Christmas?"

One of them glanced at the others, as though to prepare them for whatever "joke" was going to tumble out of him. "Get rid of age of consent laws."

"A wish like that sounds like you should be on the naughty list," I said.

"I'm not the naughty one."

"You libertarians!" I said, wagging my finger.

"How'd you know we were from the libertarian wing?"

I laughed. "Santa knows all!" And it was literally the easiest deduction anyone had ever made. I moved on. As I looked at face after face, I was wondering if I wasn't barking up the wrong tree. These weren't the conspiracy goons who could be wound up by bullshit into doing the will of the state. These were the shakers, who did the winding up as it were. They knew everything was a grift, and so they didn't burden themselves with things like "belief" or "desire to do good" or "terror of an afterlife that might judge them based on works."

A hard hand fell on my shoulder, steering me into a 180. It was an unconscious act of domination, done without any special intent. This was a hand used to moving people around at whim. It squeezed an agonized groan out of me as the fingers pinched one of my many hurts.

"Santa's a little soft!" laughed a familiar voice.

I slapped on a grin and hoped this beard would hide my face as I was brought eye to eye with an old enemy. Kirk Shelley was a member of the Thule Society, which is a nice way of saying he was a Nazi. A couple years back—I think, time gets a bit hazy sometimes—I managed to get him locked up for a murder that he'd tried to frame me for. Safe to say that if he recognized me, I wasn't going to be his favorite person.

As for what he looked like...pretty much your platonic ideal of a fascist street brawler who was making a go at appearing respectable. His Nazi ink could just be covered up with long sleeves, and was mostly in the semi-deniable area of Norse runes and the like. "It's not a Nazi tat, honest, wink wink, now let's talk about the [name the marginalized group] problem." He'd shaved his head, I suspect more because he was going bald than for a statement, and grown out a reddish beard now shot through with gray.

"Santa might have pulled a muscle sliding down a chimney or two," I boomed in my best Santa voice. The screwdriver was going to make that hard to keep up.

"Can't be showing weakness, can we?" Kirk said. He had the eyes of a crocodile, and I was the doomed goat he was about to drag into the brackish depths. He wasn't quite focusing, and that, coupled with a slight sway said he was a little drunk.

"Ho! Ho! Ho! Now what do you want for Christmas, big fellow?"

"Oh, I can think of fourteen words."

White supremacist code. Cute. "Well, that's a-okay with me," I said, shooting him that sign that fascists had "ironically" taken as their own.

Kirk laughed. "You already got me what I wanted with that presidential pardon."

Well, that explained what he was doing on this side of bars. "As much as I'd love to take credit..."

Kirk clapped me on the back hard enough to make me cough. My ribs ground together, and I had to catch myself against a table. Kirk didn't bother to hide his glee at my obvious pain. "Good man! Now get all the good little children their toys."

I staggered off. It was hard not to take Kirk's presence as some kind of ill omen. If he was in this room, he'd moved up in the world, which was never a good thing. It didn't take a fortune teller to know that getting the tablet out of this place would be done through Kirk. Through sheer meanness, evil intent, or plain rotten luck, he'd find a way to be between me and my goal. And then it hit me: I had an Assassin on the team, and they're great at removing obstructions. Problem solving. It's a good thing.

I slunk through the crowd, being stopped periodically by a fascist or a plutocrat or a fascist plutocrat in order to hear their Christmas wish. Most of them were relatively normal—a lot of requests for more tax breaks—but some got downright bizarre. One guy asked for a sinkhole on his property, but specified that it not be "one of those wet ones." I told him to check his stocking.

I ran into Lara first. "Hey there, Mrs. Claus," I said in my normal voice.

"I haven't seen one person from the thing," she said.

"Me neither. Have you seen Hasim?"

"I think he went that way. Your familiar's been following him around for some reason."

"Pud Galvin knew what I needed before I did."

"What?"

"There's a guy here Hasim needs to kill."

Lara snorted. "He could probably clear out half the room and I'd feel a hell of a lot safer."

"Ladies and gentlemen...mostly gentlemen," said a man standing by the closed tent on one side of the room. He was an old man, bald and liver-spotted, wearing a suit that cost as much as a car. "It's important to remember the reason for the season. With that in mind..." he drew a cord and the tent fell open, revealing a little fake manger. A door opened up next to them, and actors in full Bethlehem regalia took their places. Joseph and Mary with baby Jesus, and the three wise men lined up behind them, boxes containing terrible gifts for a new family. Lastly, a few farmhands brought out some livestock to really give the manger that seal of authenticity.

I had to admit, it looked pretty cool. And I was appreciating it, even if my eyes kept going to one animal in particular, like my brain was trying to tell me something. It was just a goat, after all. Nothing too interesting about one of them. Your regular brown-and-white, not-even-chomping-on-a-tin-can goat. It hadn't offered anyone a chance to live deliciously. It bleated once, and I assumed it was in response to being in a room full of strangers.

That was when Pud uttered a horrible shriek. Through a suddenly spooked crowd, I saw the little shape in the Rudolf costume charging the goat. I had enough time to swear before pandemonium broke out.

chapter
fifteen

PUD LEAPT ON THE GOAT, and blood spurted into the air. Screams split the fancy party. Hasim jumped on Pud, throwing a sack over his head and wrestling the little monster away from the wounded animal while some attendees ran for the exits and others crowded around to see what the hubbub was.

"Why did we bring a chupacabra?" Lara asked.

"Did you want to leave him in the car?"

"We could have cracked a window. Put on his favorite music."

"Oh, real good. Do you even know what kind of music chupacabras like?"

"How the fuck am I supposed to know that? He's your spirit guide!"

"R.E.O. Speedwagon?" I hazarded.

"Why does that feel like a good guess?"

We stood fast in the surging crowd. The place had an every-man-for-himself kind of energy, which suited me just fine. Kept us from being singled out or ganged up on. Lara and I craned our heads as we hunted through the people rapidly exiting the room.

"See anything?" I asked. I didn't recognize anybody, but I couldn't be sure if that was just because I hadn't looked at the pictures Riley found recently enough, or all the cranial trauma had done a number on my short term memory.

"I don't...wait. There," Lara said.

"Where?"

"*There.*" Lara pointed across the room at a woman now slinking out of the back exit. She was blonde, maybe in her twenties, pretty in a mean sorority girl kind of way. She was dressed in a clingy pink dress and she wore an ostentatious lily behind one ear. Most importantly, she carried a purse big enough for a tablet. I didn't have to remember her from the D.U.M.B. to recognize the first clumsy attempts at an identifier for a clandestine meet. As obvious as she was, I don't think we would have spotted her without the momentary parting of the crowd.

"Let's get her," I said.

Lara and I made a beeline for the exit the woman slipped out of. Riley fell into step next to us, glancing up from her phone. She was alternating between standing on tiptoes and craning her neck around to glimpse through gaps in the crowd, but she wasn't going to see over anything without stilts. "I think I recognized someone."

"Way ahead of you," Lara said.

"Let's find out if she's naughty or nice," I said. Both women stopped and shared their acute disappointment in me through a glare that could have withered saguaro. "Look, if you think I'm gonna wear this thing and not get some Christmas lines out of my system, you two are sorely mistaken."

Riley sighed. "We're talking about the blonde in the pink dress with the flower in her hair, right?"

"Yeah. Why?"

"Because I didn't want to have a misunderstanding that careened out of control."

"You're right. We wouldn't want to lose control of this evening."

We followed the blonde in the pink dress through the door, into the hallway, carpeted in the same corporate pattern as the rest of the hotel, with pots of snake plant at regular intervals. Windows, turned into mirrors by the dark outside, covered one wall. The blonde was down the hall, her phone out. She looked up at us and frowned before cautious recognition bloomed on her face. Putting her phone back in her purse, she squared herself. I don't think any of us were ready when she said, "You're the Russians?"

"Da," I said. "Vee sure are."

Now, despite the fact that I hung out with Vassily "the Whale" Zhukovsky more often than anyone should without being murdered, my Russian accent wasn't great. I pretty much sound like a bad impression of the Count from *Sesame Street,* mostly because that's how I came by the accent to begin with. I'm not proud of it, but accents were never really my specialty.

Lara, on the other hand, could do regional shit. "Yes. And you must be the seller. Thank you for wearing the lily in your hair as we asked." She did the perfect Southern Russian, just strong enough to be noticeable, but without overwhelming her words. I'd be willing to bet that had she done that for Vassily, he would have checked to see if they were from the same town.

Lara referring to the young woman as the "seller" was an easy deduction to make, and it was a good one. After all, if she got the tablet she identified as a patriot. And before you point out that selling government information in the form of a computer to agents of another country is textbook treason, I'd like to point out that there's nothing more American than grifting a few extra bucks from whatever source will hook it to your veins.

The seller's shoulders relaxed just a bit. She wasn't out of the woods yet. She was still in the middle of an illegal deal with Russians, but at least we were the right Russians. Her hand went to the flower in her hair. "Oh, of course. It's not easy finding a lily in Denver in the winter."

"That was the whole point," Lara said.

We approached, and she tensed ever so slightly. I let Lara take the lead here. The last thing this woman needed was a creep in a Santa costume when she could deal with Lara at her most matronly. Besides, all this running around was beginning to make the screwdriver feel more like a power drill. I needed to catch my breath, but not too deeply. At least I wouldn't have to deal with it for too much longer. We'd be finished soon.

Lara held out her hand. "The merchandise? We wish to see if it's what we asked for."

"Oh, of course!" The seller reached into her purse and withdrew the tablet—the same one Riley had pulled from the evidence room at the

D.U.M.B. The memories of that heist were tattooed on my temporal lobe. Lara handed the tablet to Riley, who turned it on, tapped at it, and then nodded.

"Good," Lara said.

"Hey, can I ask you something?" the seller asked. "Why are you dressed like Santa?"

"Oh you know," I said. "America."

"Oh."

"You were at the action?"

"The...action? Oh, yes. I was there. We put the fear into the deep state, I can tell you that. We're taking this country back for real Americans."

"The patriots are already in charge," I said. "President, Congress, Supreme Court."

"There's always deep state operatives to be found. *Always.*"

Riley coughed. "Sorry, something in my throat."

"You don't sound Russian."

"They train us in accents?" she tried.

"*They* sound Russian." She pointed at Lara and me.

"They don't train us very well."

The seller frowned, steeling up. "My money?"

"Yeah, about that..." I said.

"There is seller!" boomed through the hallway behind us. Now *that* voice sounded Russian.

Three men in tracksuits came straight for us from the same doorway we used. They had that heavy-lidded and ham-handed look of professional goons, the ones who were in the Goon Local and had all their goon dues paid up through the first of the year. None of them had a modern gym rat body. They had the physiques of 19th Century circus strongmen, big lumps of gristle and fat that knew violence better than they knew their own families. We might have had a shot against them had Hasim and Pud been with us. We didn't, so our chances roughly akin to a toddler facing off against a chimpanzee in a face-eating contest.

"Shit," I muttered. "Run."

"Wait, what?" Riley asked, still clutching the tablet. Lara, though, didn't hesitate. She grabbed Riley's hand and bolted. I followed a second later. The screwdriver dug brutally into me, slowing me as sure as if I'd been harpooned.

"Hey!" whined the seller.

The three Russians ran after us. True to form, they mostly moved thanks to momentum, picking up speed like semis whose drivers had crashed after mismanaging their amphetamine and carbohydrate intake. All of them had the same looks in their eyes, this faint annoyance that they had to run, but an undeniable interest in what happened after.

But here's the thing. We had Shub-Internet.

The two infected phones were safely stashed in the van, turned off and effectively invisible. Riley clutched the tablet to her chest, the final and largest piece of the god. We had it. We'd won. Assuming we could get away from these Russians, of course.

"They stole the tablet," the seller said. "Get them!" The Russians weren't listening, but I was happy that she could at least feel involved in the whole thing.

We rounded the corner, and I knew I wasn't going to make it very far. Attempting to move quickly in a Santa suit is nearly impossible when you're at full health. Me, I was suffering from a year of malnutrition, a beating by an angry mob, and a torture session on top of it. I wasn't going to outrun my past, let alone three Russians who were, at the very least, dressed for it.

The corridor split, leading through the kitchen. I figured now was as good a time as any. Lara and Riley were ahead of me, and without any conversation would make it to the van before the Russians knew what hit them. *We* had to recover Shub-Internet, not *me*. So I stopped.

The lead Russian bowled into me, unable to stop that forward momentum that had been moving him along so effectively. I went sprawling, tumbling over the carpet, and slamming into one of the potted plants. A bright bolt of agony lanced through my side. My breath left me, and I felt suddenly like I was trapped, the Santa suit becoming Shelob's web. I tried to fight free of it, but I couldn't, and my Samwise was out front corralling an enraged chupacabra.

No, it wasn't a web—it was rope. Tying me to a plank. I couldn't move and any second the water would tumble over my face and *I can't breathe, oh god I can't fucking breathe.*

The Russian lifted me up and the track lighting was blinding as he checked my skull integrity against the wall. The pain this time was a relief, because at least the air was there, clear and smelling of industrial cleaning products.

"Is that him?" asked one of the Russians.

The one holding me yanked Santa's beard down. Half my face was purple and I carried a few new cuts, but he must have liked what he saw. One of the others pulled something up on his phone and put the screen next to my face. "Looks like him."

"Misha said to kill him."

"Misha didn't say to kill him in the middle of hotel."

"You got phone?" demanded the Russian holding me, his breath stinking like a fish farm.

I was about to get it when three words echoed along the small corridor, leaving me to wonder just how many of us were now completely fucked.

"*Be not afraid!*"

Ask a stupid question, get a terrifying answer I suppose.

THE MAN COMING down the hallway wasn't all that much to look at. Not as broad as any of the Russians, and he had a look like he spent his summers playing guitar at a church camp by a lake. He had a shoulder-length mane of brown hair, except for a patch by his temple, where a nasty scar ran partway around his head. His beard was considerably rattier than the hair. He was dressed in a pair of slacks, loafers, and an ugly Christmas sweater featuring a bunch of grinning yellow Minions. I wasn't happy to see him. The last time we'd met wasn't under the most ideal of circumstances. His name was Gabriel. "Like the angel?" you might ask. Yes, exactly like the angel.

Now, there are two schools of thought when it comes to guys like Gabriel. The first is that they're deranged fanatics who cut off their own junk in order to never succumb to sensation, and now all that build-up of testosterone and frustration has nowhere to go, and so they develop low-key superpowers. The second school of thought is that they're exactly what they say they are, which is an angel incarnated in human form. I leaned pretty heavily toward the first, because I found it scarier. Seriously, if he'll cut off his own junk, what do you think he'd be willing to cut off of *you*?

One of the Russians laughed. "Why are we afraid of you?"

Gabriel smiled. "While I might not entirely approve of a pagan idol like Santa Claus, I am going to have to ask you put him down."

The two Russians who weren't holding me went out to meet Gabriel. They enclosed him like veteran bullies, certain they were about to have some fun. "I think you should find somewhere else to go."

"Nonsense. I'm right where I need to be. Now, are you going to let him go or not?"

One of the Russian's hands came down on Gabriel's shoulder. I winced. Nothing good was going to happen to these men from this point onward.

Gabriel grabbed the hand and twisted until the sound of cracking breadsticks came out of it. The Russian howled. Gabriel took the opportunity to punch the other one in the throat. That Russian staggered backward, clutching at his neck and gasping. Gabriel turned his attention to the one whose hand he'd broken, and hammered him in the face once. The Russian hit the floor and sucked carpet.

The final Russian dropped me. He did a little bit of math, decided he didn't like the answer, and broke into a run. Gabriel gave a good-natured laugh like the minister had just told a funny story about the time his wife mixed up his lunch with that of his seven-year-old. "Are you all right?" he said to me.

This is silly, but for whatever reason, Gabriel checking on me inflated a well of emotion that closed my throat and made me blink back tears. It was a sucker reaction, and I corralled it, but for a split second, I was vulnerable. Not that I deserved it. In any case, I was all right, for a given value of that concept. Breath actually inflated my lungs. Shallowly, sure, and it hurt like hell, but I was getting back to equilibrium. The feelings, like whipped dogs, retreated back into their dens. I needed to be cold and sharp if I was going to get the job done.

The seller poked her head around the corner. Her indignant eyes widened as she saw the two unconscious Russians on the floor and the beatifically smiling angel standing among them.

"*Be not afraid,*" he said to her.

Wisely, she was quite afraid, and darted away back the way she came. Whatever she thought she would gain from the sale of the tablet was forgotten.

Now I was alone with Gabriel. Out of the frying pan, into the deep fryer, as they say.

The angel fixed his attention on me, his gaze exquisitely empty. A frown rippled over his face. I prayed to the lines of code we'd locked up on three devices, because if you're going to pointlessly pray, you might as well do it with a god who could be tricked with porn. *Please, O mighty Shub-Internet, don't let this psycho recognize me, and I'll give you all the depravity you can eat.* Gabriel crossed the short distance between us. He smelled like hot chocolate with marshmallows. He reached up with one hand and moved my beard aside.

"Robert Blank," he said. "Coincidence is the Lord laughing."

"Hey there, Gabriel," I said, remembering that you do not call him 'Gabe' under any circumstances. "How are you?"

"I'm well, thank you, Robert. It has been, what, three years, two months, and sixteen...no, now seventeen days."

I tried a laugh. It didn't go well. "But who's counting, right?"

He smiled. "You think I bear you ill will?"

"The thought had crossed my mind."

"For betraying the Inquisition and turning me over to the government to be locked away in that military base."

While that was probably the most uncharitable reading of the situation, it wasn't entirely incorrect. I'd worked for the Inquisition for years under the name of Michael Hagen, doing whatever weird thing they needed of me. Same as I'd done for every other secret society out there. Later, as a fixer for the criminally insane, I might have helped lock Gabriel up. I might have even delivered him to his eventual prison, which is how I knew the basic layout to begin with.

"When you put it like that..."

"Are you frightened?"

"A little, yeah."

"Be not afraid. I bring you good news that will cause great joy for all the people."

"That's a relief." I was not relieved.

Gabriel smiled, his hand kneading my shoulder. His grip felt like a cement mixer. "You are concerned. Yes. I understand now. You think I am still affiliated with the Inquisition. I am not."

"What happened?"

"I haven't submitted a formal resignation, if you're wondering. I have new friends." He leaned closer, whispering, "Did you know that the Catholic Church has been associated with child abuse?"

"I might have heard something about that, yeah."

Gabriel shook his head in wonder. "I had never heard."

"If you don't mind my asking, when did this happen?"

"Yesterday. I was having a normal day, praying with the Lord our God, when I heard a commotion outside of my cell. Imagine my surprise when the door opened and instead of a guard with my gruel for the day, it was a collection of patriots. They were Christians, of course, and as such, accepted me as one of their own. I had never experienced such love on the earthly plane."

"Can I guess? One of them took you home and showed you things on YouTube."

"Yes! How did you know? I learned all about the Cabal and the awful things they are doing to children even now. Imagine! Torturing a babe for adrenachrome!"

Great. They radicalized an angel. "Yeah. It's pretty messed up."

"Ah yes, your gift for understatement. But do I detect a subtle hint of camaraderie?"

"Uh yeah...I had a similar path to awakening."

"You have taken the red pill!" Gabriel said. And I don't know what it was about an angel using a far right meme, but it made my skin crawl.

"You bet. And I never looked back."

Gabriel released his grip. "What a fun coincidence!"

"It sure is."

He frowned at me. "Is that why you're dressed like Saint Nicholas?"

"I was trying to dress like Nicolas Cage, but the guy at the costume shop misunderstood."

Gabriel laughed, unsure of whether he should be or not. "Come along, Robert. The two of us are in the same whale."

"I don't know what that means. Hey, can I ask you something? How did you get from the folks that pulled you out of the military base to here? Seems like a different class of people."

"The grace of God, my friend. I merely reached out with my new revelations and was invited."

"Makes sense." If I were a bunch of wealthy fascists, I'd jump at the chance to get my own angel too.

Gabriel steered me with the natural confidence of someone who never gets told no. "Come with me. There are some people I want you to meet."

"Who?"

"There are enemies of the Cabal here."

"A whole ballroom."

"Yes, but there are those who are perhaps more equipped to help this country see the military tribunals of the offenders that will bring about the healing we so desperately need."

"Oh, good."

"I imagine that if they were enthusiastic about my services, they might feel the same way about yours. I seem to recall you having a bit of a reputation in the City of Angels."

"I don't want to toot my own horn."

"Toot away, my friend. Toot away."

He guided me back along the hallway to the ballroom. The place had mostly emptied out, leaving only the detritus of the party. The manger had been splattered with blood. I didn't think I should bring up that his gathering had been anointed with the blood of a sacrificial goat. That didn't seem like information that would help me too much.

A couple of the stockbroker types were raiding the bar. "Excuse me, fellow patriots. Did the higher-ups already adjourn?"

The stockbrokers exchanged amused looks. One of them straightened up and in a bizarre trans-Atlantic accent that never sounded even remotely like Gabriel said, "They did indeed, good sir," and the three of them all giggled like assholes. Gabriel didn't notice, or maybe it was that divine grace I'd heard so much about.

That's right when I realized we were an angel and Santa Claus hanging out together. For a good joke, we'd need a third. "Hey, you wouldn't happen to know where the Easter Bunny is, would you?"

"The Easter Bunny is dead," Gabriel said with chilling certainty.

I thought it might be a good idea not to run my mouth around dangerous men. It's a shame I don't have more self-control in that regard. "Excuse me for just one second." I went to the bar and mixed myself a cocktail, if straight whiskey can be considered a cocktail. I gulped the first one down like water and poured another.

"Whoa, slow down there Santa," one of the assholes said.

"Careful, motherfucker or I'll shove a lump of coal up your ass," I said to the guy. Maybe I was more intimidating with a beard, because he was scared. I lumbered my way back to Gabriel. "Let's get going."

"You should not pollute your body with such poisons," Gabriel said.

"I thought Jesus loved wine."

"That's not wine."

"No. No, it's not."

Gabriel didn't have much else to say. He escorted me out of the ball-room, leaving behind the American Psychos raiding the bar. At the elevator, he punched the penthouse floor button, scanning a room key on the elevator's scanners. Gabriel hadn't always been what I'd call classy, but the Inquisition had a ton of cash. The Vatican had been bankrolling them for centuries. Why stop now? It wasn't like heretics were suddenly in short supply.

The elevator opened onto a room that could not have been more clear about the central message that I didn't belong in it. Every inch of it screamed the kind of wealth that you got a thousand years ago when you put the right village to the torch. Everything had a burnished, candlelit, leatherbound look to it, and the room smelled like expensive cigars and nepotism.

The men in the room were no better—and they were all men. They were men in the way that only the bygone era could manage, which is to say they were more toxic than an oil slick and twice as valuable in Texas. You might be thinking, "Hey, Bob. Don't rush to judgment. These fellas might be pillars of the community." Trust me, they weren't. Evil ages you, and if any one man in that room started hanging out with Emperor Palpatine, old Sheev would be known as "the baby-faced one." Even the younger ones, the tech moguls in their fifties, had the kind of warped and soggy features from too many plastic surgeries and quack diets. Everybody in the room had the head weaving and tooth grinding you only get after a profoundly abusive relationship to uppers.

And I recognized some of them, so I knew their crimes. Nicholas

Costa of the Knights of Malta chomped on a Cuban cigar while chatting with a martini-drinking Frank Brittain of the Thule Society. Wilson Donner of the Goys from Brazil sat in a leather chair like a throne, while nearby Jack Calhoun of the Warmer Earth Society regaled him with a loud story about making another billion here or there. And over by the fire, that was Jurren ten Boom, the guy behind that app that delivers water to your door invading the space of Hans Johnson the social media guy who collected genocides like Pokemon.

Every man in the room was responsible for more death and misery than any one person could track, and all of it would have been justified with a shrug or a gesture toward how much cash it had put in their ledger. This was pure black tar evil, and it was all in a single room, ready to freebase. I had a brief fantasy about the havoc Hasim or Pud could have wreaked. But no, it had to be me up here.

When we came in, we caught a few looks. Gabriel wasn't dressed for the occasion, and I was Santa Claus. My entire body shivered with the urge to hurt these men, and they were old and frail. I could probably take a few of them. But I was also standing next to Gabriel, who could kill me with a dirty look. And there was the simple fact that at one time or another, I had worked for every one of these monsters. Wasn't like my hands were clean.

"Gabriel, what are you doing here?" I knew that voice too. See, there's a lot of evil in the Information Underground. That's kind of the way it works. People do bad things in the shadows and everyone suffers except for a few who get to add another couple zeroes to their ledger. In the rich tapestry of psychopaths that make up the world in which I lived, there was one man who was worse than all the others. One man I was comfortable calling the Prince of Darkness. That man was Irving Quackenbush, one of the worst human beings ever shat out onto this Earth. Irving Quackenbush ordered genocides the way normal people do Sudoku: distracted and sometimes on the toilet. Irv had wiped out entire ethnic groups in his pursuit of profit, and like the worst kinds of monster, was smart enough to confine his attention to the parts of the world with more melanin, so no one paid attention.

Irving Quackenbush was old, but still more or less intact. He walked with a cane, but he barely stooped. His head still had a few white hairs clinging to the liver spots, but most had given up. His face mostly looked like a Jack-o-Lantern a couple months past Halloween. His suit was tailored to his skinny frame, all dark colors that looked at once classy and conspiratorial.

"Mr. Q," Gabriel said with a grin, turning to me to make sure I heard it. My stomach turned over, mostly because I nearly answered to it. "I have someone I would like you to meet. Robert Blank, meet Mr. Quackenbush."

A ripple of recognition fluttered over Quackenbush's features. "Mr. Blank, really. I've never had the pleasure."

"Hi," I said, unsure of what else to say. What do you say to the Devil? It's pretty much either "Hi," or "How about a fiddle contest?"

"What is a man of your talents doing so far from home?"

I swallowed. "Oh, you know. Here for all the patriotism. Wanted to help out with the...thing...at the airport. Happened to run into an old friend here..."

Quackenbush nodded. "Gabriel? If you would be so kind as to leave us?"

"Yes sir. Where we go one, we go all."

"Of course."

Gabriel patted me on the shoulder, and I swear he jogged something loose. Or maybe I just hurt everywhere. He returned to the elevator, and I didn't think I could be sad to see him go, but I kind of was. Sure, he was a supernaturally strong psychopath, but he was a relatively friendly face, which none of those present were even close to. More of those present had started taking note of me. You never want to be the one person at a cult meeting everyone stares at. That's how you end up on an altar.

"Mr. Blank, if you would come with me?" I followed him into the next room, grateful to get the eyes off me. He opened up the doors leading out onto the balcony. The storm had abated, leaving the streets covered in white, and a silence hanging thick and heavy over the city. The air was frigid this far up but I was in a Santa suit, so all things considered, I was dressed for it. He stepped out onto the balcony, acting like it was a balmy seventy degrees out there.

I hugged myself. Didn't help. Christmas lights glittered over the city. "Christmas," I said.

"Ah yes, Merry Christmas." He shook his drink, the ice making crystal sounds against the glass. "Mr. Blank. It isn't just anyone who can vanish the way you did. One minute, you were the best fixer in Los Angeles. The next, you were gone. I assumed that you had been killed. You do have an uncanny knack for amassing enemies."

"It's my sparkling personality."

"And when you reappear, it's a thousand miles away in another city where I just so happen to be at the time."

"Hell of a coincidence."

"I don't believe in coincidences."

There was that pattern recognition again. Belief in coincidence is vital to sanity. Start seeing connections between everyone and everything...well, that's how you drive yourself crazy. I don't think Irving Quackenbush was crazy, exactly. Personality disorders, sure. But I think there was just enough irrationality in him to let him pretend he was entirely reasonable. If you're constantly surrounded by a web of conspiracy, it's a great way to justify the next awful thing you want to do.

"I had no idea you were here, sir," I said. "I was here for the action at the Denver airport. It was posted all over the patriot groups."

"You're trying to tell me you were there as a true believer?"

"You bet. Just trying to make America great, drain the swamp, build the wall, fist the alien. The usual."

"I don't believe you." Quackenbush decided. His gaze felt like Superman's heat vision. One look would flay me open. "I might assume that a fixer such as yourself is too savvy to fall into something as transparent as this Q nonsense. But I don't have to assume, because I know you couldn't have."

"No one is immune to it."

He offered a reptilian smile. "You are, because you invented it."

Maybe it was the cold, or the lack of sleep, or the hunger, or the booze I had laid out on top of all of that, but the world felt like it was beginning to sway. "No, I didn't."

"Don't lie to me. You can pull the wool over the eyes of a blunt instrument like Gabriel, but I know something you do not."

"What's that?" I managed.

"Who do you think hired you to create Q in the first place?"

Now I did feel like I was falling, tumbling off the balcony into the frozen night. "You?"

"Don't be so surprised. I don't have to tell you how important Quackenbush Security is to the world at large. I have the resources for such an operation."

"Why?"

Quackenbush turned to the balcony, as though he was addressing a great throng of supporters. They were all ghosts. "Roosevelt ruined this country. Did you know that? Before him, a man could make something of himself. When we were at the cusp of being truly great, Roosevelt bowed to the will of the parasites. He invented Social Security. He created work that didn't need to be done in order to lie about the hand-outs he was giving. A group of patriots saw what was happening to their beloved country and resolved to take it back—but they were betrayed by the very man they chose as a figurehead."

"You're talking about the Business Plot."

"I dislike the name."

"A bunch of capitalists got together to oust Roosevelt, and install a retired Marine Corps general as a fascist dictator."

"An oversimplification, but yes. Only the man chosen, Smedley Butler, betrayed those patriots. And the country began to spiral."

"Spiral?" I admit, I didn't think things were going great, but I doubt Irv and me had the same ideas about why.

"This country was founded on a simple principle—"

"Not paying taxes?"

"Taxation is theft. You see, this country was built so that the smart, the strong, through hard work, could prosper. The ones who weren't smart? Weren't strong? They would fail, and this was good and natural. Upsetting that natural order pushes parasites to the top where they inevitably are overwhelmed and fail, and grinds the truly great under a boot of oppression."

"Yeah, you seem oppressed."

"My money, taken from my pockets, so that some illegal can have a sixth child? Who, of course, is American just because her mother had the low animal cunning to navigate a river."

"When our ancestors showed up here, this country was occupied. We killed them. Then we imported people from Africa in chains."

Irving smirked. "Slavery and genocide, yes. I know, very sad. Have you ever considered one simple point? You can't commit a genocide upon or enslave a superior people. It's impossible. These alleged crimes you pretend to be so upset about, while doing nothing to address those so-called injustices, were only possible because these people chose to live in the dirt. They were barbarians and we brought them civilization. Some of them died." He shrugged. "A fine price for the gifts we brought."

I admit, I've coated myself in a shell made of pure cynicism. You don't make it very far in my line without one, but sometimes you encounter a racism so pure it staggers even someone as dead inside as me. "Holy shit," was all I could manage.

"I suppose you think it's a coincidence that Europe colonized the world."

"I think it was mostly thanks to the great Khan's alcoholism."

"His people never could handle drink," Irving said, bringing his own to his smirking lips. He returned to the earlier point, not quite done twisting the knife. "Patriots, who had succeeded in our great culture, would put the country back on track, fix what the traitor Roosevelt had broken. Smedley Butler was glorious, did you know that? A butcher for freedom. But somewhere along the line, he developed sympathy for the parasite."

"They tried a coup, and you failed," I said. "Wasn't like they were executed, thrown in prison. They just kept being incredibly rich, successful, and influential businessmen. Hell, Prescott Bush got his son and grandson made president."

"They were banished to the shadows, when they should have been in the sun, restoring the promise of this once great nation. They made one mistake, and one mistake only: trying to do it all at once. Why put everything on the back of a single action that can be stopped by one man? Instead, why not work subtly over the years? Undermine

Roosevelt's treasons at every turn, until the very parasites he uplifted begged to have their life support removed."

"Still, why hire me to make Q?"

"This country wasn't ready in 1933."

"Ready for what?"

"A sure hand on the tiller."

"You mean a fascist dictator."

"The Depression was too near a memory. Americans had grown weak, dependent on government to save them, when the truth is that some people cannot and should not be helped. These people were draining resources that should go to those with the ingenuity to seize them. Our government is enslaved to the whims of the electorate, idiots who can't see past their next meal. They would see a strong leader, one who could put this country back on a path of strength and would make connections to the war we had only recently fought."

"They'd look at your fascist and see Hitler."

"Hitler was a failed art student. Do you know how incompetent you have to be to fail at art? Anything can be art if you know how to sell it. He was never fit to run a country, even if he did get a few things right. The country was not ready then, but now? We have come to accept that some people produce value and some consume it, and the former should be empowered and the latter allowed to wither. We are no longer shielding lessers for cosmetic differences like race. Enough of the populace is ready to pick up arms and assert their birthright. The country is ready. All it needed was a little push. So I hired a number of operators like yourself to lay the ideological groundwork. I told you to make things up and put them on the internet. Most of those lies vanished like farts in the wind." He fluttered his fingers, watching the lie vanish into the chill Christmas air, then turned to me, his eyes like a dying star. His gnarled finger pointed at my heart. "I wasn't surprised when it was your lie that took root. Your lie gave us the fuel to see this thing through. *Your* lie finally made the parasites beg for the boot like they should have in '33."

Nothing was under me. Vomit clawed its way up my throat. "No. See, there's still hope. I can scrub Q from the internet. I know how. I have all the tools I need. I can kill it."

Quackenbush spread his hands. "What good will that do? Q has already done far more than I ever hoped. It's free of the internet now, spreading among the populace unaided. It created the movement I wanted, and eliminating the theory itself will do nothing. I have a heavily armed mob howling for the blood of my enemies and we run the government. Those fools are ready to dismantle every part of this country and cry out in pain when they suffer for it, and they will never connect their actions to their delusion. All that remains is crushing whatever remains of dissent, and there is precious little of that. We can be comfortably ruled by a single man who will feed the rubes Christianity while we squeeze every drop of blood from you. We will live like pharaohs, as is our birthright." His lips skinned back from his teeth, and he toasted me. "You're merely trying to cure the cancer of a dead man."

The city was quiet below me. I was completely alone, with only this ghoul as a companion. This rich man who had lined his pockets by systematically making the world a shittier place. I'd been a pawn, a pawn that had jumped off the board and by the time I climbed back on, my king was in checkmate. And now all I had was Irving Quackenbush watching me with a smug look on his shrunken pumpkin face, ready to make even more money by killing as many people as he could. Money he didn't even need.

I didn't hear anything behind me, but I assumed there would be a gunman. He would have crept over the soft carpet of the room, leveling his pistol, ready to splatter my brains all over downtown Denver. No reason not to. I had a lot of regrets, sure. Mostly I wished that the last thing I saw wasn't Irving's serpent smirk. "So," I said, "I imagine you're going to have me killed."

Quackenbish laughed. "Kill you? Whatever for? Mr. Blank, it doesn't matter whether you live or die."

chapter
seventeen

I DON'T REALLY REMEMBER the walk to the elevator. I existed in a numb haze knowing that the only thing around me would be screaming. Mine, of course. The thing that had torn me out of despair was entirely pointless. That's a tough thing to hear, made worse when the person saying it used such a maddeningly reasonable tone. Quackenbush wasn't taunting me. Sure, he enjoyed twisting the knife, but that wasn't the purpose behind what he'd said. No, he was stating a simple fact. He was *educating* me, trying to get me to put aside childish things and grow the fuck up in an uncaring world.

In the stories we grow up with, there's always hope. A fool's hope, like a certain old man said, but hope nonetheless. There's always a daring plan with long odds. There's always a proton torpedo to be fired at the exhaust port just above the main reactor. Always a crane kick to be landed on the bully's chin. Always streams to cross that will defeat the marshmallow god. So naturally my mind was frantically groping for the magic bullet that would give me victory at the moment of defeat. My mind, desperately unraveling the riddle of hate.

And let's be clear for a second: my original plan was madness. Releasing a digital god to devour a conspiracy from the online world wouldn't be anyone's first impulse. To be told without a shred of doubt, that everything I had done, from pulling myself out of a mire, to assembling a crew and stealing that god from the D.U.M.B., to being tortured by a weasel for the entertainment of thugs, was utterly pointless...well, it was a bit much to take.

The elevator slid open with a jaunty *ding*. Kirk Shelley stood dead center in the car grinning like a muppet. "Let's go, Bobby," Kirk said. "Oh yeah, I know who you are. Mr. Quackenbush called down and asked that I escort you out of the building. Specifically wanted *me* to do it, too."

That meant another beating on top of the unhealed agonies of the last few. Maybe if I was really lucky he'd pop a couple organs like water balloons.

I stepped into the elevator and turned my back on Kirk. Might encourage him to get on with it, go for a hit on the head that might make me forget. He leaned past me and hit the button for the lobby, rancid breath on my neck. The doors shut on the meeting of the new Business Plot and they got back to deciding how many people should die in order to maximize short term quarterly gains.

"I knew it was you downstairs," Kirk lied. "I just figured it would be more fun to give you enough rope to lynch yourself.

"That's thoughtful."

"You're probably worried. Think that I'm gonna pay you back for those two years in prison."

"You were inside for two years?"

"The longest two years of my life."

"You murdered someone. It was on tape."

"The sentence was longer, but pardons don't care if you have two years or two decades."

"Of course."

"We need that kind of thing anyway. You know how conservatives are oppressed in this country."

"Waiting two whole years for a presidential pardon! Will your people ever be free?"

"Snark all you want, but things are changing for the better."

The elevator opened up on the lobby. Just a Santa going for a walk with a white nationalist murderer. Nothing to see here, folks. We went outside in the frigid air of Christmas night. I had no idea where I was going, merely that I was no longer welcome in the hotel. I could add that to the list. All I knew for certain was that I had nowhere pressing to be and nothing important to do. My plans had come to nothing, and all that remained for the evening was a vicious beating at the hands of a Nazi I'd once administered wholly inadequate justice to. Goes to show how well my schemes worked.

"Left turn," Kirk said. He was talking about the alley running alongside the building.

Getting beaten up in an alley was part of the job description for whatever I was calling myself at any phase in my life. There was something almost sentimental about the whole thing. I could ruminate on all the various alley-beatings I'd suffered in my days. In a golden autumnal day in my mind, I could peruse the albums of my precious memories.

We got down about halfway and Kirk said stop. I turned, giving myself enough room between my back and the wall that when I fell, I'd have somewhere to go rather than right into brick. But Kirk didn't throw hands. He kept grinning his maddening grin.

"You know, during my time inside..."

"Two years," I said.

"It's a long time," he snapped. "During my time inside, I thought a lot about what I would do if I ever caught my old associate Otto Maddock." That had been my Thule Society name. I'd been going through a *Repo Man* phase. Don't judge. "Later, I found out your real name. Mr. Quackenbush showed me a ledger with all the names of his operatives. Explained to me what you were doing back in LA. That you were a traitor to everyone you ever spoke to."

"Paid well," I said. "Kind of."

Kirk pulled a pistol from his jacket. Its plasticky black finish swallowed the diffuse light from the street. The most intense wave of relief washed over me at the sight of the weapon; I just wished someone else were holding it. I pictured Mina standing behind it and I felt a bit better.

"Mr. Quackenbush doesn't want you dead, but I don't think he'll be too upset one way or the other," Kirk said.

I focused on the other side of the alley, where the old bricks glistened with melting snow. Not the worst sight to go out on. To be honest, I'd been expecting to be shot like this for a long time. If Kirk would keep his fucking mouth shut it'd be tolerable, but that's the thing about bullies. They never can.

"Good riddance to trash—"

"Hold it right there!"

I didn't think that any sound could truly surprise me, but that one did. I knew the high, childlike voice with the Dracula accent. I had trusted the owner of that voice, and she me. She was one of the few people I considered more than an acquaintance, though her status as Mina's best friend meant I assumed her to be lost to me. Except here she was, saving my rotten life.

Kirk and I turned, and I like to think we both felt the same kind of embarrassment. Like we'd just been walked in on having terrible sex, and now we were going to have to explain what that yak was doing here and why we'd bothered to shave it.

The figure coming up the alley was hobbit-small. She was a compact wad of muscle and tendon, trained for the kind of physical feats they give medals for. Literally. She had a gold and a bronze one. She stepped into the light, revealing a pretty and unmistakably Slavic face, her brown hair pulled into a high and tight ponytail. She wore a bomber jacket with fur at the neck, and leggings that showed off gams, that while short, had more muscle on them than Jeffrey Dahmer kept in his fridge. Her name was Oana Constantinescu, former member of the Romanian Olympic gymnastics team and pocket-sized badass, and I never thought I would see her again.

"Let him go," she said to Kirk.

"You're fucked now," I told him.

"Shut up," he barked at me. He turned his attention to Oana. "This doesn't involve you. Take a walk."

"Mr. Quackenbush doesn't want him hurt." For a moment, I knew true despair, but then what had to be going on dawned on me. This was an undercover op. Oana had been an enforcer and dirty tricks specialist for V.E.N.U.S., a feminist conspiracy. She'd only cut ties with them when they showed their feminist bona fides weren't bona and might not even have been fides. They'd tried to use Mina as a bargaining chip, and Oana, what with being a good person, walked.

"This is better long term," Kirk said, "and I don't answer to the likes of you."

She took another step. Oana's Olympic days were long past, and Kirk had at least a foot and maybe a hundred or so pounds on her, but I think even he knew that she would roll him up like a rug if they decided to slap leather. "I'm not telling you anything you don't know. Mr. Quackenbush didn't say kill him, so you don't kill him."

Kirk seethed. "Fucking fine. You want him alive? You deal with him." He stalked for the mouth of the alley, pausing when he was right next to her. "Don't let me catch you alone."

"You know where to find me."

Kirk left, probably to go do whatever frustrated Nazis do. Nothing good. With any luck, he'd run into Pud Galvin.

"Oana, what are you doing here?" The relief in my voice came out in frosty plumes. It wasn't that she saved my life. It was that she had stepped out of my former one. If she was here, that meant the past wasn't too far away, and maybe I could grab it. It's fair to say that between my persistent hunger, the booze, lack of sleep, and maybe some of the torture, I wasn't exactly thinking clearly.

Her smile was filled with pity. "You don't look so good, Bob."

"I've had a tough couple of...time units?"

"You should go," she said. "There's too much happening right now. You don't want to screw anything up."

"This is an op! I knew it. Is...anyone else here?"

"You mean Mina. She is at home the last I heard."

"Last you heard?"

"She and I haven't spoken in months."

"Deep cover?" I asked hopefully.

"Bob...the men here...we're doing a very important thing. The Cabal is on the ropes. We just need a last push to take them down."

My head pounded anew. My stomach fluttered like a jellyfish. The world tipped and heaved, threatening to throw me into the churning water. Oana was still talking, but I couldn't hear her over the blood howling in my ears.

It couldn't be true. It had to be fake. All I managed was a plaintive, murmured, "No."

Oana cocked her head. "All we were doing with our lives was a lie. The conspiracies we served only kept the Cabal safe. Shielded them. I did my own research, and soon, they found me. I work for Mr. Quackenbush now. I know what you're thinking. Kirk Shelley is unsavory, but he's on the right side here. He's a useful tool. Eventually, I'll take care of him, but for now, he does what he is told."

"Not you."

"Did you forget where I grew up? I lived under communism. I know what kind of evil it can foster. Here, it made the Cabal. So I'm doing what needs to be done."

"Is Mina...?"

She shook her head sadly. "Mina works in the industry. I know she's not with them, but she can't believe she's close to so much evil. She even told me that *you* made Q up." Oana laughed. "Could you imagine?"

"Oana please, not you too."

"It's okay, Bob. The patriots win." She handed over an envelope from her jacket. It was still warm when I opened it. A plane ticket, a couple bills, and even a brand new ID with the name Robert Blank. I turned them over in my hands, willing them to change to a note that would tell me this was an op. She was performing for surveillance. I knew it wouldn't; her expression had a fanatical surety, and pity for a friend who couldn't see the truth. "Go home. There's nothing you can do. We have everything in hand."

I don't know what happened next. There was only the pounding in my head and the darkness all around me. I could only think over and over, that I broke my friend. I'd taken away her rationality without even a thought. She was gone now, lost to those fascist monsters upstairs. And the worst part of it was that if I could break Oana, I could break anyone. Except for the one person who deserved it. I was standing across a crack in the world of my own making while being reassured that it wasn't there at all.

"Bobby?"

I only realized at the sound of my name that I was sitting on the frozen curb, staring at a section of icy concrete. My ribs felt like they had been kicked to pieces all over again. The screwdriver was in deep, but part of me needed that pain.

Hasim stood over me, concern painted all over his face, and since he was still dressed like a North Pole elf, it was a pretty funny image. Riley was close by with Pud, and Lara a little more distant. All of them were varying shades of worried and scared. Other than us, the streets were empty. It was as clear and cold as glass.

"What?" My voice was gummy with unshed tears and congealing blood.

"I have all three devices," Riley said hopefully. "I can put Shub-Internet together. We've got it."

I clambered to my feet, stumbling as the world shifted. My head kicked like a mule. "Why would we do that?"

"What?"

"Why? What the fuck good is Shub-Internet going to do?"

Riley shifted, glancing to the others. She looked like she thought she was being tested with a trick question. "That was the plan, remember?"

I laughed, the screwdriver turned, but it was far away now. Thanks, alcohol. "The plan, right. Gotta stick to the plan. So let's say it works just like we think. We let Shub-Internet out and it actually does what we want. Fabian uses one of his spells or whatever and the big scary Lag Monster eats up every last mention of QAnon online. What then? You ever fucking think of that?"

"Hey," Lara said. "Don't throw that shit at her. She's trying to help."

"Trying to help *what*, Lara?"

"Trying to help *you*, motherfucker."

"That's rich. Look at me. Fucking *look at me*." I held out my arms. I was a badly beaten and malnourished man in a soiled Santa outfit. "Is this the kind of person you think you can help?"

"Hey, man. It's okay," Hasim said. "Settle down and let's talk this thing out."

"Oh shut the fuck up with that."

"Hey!" Lara barked more forcefully. "What the fuck is this?"

I leaned in close to Lara. She didn't give me an inch. "There's nothing we can do. The damage has been done. No, wait. *I did the damage.* I broke every goddamn thing in this world and there's no way to put it back together. You know when I thought there was? I was drunk and fucking *ergot poisoned* after sleeping in a park for God knows how long. I was trying to tell myself that I could fix things, but that was stupid, it was always stupid."

"Calm down," Lara told me in her sternest teacher voice. "I hear what you're saying, but let's calm down and figure this out."

"There's nothing to figure out. The thing I thought we could do? I don't even know if it's possible. But the thing is, it doesn't matter. The toxin, the memetic disease, it's already out there in the ether. Fucking Paul Mallon tried to tell me this back on his cult compound! Q isn't even a thing anymore. And it's not like there isn't a precedent. When Jesus was gone, did that suddenly make Christianity stop?"

"Dude, this is not a religion."

"Yeah it is! You just don't want to see it as one because then you're going to look in the mirror, all three of you, and have to reckon with the dumb shit you believe."

"That's enough," Lara said.

"And that's the other thing. This whole Information Underground shit, all of us in our little secret societies running the world, what were we doing? We were giving *them* cover." I jabbed my finger at the top floor of the Ritz where the Business Plot should still be drinking strong. "They always need conspiracies to blame. Oh, it's never the real ones. It's never the rich sociopaths fucking the world over for a buck. Nah, it's the Jews, or the Muslims, or the Mexicans. It's whoever they think they can drive out and scapegoat. And you know what? *We helped with that.*"

"I don't think I need to take this off some white cis motherfucker," Lara said.

"Good. Walk the fuck away then. We should. We were wasting our time."

"You know what? Fine. I'm fucking done." Lara walked away into the snowy night.

"Lara, wait." Hasim caught up to her, and the two of them argued, their voices just out of hearing, eaten up by the cold.

Riley took a wobbling step to me. "B, I'm not sure what happened, but maybe we should get you something to eat, some rest maybe..."

"You know what I can't figure out? I know why *I* did this. I was desperate enough to believe anything. What I can't figure out is why someone as smart as you did."

"B..."

"Not so smart after all, I guess."

I walked away, leaving my crew behind. Pud howled, his wails echoing through downtown Denver.

chapter
eighteen

BLAME THE DRINK, blame the concussion, it doesn't much matter to me.

I used Oana's poison ticket. I flew home in a daze, all my injuries pounding in time with a sluggish heartbeat. My consciousness prairie dogged its head a few times—oh, here's Blucifer, here's the drink cart, here's the couple obviously getting into the mile high club because that was last year's New Year's resolution—but mostly I remained mired in the bog of my self-loathing. Pressure gripped me like a vise, grinding all the broken parts of me against one another. Also, I don't recommend flying in a Santa suit. Even on the night after Christmas, security finds you more interesting than you'd like. The ID Oana gave me staved off the worst of it. Small favors, I guess.

I trudged to long term parking and extracted the Belle, chewing up the last little bit of money Oana had given me. Didn't really matter, though. Where I was going, I didn't need money. Corn mash whiskey and ergot were free.

It had been a mistake to leave my exile; never should have left the numbers station in the hills. Not the most heroic outcome, but sometimes a mistake is so big that there's no fixing it. It's best to leave the world to play with the pieces.

The sun was crawling out into a smoggy sky as I pulled into Griffith Park. I wondered what Mikhail would say about my brief and ill-advised foray back into the world. I'd take my lumps and then I'd drink myself into a stupor. I could handle that for a long while. Mikhail's shack was right where I left it, always about an inch from tumbling into a stack of garbage. I pulled up next to it, and got out in the plume of dust. The still beckoned me over, *Welcome back, cowboy. What can I get you? A new world, one where you're not memetic Typhoid Mary? 'Fraid that's off the menu. Howzabout a snort of the old poison? It's just like you remember, and it'll take you into a dreamless sleep where you never did a damn thing wrong.*

By the time I staggered through the shack's doorway, I was halfway to the promised oblivion. Mihail was hunched over the radio reading off his seemingly random string of nouns and numbers. I collapsed into the wire frame cot like a sick Christmas tree at the last axefall, closing my eyes against the sudden wash of nausea, and stared at the makeshift ceiling. There was something both comforting and awful in the familiarity, like being beaten by a parent.

Darkness closed in around me, and I think I slept.

I woke up, early morning light bleeding in through the holes in the walls and ceiling. I was on my back, breathing shallowly. When I moved, every part of me made certain to explain why that was fundamentally a bad idea and that I should think about a new existence as a sessile organism. Never one to listen to common sense when drink was in the offing, I turned onto my side to begin the process of getting up and found Mikhail staring at me.

"You're back," he said.

"What the fuck? Have you just been sitting there like a serial killer the whole time?"

"You've been out for almost twenty-four hours."

"That's not a no."

"You're dressed like Santa Claus."

"Yes, I know."

"*Why* are you dressed like Santa Claus?"

"Because, Mikhail, I'm in the Christmas spirit. Can't you tell?" I fought to sit up and finally managed it, covered in sweat and trying not to gasp too much. I reached for the bottle of shine and found that it had tipped over in my sleep and that was why Santa smelled like gasoline.

"Did you do what you set out to do?"

My laugh turned into a grimace. "Nope. Don't even think it was possible at all."

"You seemed so confident the other day."

"Yeah, well, it turns out that I'm an idiot. The funny thing is, you'd think that more people would know that."

Mikhail stood up from his squat, his knees popping like champagne corks. He looked like he was considering his words carefully, though I couldn't imagine why. "Wasn't possible, huh?"

"At first, I thought all I had to do was kill a man. Not even a good man. The kind of guy who makes the world worse every day he's breathing and laughs if it bugs you. No, it had to be an idea. Problem is, ideas are harder to kill than cockroaches in power armor. I thought I could do it just because I wanted it bad enough. Wishing for something doesn't make it so. They're all wrapped up in each other, the man, the idea, feeding on each other and this culture that says anything is fine and dandy as long as you can make a buck off it. And if you can make a billion? Well, friend. That's doing good."

"You thought you could kill an idea."

"Every now and again I pull a miracle out of my ass. Usually when my back is against a wall."

"Of all the things to kill, why Q?"

"Kronos could eat his kids, right?"

"What?"

"Sorry. Because it's a fucking poison that's eating this country alive. Only that's not quite true. It's poison that's been there all along, and it just woke the fuck up and now it's picking its teeth with our world."

"I thought it was a bunch of patriots who didn't like child molesters."

I laughed. "Seriously? Who's their savior? A guy who bragged in an interview about barging into a dressing room to ogle naked teenagers. A guy who hung out with one of the most famous pedophiles ever."

"Teenagers...that's ephebophilia, not pedophilia."

"How the fuck do you know *that* and not know who Kronos is? Anyway, not the point. The point is that if they're so mad about sex trafficking, they sure did pick someone who should have 'Most Likely to Sex Traffic' under his high school senior picture."

"Your country *rewards* that? I grew up hearing about the decadent west, but this—"

"Did you hear about hyperbole during all that decadent west stuff? Okay, the point is that in their whole alleged crusade, they picked a figurehead who is pretty obviously guilty of multiple counts of sexual assault. There has to be a better choice than him. Billions of them. And it's not just him. Whenever one of theirs gets popped for anything it's always dismissed, ignored, excused while the people they hate get tarred with zero evidence."

"This country is corrupt."

"You'll get zero argument from me there. Talk about the real shit, that's all I ask. The whole pedophilia Satan worshipping thing is just cover. Cover that protects you from looking inward. In this country, you can be as angry as you want, you can hit and kick and that's strong. But the second you look inward? You're weak. So it's cover that points the anger out like a gun, rather than in where it might actually do a little good. That's all it ever is." I slumped, exhausted and annoyed with myself for getting worked up over something I couldn't change. "How did we get on that?"

"You tried to destroy an idea and couldn't."

"Right," I said. "It was dumb of me to think I could do that. I really thought that I'd figured out how, but the truth was, I *wanted* it to be true, and so it *was* true. I was drunk and as it turned out, poisoned. I didn't even start out with that plan. No, I was going to go kill Paul Mallon, and of course that was a dead end, so I picked up that insanity with Shub-Internet."

"Shub...what?"

"God of the Internet. It's..." I waved my hands around and thought about what Riley said. Then I thought about the last thing I said to her and reached for the empty bottle. The walk out to the still felt impossibly long, but you know what they say about how the journey of a thousand miles begins.

"You're done trying, then?"

"Oh, I'm done. Completely."

"Good," he said, shambling to his workstation.

I probably could have left it there. His chair squeaked, followed by the click of the broadcast starting, and then the distinct Russian words followed. I focused on the hole in the ceiling, where a piece of clapboard and aluminum didn't meet flush. Through it was a swatch of faded blue, like old denim. *Good*, he had said. *Good.*

"Misha?" I asked.

"Yeah?" he answered, interrupting the broadcast.

"Misha is a nickname for Mikhail."

"I know."

I clambered to my feet, as the screwdriver drove ever more deeply into my side. I was having trouble seeing where I was, but I wasn't looking here. I was looking at where I had been. "Pretty big coincidence that the same day I break into a military base, a whole bunch of Q nuts descended on it too. And only one person in this world who wasn't there with me knew I was going." The chair squeaked and Mikhail turned fully. His eyes were almost invisible under his heavy brows. "That I was going to destroy QAnon."

Mikhail's bony hands clenched into treelike knots. "There is no QAnon. There is Q and there are Anons."

The ice behind those words hit me full force. "Why?"

"Someone is finally going to take down the Cabal. Someone is going to protect the children and make this country great, and you want to stop them."

"How? How the hell were you into it under my nose this entire time?"

"You think it's hard to get something past a man who spends all his time wandering around in the hills and the other half blind drunk?"

He was right about that. He could have landed a passenger jet on my face and all I'd wonder is when my mustache got so heavy. "I made it up! I made it all up! *I told you I made it up!*" Over the protestations of my entire body, anger shot me to my feet.

"Two things I know about you. One, you lie a lot. Two, you know things. So if there was one person who would know about the Cabal, it'd be you."

"You sent cultists to kill me."

Mikhail didn't blink. "I did what I had to do."

Rage wrapped me up in a burning blanket. I couldn't think, let alone speak. All that was left of me was the wrath that would eat me up.

I charged Mikhail. I was damn slow—the sleep, the hurts, the Santa suit, all of it slowed me until I was trying to fight in treacle. He leapt up, quick and mean as a cobra, but couldn't get out of the way before momentum crashed me into him. With a grunt, he slammed into the radio equipment. My air went out in a gust centered around the pinpoint in my ribs. Suddenly my legs were buckling and my arms didn't go all the way up.

He pushed at me, but I had leverage on my side. Pretty much all I had. My hands crawled from his shoulders to grip his neck. I squeezed, and for a bright moment I thought I might actually be winning this thing. But we all know how those thoughts turn out.

Mikhail flailed away, and he got lucky. Throw enough and something will connect, especially when if I were a video game boss my entire anatomy would be flashing red. His fist came down right on the swollen mass of pain that was my right side. He pushed out what little air I could breathe and installed the feeling of broken glass through my body. I lost my grip on Mikhail, and he shoved me backward. He followed up, slamming again into the throbbing red splotch that was my ribs.

Right about here, it should be pointed out that neither Mikhail nor I especially knew how to fight. I spent most of my time avoiding the fights I could and losing the ones I couldn't. Mikhail seemed to have a similar experience. There was nothing pretty or even dignified about our violence, and I suppose it was sort of honest for that at least.

I went down in a heap, and Mikhail fell on top of me. I braced for the water that would suffocate me. Turned out I didn't need it. The weight on my chest, coupled with the pain, was as sure as drowning as the water had been. I tried to breathe in, but the agony gripped me, tried to grind me up. I opened my mouth, but nothing could come in. I was slipping.

Mikhail never stopped. Whatever switch had flipped in me had flipped in him as well. He had betrayed me to that mob, and in his mind, it was only because I had betrayed everything good and right in the world. I was helping a universe of the worst monsters. Anything he did to me was not only justified, but demanded by basic morality.

The blows didn't hurt all that much. I'd been beaten by professionals. The suffocation was far worse. The helplessness of needing to breathe, but being completely unable to do this thing I had taken for granted. My vision started to iris shut as I lay there gasping. That's all, folks. Wasn't how I wanted to go. Wasn't how anyone wanted to.

Then air flooded into me, burning like white phosphorus.

My senses returned from underwater, muddy at first, my brain fumbling for where I was. I lay on the dirt floor of the shack, staring up at the same gap in the ceiling. The sounds, though, those were awful. It wasn't the distant susurrus of traffic or the night songs of coyotes. It was agonized screaming and the sound of an energetic meal of ribs. The smell too, no longer the vaguely rosemary scent of the park, but of raw meat and pennies.

I sat up. Mikhail thrashed around on the floor with a chupacabra on him. The monster tore into my old roomie, ripping pieces off, decorating the shack with arterial spray. All I could do was stare. He wasn't even really drinking the blood. It was like watching an uncensored cut of a raptor just going apeshit on Robert Muldoon.

I couldn't pull my eyes away. I had to watch to the end. So I watched while Mikhail's struggles weakened. Watched when his limp hands were only quivering slightly as his life slipped away from him. Watched his gore turn gritty as it mixed with the dirt. The chupacabra turned around, his little face stained red. "Glah!"

"Pud Galvin?"

Pud loped over to me like a chimpanzee, leaving behind what was left of Mikhail, who looked like he'd been turned mostly inside out like a discarded puppet. "Ugluck," he said, holding out one claw. A bloody finger, popped off at the first joint, sat in his palm.

"I'm not hungry."

Pud stuck the finger in his mouth and chewed. Whatever was in my belly churned. After a moment, Pud loped back over to Mikhail and treated him like a delicious lobster. I sat on the floor, trying to reinflate my body, though every time I took too deep a breath I nearly passed out.

"I thought he was my friend," I said. Pud looked up from his awful feast. "Yeah, the guy you're eating. Only person who took me in after…" I gestured. "You know. You were there."

"Glah," Pud said thoughtfully.

"Turned out the only reason he took me in was that I had redpilled him entirely by accident. How's that for irony? The only person still talking to me was doing it based on a lie."

Pud dug around in Mikhail's chest cavity, surfacing with a triumphant, "Ah!"

"Okay, okay. You were still talking to me, but you're a tulpa. Or a familiar. Or the friendliest chupacabra I've ever met. I guess Mikhail was right to be scared of you after all."

Pud paused in his feast and held up one hand, his four talons splayed. "Errr."

"Fine, yes. You, and Lara, and Hasim, and Riley. Riley didn't know me before, so she doesn't count. And Lara and Hasim…I don't think they're around anymore, and that's my fault. And besides, what would they even say? 'Go to the hospital, Bobby. Stop eating ergot, Bobby.' I thought this was America."

"Hrm." Pud leaned in and made awful slurping sounds.

"They see me now, Pud Galvin. They know what I am. My stupid plan never had a chance of doing anything. Destroy an idea? How dumb can you be? We call it a virus, but that's not true. It's the closest you can get. It's not dead, it's not alive, completely inert…but it has *will*. These memetic viruses, they're built with a goal in mind. To ease a path the host already wants to take. A path that's been carved by history."

Pud frowned, and he looked almost thoughtful as he masticated some of Mikhail. "Mrg."

"You kind of solved that. Kill the host, right? No, Pud. We can't kill everyone who believes in QAnon."

"Glah."

"Because it would be wrong."

"Blerg."

MY SKIN WAS greasy with the desperate sweat of survival. When I finally managed to get up, I stumbled out the door, resolutely not looking down at the ruin of my old roommate. Pud stayed with his feast. I found my way to where the shack sat and nearly fell on my ass. My ribs give me a shank through the guts, and I stayed there, waiting for the pain to fade into something manageable. I ended up sitting there for most of the day, drifting in and out of consciousness.

Sometimes I would open my eyes and the world had changed, ever so slightly. The light turned gold, the shadows longer, the sounds from inside the shack drier. At some point, when the sky was purple and pink, I became aware of a presence next to me. That's the only way I can describe it. One moment I was alone, and the next I wasn't. It wasn't a sound, or a smell. It was knowledge.

A man stood not far away, right next to the old chair where Mikhail sometimes sat to masturbate to urban sprawl. Look, my old roomie was a weird guy. This man was dressed head to toe in black, his outfit looking like something Dr. Evil would wear to a funeral. He wasn't especially tall, his build average. He looked to be in his fifties, his white hair collected in a ponytail, with a saturnine face and a beaky nose. Silver rings set with jewels glittered on his fingers; whoever he was engaged to had sprung for quite the rock. He watched me speculatively, maybe wondering if he needed a half-dead Santa at the world's most depressing office Christmas party. I had seen him twice before, and though he filled me with dread then, I didn't mind him as much now.

"Good evening," he said. I heard some kind of European accent, but I couldn't pin it down. In point of fact, I never figured it out nor heard anything like it again.

"Yeah?"

"May I join you?"

"You've been following me."

"Not as such. Following events. They just happen to lead to you."

"Oh. Pull up a seat."

I didn't think someone that looked like this guy, someone who had the kind of money that led to things like collecting horses or stadiums, would want to get his clothes covered in Griffith Park dust. His outfit might have heard rumors of this thing called dirt, but certainly didn't give them much weight. But this guy plunked down right next to me. He seemed content to stare at the city in silence, which put me at ease. I figured he'd want something, and the money I could smell on him said it wouldn't be anything good.

"Got a name?" I asked.

"You can call me Weldon. Herman Weldon."

"Bob Blank."

"I know who you are."

"Yeah, I figured. Everybody needs a fixer."

He glanced at the shack. "Except perhaps him."

"Nope. He's extremely dead."

"It was going to happen to him eventually."

"Happens to everyone eventually."

Weldon smiled. "Eventually."

"So you know who I am. Got a beef then?"

"Do I look like someone with beefs?"

"No, I guess not."

"I thought I might like to meet you."

"That puts you in an exclusive club."

"I suppose it does."

We sat in silence, with only the sounds of Pud's feast as company.

"Don't suppose you're here about Q?" I asked.

"You know, I was curious about something. Was it named for the Q Document?"

"The what?"

"The Q Document. You're familiar with the Gospels, yes? Matthew, Mark, Luke…"

"…and the Human Torch."

"…and John."

"I've heard of them. Religion and I aren't on speaking terms."

"Interesting company you keep in that case. Mark was the first of the Gospels written, followed by Matthew and Luke in some order. This is apparent from the text, because many of the same scenes occur, though not necessarily in all three. There are parts of both Matthew and Luke that look to Mark as a source and adapt to convey the lesson that the individual evangelist thought the most important. Not always the same parts, you understand. The tantalizing aspect is that there are portions of Matthew and Luke that depict scenes—the same scenes—that are not present in Mark. Thus, a missing document has been posited. A lost gospel that provides the other source for the later ones. The accepted name for it is the Q Document. In some ways, it is a perfect name for the conspiracy you invented. In a sense, you are adding a source for fundamentalists to point to, saying, 'You see, our dogma has always believed in this.' So, satisfy my curiosity. Did you name your earth-shaking conspiracy for the Q Document?"

"*Star Trek*."

"Ah yes, my second guess."

"What about John?"

"Not based on either. Written without a documented source, and later than the others. Presumably, it's why John is so much different. The first three—or four, if you include Q—are about the life of Jesus, an apocalyptic rabbi of the kind that were relatively common in those days. John takes the messiah ball, as it were, and runs with it."

"I mostly know it from that rainbow afro guy who used to show up at football games with that John 3:16 sign."

"Rainbow afro guy?"

"It was a wig, I think. He'd go to football games and just hold up the sign. He ended up kidnapping a maid because of the Rapture."

"I don't see how these things are related. I'm not very clear on the heretical notion of Rapture, but it's my understanding that the righteous simply vanish?"

"Yeah, I think so."

"So wouldn't his hostage vanish? Along with himself?"

"I think you're looking for logic that you're not going to find."

"Humans hunt for patterns. The way an owl hunts mice, we look for things to line up neatly and when we do we ascribe significance to them that might or might not be there."

"Like pareidolia. Seeing Jesus in a tortilla or an antichrist in some chaparral."

"What a strange example."

"It's a callback."

"I see. Well, yes. I did it just now. I saw a letter, one of only twenty-six, and one commonly used for the mysterious and strange by virtue of it being relatively uncommon. Q carries a weight by itself that, for example, E does not."

"Yeah. I don't think EAnon would have gone anywhere."

"I took that and ascribed additional meaning, convincing myself that you had referenced a document that only scholars and enthusiasts consider. I tricked myself."

"People want to be tricked."

"How do you mean?"

"This world is a depressing place, but it's the only world we have. So people want to be lied to. They want to be told that what they do truly matters, that they're the hero in the stories they grew up reading. The truth, that we don't have any control, is too scary."

"You don't subscribe to the great man theory of history, then."

"I subscribe to the great surfer theory."

"Explain."

"Forces, economic, political, whatever—they're like waves. No individual person can really move them. They move because vast groups want them to. They can be directed only by concerted pushes to change what your average person sees as morally acceptable. The great men, as you'd have them, are surfers. They get on the wave and ride it to shore."

"Have you ever heard of the Kerkoporta?"

"Is that one of those probiotic drinks?"

"You've heard of Constantinople."

"Now it's Istanbul, not Constantinople."

"Correct. But at the time of this story, it was still Constantinople."

"That's nobody's business but the Turks'."

"Precisely! And the Kerkoporta is why! Byzantium, as the city was originally called, was placed in one of the most strategically important places in the world. The gateway between Europe and Asia, the border between Black Sea and Aegean and thus the entire Mediterranean, it was perhaps the most important port in the classical world. Because it was so important, Byzantium, or Constantinople as it was called at the time of this story, was under constant siege. The defenses were impregnable. On three sides, the city was defended by water, and any ship that approached had to contend with Greek fire."

"Primitive napalm. I've played D&D."

"In an age of wooden ships, imagine how terrifying an enemy that wielded flame would be. The land approach was secured by a series of concentric walls, with a number of gates allowing inhabitants in and out during more peaceful times. When Sultan Mehmet II arrived in 1453, I don't think even he believed he'd be able to sack the ancient city. And he wouldn't have. The Romans—we call them Byzantines now, but they saw themselves as Romans—were in an advanced state of decay. However, they could have defeated the Ottomans were it not for one thing. The Kerkoporta was one of the gates into the city. Not even a significant one. More of a side entrance. One man, presumably a guard, left it unlocked entirely by accident. The Sultan's army gained egress, and the Roman Empire was crushed."

"So you're saying that you don't believe in the great man theory of history. You believe in the great fuck-up."

"I wouldn't quite put it that way."

"One man can't control the forces of the universe, but one man can fuck things up so badly that, in the right circumstances, he can destroy a 1500-year-old empire."

"Well, again, I think that's..."

"You just need the right circumstances. And it helps if what you're going after is already a sick old man." A plan, a vain, fool's hope, the kind in all the stories clicked into place. I saw it, front to back in that ecstatic moment between breaths. I stood up. My side didn't hurt quite as badly as it once had. "Thank you."

"You're going?"

"I have work to do."

"Good."

"Are you staying here?"

"For a little while. I have to admit, I never get tired of a Los Angeles sunset."

"Happy trails, Herman."

"And to you as well, Bob."

I poked my head into the shack. Mikhail's corpse was entirely gone, save for his left hand and a section of forearm. The dirt where he had lain was stained and soggy. Pud ran his snaky tongue over his lips and regarded me.

"Time to go, buddy."

Pud lifted one haunch and released a rib-rattling fart.

"Yeah, I think so too."

I dropped the Santa jacket on the cot, but I left the pants on. I was getting used to them, and the suspenders actually made them fit reasonably well. Pud and I piled into the Belle. I stayed there for a time, knowing that this really was the last time I'd see the shack. I wasn't sure how to feel. Sure, it was sad and desperate, but it had been there for me when nothing else had. He had been someone before Q. A spy, sure, but who am I to judge? I'd taken that away with my conspiracy, burned that man away, leaving someone who thought nothing of condemning a friend to be torn apart by a mob. That Mikhail hadn't been my friend, but the pre-Q Mikhail had been. The one my virus destroyed. Pud Galvin had eaten a husk.

No one ever came up here. Eventually some hiker, long off the good trails, would find the shack, the still, the plot of corn. It would all be overgrown, the weather eating away at the edges, a coyote snoozing the day away in the dusty shade. The hiker would wonder what the radio equipment was for, who could have been squatting in the park and what became of them. Eventually it would be one of those weird mysteries that happens whenever some piece of the Information Underground slinks into popular consciousness. And eventually, as with all interesting places in the hills, would become the site of some pinup photoshoot.

The last thing I saw was Weldon, sitting on the overlook, staring out over the sunset. Then the Belle threw a veil of dust into the air, and my old home was gone.

I didn't have a ton of time, but I had a stop I had to make across town before I could finish this thing. The car knew the way to go. It couldn't forget.

By the time I arrived at the edge of the canals in Venice it was full dark, which was the way I wanted it. There was a time when a madman thought he'd recreate the Italian city of Venice here, complete with canals instead of streets. It didn't take off, and I can't imagine why in a place wracked with drought. Anyway, he managed a couple square blocks. They're pretty cool.

I pulled up at the edge of the canals, in front of a small house, and turned off the car's engine. Lights glowed in the windows, but I found myself unable to look closely. "Hey, Pud. You see any paper back there?"

Pud passed up a Burger King bag. I sighed. "Yeah, I suppose actual stationery would be a bit much to ask." I scrounged around until I found a pen I'd stolen from Medieval Castle and stared at what was now a blank page. The feelings that compelled me to make the drive over here and actually pick up a pen and paper were now jammed up at the bottleneck of my hand. I knew what I felt, what I needed her to know. What I didn't know was how to *say* any of it. The simplest concepts, stuff like water being wet or private militaries being bad, were entirely beyond my abilities. That's how these things always went. Everything is easy until you try.

I don't know how long I stared at the blank page, but the light went out in her house and that made things easier. I pressed the old bag on the dash and put the pen to it. Pud's breath was hot on my neck, and it stank of Mikhail meat. "Hey, buddy, it's tough doing this with you looking over my shoulder."

"Burg." He settled back on the car seat.

I started to write.

Mina,

You were right. I don't know if I ever said that. I don't remember things all that clearly. It gets all wrapped up in what I was feeling, so it's this gray slush. You said that there should be a line. I spent my life not really having one. I worked for everyone under this idea that it would all sort of balance out in the end, and if I took every job, that meant if things ever got really bad, I'd be in the perfect spot to do something about it. Turns out that was just something I told myself so I could get paid.

This was a step too far. I fucked the world worse than most people ever get the chance to. And now I know there's no real way to unfuck it.

But I think I figured something out, a way to put things relatively right, or at least less wrong than they were. So I'm going to go do that. And for once, this won't be half-assed. I'm using my entire ass, and with any luck, a few extra asses. I'm regretting this turn of phrase already.

I hope you read this note. And when you're done with it, I hope you burn it and never think of me. I couldn't handle you hating me. I just need to soften it to minor dislike or even indifference if I'm going to get some peace. I'm sorry about my choice of stationery too. I'm sorry about a lot of things.

You were right. About pretty much everything since I met you. It's hard remaking the world from a position of justice, so you made a hard road for yourself. Maybe next time you walk it, there won't be as many roadblocks.

I drew a small rabbit at the bottom, folded it up neatly, and walked it across the street to her mailbox. What had been our mailbox. Maybe she would read it. Maybe she would think it was trash and throw it out. At least I had written it. That meant something.

chapter
twenty

RILEY'S STREET WAS ASLEEP. I pulled to a stop in front of her house, noting the car that looked like a geometric blueberry sitting in the driveway. I stared at the front door, running through the plan and the apology in my head. Say what you will about me, but I had managed to fuck up my friendship with Riley in record time.

Pud made a purring noise.

"I know, buddy. You like her."

"Glah!"

"Well, you're gonna have to get used to it if you keep hanging out with me."

Finally I got out of the car, looked at her house for a little while longer, only then realizing that I was greasy with flop sweat. I forced myself to the front door and I knocked as though a colonoscopy made of fire was waiting for me on the other side. No answer. I knocked again, louder. Still nothing. I peered into the frosted windows on either side of the front door, but couldn't see anything clearly as the designers of those windows intended. Maybe some light glowed inside, maybe not. I wasn't sure how much I needed to trust my senses right at the moment.

Pud romped through the foliage in the front yard, and judging by the frantic rustling sounds, he was pursuing some hapless animal. "If you get skunked, there's no way I can afford tomato juice," I told him.

He didn't listen. Probably why one should always train one's chupacabra.

After a moment's consideration, I limped around the side of the house. Flowerbeds pressed up against the siding here, and light bled around the drawn curtains of one window. I steeled myself and knocked, hissing in a stage whisper, "Riley! Riley, are you home?"

Muffled bumps, a few thumps, and some cursing greeted me. A moment later, the curtain raised, the window opened, and Riley, wearing a green silk robe, leaned into the frame. I realized, now that I could see the cotton candy colors of the room behind her, that this was what I had started to think of as her boudoir. Riley's face was made up and her hair lightly tousled. She looked a bit like she was wearing a costume. Except for the annoyance on her face. That was entirely honest.

"What do you want, B?" she hissed.

"I have an idea."

"An idea? To hammer on my window in the middle of the night?"

"I knocked at the front...I had an *idea*. To do what we wanted to do kinda!"

"Riles?" called a high and breathy voice from inside. "You coming back or what?"

"Just a sec!" Riley leaned in. "Right now. You have an idea *right now*. You couldn't have had an idea tomorrow morning or in Denver."

"Uh...I interrupted something."

"A bit!"

"Riles? Are you talking to someone?"

"Get the hell out of my window. Go to the front and I'll let you in," Riley said.

"Cool, yeah." I peered in past Riley and met the eyes of a pretty young woman presently tied to Riley's bed. "Hey."

"Hi!" she said brightly. "Are you a friend of Riley's?"

"We're not doing this right now," Riley said. She turned to the woman on the bed. "And if you keep talking, the gag is going back in."

"She seems nice," I said.

Riley pointed to the front of the house, glaring at me. A moment later, moving with fast annoyance, she opened the door. "Wait here," she said, pointing at the sofa, before practically running back to her boudoir.

"Is it cool if I raid your fridge?"

"Whatever!" she called over her shoulder.

"Uh, Riley?" I asked. She turned, her hands at the ties of her robe. "What's the deal with..." I pointed at the bedroom. "Do you have like an OnlyFans, or what?"

A smirk tugged at the corner of her mouth. "You interested?"

Suddenly, I felt very hot and had trouble looking at her. And yeah, I was a little, which was a weird sensation after so long *not*. I shrugged. "I mean, a little."

"This is a conversation that I'll be happy to have in about an hour, okay?"

"An hour?"

"I'm a professional."

"Do you play board games after or...and you're gone." She'd disappeared into her boudoir and slammed the door behind her. The sounds that emanated were of the sort that a gentleman does not describe, so I probably shouldn't either. I opened up the door for Pud, who was scratching and whining, and he shuffled in. Whatever he'd been hunting was long gone. Probably good. He had just eaten a whole person. I didn't want to make him sick. Me, on the other hand, I could eat. My appetite had returned along with traces of my libido, checking out what I'd done with the place while they were gone. They were not going to give me my security deposit back.

Judging by the contents of the fridge, Riley's diet was depressingly clean. Eventually I settled on some carrot sticks with a vat of hummus. Not the greatest snack in the world, but my eating habits had been sporadic enough that it didn't much matter. I could've eaten particle board and been happy.

I settled down on Riley's sofa with my snack, and stared at the wall, listening to the music from the other room. The couch hugged me, and I barely felt my hurts. I thought that an hour had been an exaggeration. Apparently not. They reached a crescendo, and then things went quiet. Not too long after, the door opened.

"I'm going to jump in the shower," Riley announced. "I'll be with you in a second."

The other woman came out into the living room, now dressed in a sweater and jeans, her strawberry blonde curls pulled into a bun. "Hey," she said. "You're a friend of Riley's?"

"Uncle. The Grangerfords have started up the feud again, and I need Riley to come on home."

"Oh," she said, nodding. "Sounds serious."

"Baby carrot?"

"Thank you!" she said, taking one. "I always get so snacky after sex."

"I thought it was cigarettes."

"Ugh, no. Everything smells *amazing* and the first thing you want to do is stink it up? No thank you." She plopped herself into one of the chairs. A bolt of realization hit me, and I located Pud in the kitchen, laying down under the breakfast table. She smiled at me, adorably pooped from her exertion.

"So who are you with?" I asked.

"Oh, I'm single."

"No...like...are you a Servant of Shub-Internet too?"

"A what? I was raised Lutheran, if that's what you mean."

"Kind of?"

"I used to be a Girl Scout."

"Got any cookies?"

"Oh God, I wish. I would murder an entire box of Thin Mints. You know how it is with..." Her eyes went wide. "I was about to talk about banging your niece. I'm sorry!"

"He's not actually my uncle," Riley said. She stood at the mouth of the hallway, wrapped in a towel, with another turning her hair into a beehive. "He's just this weird friend of mine."

"Like, how weird?" the other woman asked, leaning forward.

"I'll tell you later, but I gotta talk to him now, 'kay?"

The other woman got up. "I'm Skye," she said to me.

"Bob."

Riley took Skye out to the porch, after a quiet conversation and a chaste peck on the lips, Skye left. Riley returned to the living room.

"She seems nice."

"You want her number? She'd probably be good for you."

I shook my head. The room was hot again, and my Santa pants were uncomfortably tight. I didn't need to be thinking about any of that. It was irrelevant. "That's...ah...that's not why I'm here."

"Your loss. Now what are you doing pounding at my window in the middle of the night?" Riley folded her arms, looking sternly down at me. I felt about two feet tall.

"I'm sorry about before," I blurted. Wasn't how I planned to apologize; it just came out.

She frowned. "Sorry?"

"For leaving you in Denver. For insulting you."

The frown brightened into a laugh. "I thought you needed to blow off some steam. And believe me, that's pretty far from the worst thing a white guy's ever said to me."

"I'm still sorry."

Her gaze softened, deepened. "I met you, what, a week ago? I'm here, minding my own business, and you show up at my front door. You don't look great, and you smell worse, but there's this glint in your eye like you know something. I thought there might be something to you. When I was really little, I used to watch this show, *Behind the Music*. The first act they'd be all about how this old musician was incredible. Inventing some genre, packing stadiums, doing things no one had ever thought of before. Then in the middle of the episode, they'd lose themselves to alcohol and pill addiction, right? When you're not around, that's how Hasim and Lara talk about you. Like you were the greatest guitar player alive in the second act of a *Behind the Music*."

"You probably shouldn't have watched that show when you were really little."

"They told me stories that couldn't possibly be true. The thing is, I believe them because I saw who you were when we were in that military base. You were fucking around for like half of it, and you were still saving my life. *That* guy was whoever Hasim and Lara knew. So if that guy comes to my door and says he needs something..." she shrugged. "Here I am."

I coughed, mostly because I didn't want to start crying. "Thank you," I managed.

"Tell me, what's this idea of yours?"

It took me a second to compose myself. "You still have the three pieces of Shub-Internet?"

She nodded. "They're on the altar in my bedroom."

I outlined my plan to her. Well, most of it, anyway. I held one part back. "Can you do that?"

She frowned, nodding. "I can, with some caveats."

I got up, but found myself swooning. "Let's go. We need to talk to Hasim and Lara."

"No, B. You need rest."

"I slept last night."

"You're still pretty banged up, and keep refusing a hospital. You're going to get some sleep."

"We don't have time!"

"We have enough for you to sleep. If that plan is going to work, you'll need to be on your game, which means sleep. My couch is nice and comfy. In the morning, you're going to eat a real meal. *Then* we can go talk to Hasim and Lara."

I started to protest, but Riley pushed my shoulders down and it was either a second later or I'd already lost consciousness, but a soft blanket was thrown over me. I thought I should probably tell her that I'd lay down for a second, maybe rest my eyes, but we really should be getting moving. The next thing I knew, though, sunlight was streaming through the windows, the whole house redolent with good coffee. I stirred, but quickly found that I had a chupacabra curled up on my feet. I couldn't move him. He was too cute.

Riley peered over the arm of the couch, holding a steaming mug. "You're up!"

"How long?" I croaked. My body was heavy, but the aches weren't quite as bad as they had been. The screwdriver had been replaced by an allen wrench and wasn't boring into me with quite the same gusto. A bolt of panic shot through me as I thought I might have slept through the new year. Pud squawked, glared at me, walked in a circle and settled back down.

"Six hours or so? You look like you could use more."

"It's New Year's Eve, right?"

"Ugh." She rolled her eyes. "Yes."

"Don't like New Year's?"

"Most pointless holiday there is, if you ask me. I don't know how you take it," she said, changing the subject with a proffered coffee mug.

I pushed myself into a sitting position, wincing as the old aches reminded me I wasn't fully healed, and extracted my legs from Pud, who opened one eye to watch me balefully. "Liquid form is fine." The mug was black, decorated with a field of white tombstones, and felt good on my hands.

"Listen, I thought I was going to make us breakfast, but then I remembered that I don't cook."

"I can cook," I said. "You have food and whatnot?"

"I went to the market while you were asleep. I think I did okay. It was only when I got back here that I instantly felt overwhelmed. Anxiety is fun."

"Just to remind you, you were getting anxious over cooking breakfast for a man who has lived in a park for the past year and is still wearing stolen Santa pants."

"It doesn't have to make sense."

"No, it doesn't. Let me wake up and I'll figure something out."

Riley might not have been a good cook, but she was a hell of a shopper. I made us a decent scramble out of what she brought home. I didn't want to start tugging on that thread, but it was a real meal in a way that I hadn't had since my exile. Went a long way toward making myself feel human.

"How long is this trip?" she asked.

"Overnight."

"How should I dress?"

"Comfortable for the road. For the op, you have two options. Either black pants and a white shirt and black bowtie, or something tight and low cut."

"I think I have most of the first one."

Riley went into her room, and when she came out she was dressed in a t-shirt covered in faded tentacles, tight jeans, and some ballet flats, a bag slung over one shoulder.

"The devices?" I prompted.

"What? Oh, right!" She scampered off and returned with the two phones and the tablet, stuffing them into a laptop bag.

"You have all the hardware you need?"

She unzipped the bag and touched each thing as she named it off. "One machine for Shub-Internet, a working machine for me, your phone, my phone, the tablet, and the pineapple." The pineapple, as she called it, was a flat box with four thick antennae, looking a bit like an Imperial cargo ship.

"Let's go," I said. "Things are going to get weird."

"This is why I hang out with you."

We loaded up the car and drove to Lara's. I could have gone to Hasim's first, but I wanted to rip the band-aid off. I had the feeling that Hasim would be relatively easy to apologize to, what with his present existence heavily focused on amends anyway. We pulled up in front of Lara's place and what I'd felt in front of Riley's was multiplied by factors in the thousands. Lara is an intimidating person in the best of times, and I knew she wouldn't let me off the hook as readily as Riley had.

"Are you going to get out of the car, or just stare at her house?"

"Staring's not an option, huh?"

"I was under the impression we were on a bit of a time crunch."

She was right. It was eleven. We had to be in Monte Rio before midnight. It was a seven hour drive, and there would be stops along the way. I got out and looked down at myself. The bloodstained undershirt and Santa pants combo wouldn't fly where we were going, either.

Riley and Pud joined me at the top of Lara's walkway. Riley gave me a little push. "Come on."

I decided that moving quickly was the only way to do this. With a few quick steps I was at Lara's front door, knocking. A moment later, the door opened, and she came out, barely looking at any of us. She was dressed in white, as per usual, and made up. Subtly, sure, but I knew her well enough to notice when she wanted to look special. "You're right on time, I was won—" She trailed off when she saw who was standing on her front door.

"Hi," I said. Riley waved.

"Oh, hell no," Lara said.

"I have a plan."

"*You* have a plan?" She glanced around. "Goddamn it. Come in, but you're leaving soon." She opened the door and let us into her house. She didn't invite us to sit down, which didn't really bode well. "I don't want to have this conversation in front of my neighbors. What do you want, Bob?"

"Okay, well, first off I'm sorry about Denver."

"Fuck Denver. Why are you on my doorstep?"

"Well, I—"

A knock on the door interrupted us. Lara rolled her eyes in frustration and I swear a blush crept into her cheeks. She muttered a curse and moved past us to open the door, revealing Hasim, dressed like he was headed to a job interview. His hair and beard were both neatly combed. "Hey, La—Bobby?"

"Yeah, he just *showed up*," Lara said.

Hasim paused. "You look amazing."

"I know," Lara said, doing a little curtsy. "But thank you."

"You," he said pointing at me. Lara stepped aside for him, and Hasim closed the distance between us. I figured he might deck me. Why not? I deserved it. If he did, I hoped he'd pick the left side. That was in a bit better shape than the right; might even me out. He paused about a fist's length distance, and then grabbed me in a bear hug. "Don't do that again, dude! You scared me!"

"I'm sorry about that." He kept hugging. "Hasim, I'm pretty sure I have some internal injuries."

"Oh shit," he said, letting me go. "Sorry about that. Hey, Riles. Glad somebody's looking after this chump."

"He's made it pretty clear it won't be him," Riley said.

"What the fuck are you doing in my house, Bob?" Lara said.

"Yeah, I mean, glad to see you but why are you here?" Hasim asked.

"Wait. Why are *you* here?" I responded.

"Is this a date?" Riley asked, clapping her hands.

"We were having lunch," Lara said primly. "And now we're not. I'm getting something to drink." She stalked into the kitchen. Riley bounced after her.

"Oh man. I hope this isn't fucked up," Hasim said.

"She said yes," I said. "If it's not happening today, it's still happening."

"Yeah, dude. I wanted it to happen today. Get the new year off on the right foot, you know?"

"I'm sorry," I said.

"About what?"

"Denver. Q. Messing up your date. Pretty much everything."

"We all make mistakes."

"Those are some pretty big mistakes."

He shrugged. "So were mine. You make amends a day at a time."

I cleared my throat. "Listen, if you're going to be dating Lara, I want you to know she's special. If you hurt her..."

"...you'll kick my ass," Hasim sighed. "I know."

I laughed and immediately regretted it, cradling my busted rib. "Nah, she can take care of herself. I was gonna say, if you hurt her, I'll be very disappointed in you."

Hasim stared at me in horror. "That's so much worse, dude."

I patted his arm. "I know."

Lara returned with a mug of coffee, trying to hide her mild embarrassment under a cloak of general anger. Riley followed, grinning like the Cheshire Cat who swallowed the Cheshire Mouse. "Okay," she said. "You've got my undivided attention. Talk."

I laid out the plan in the simplest terms I could, bringing everyone up to speed on exactly what I'd learned at the Denver Hilton. Whenever I got to the technical stuff, Lara glanced to Riley to get confirmation, and she'd either correct me or elaborate on a point I'd made. Just as with Riley, I held one little bit back. They didn't need the whole thing, just what *they* were doing. When I was finished, Lara nodded to herself, sipping the coffee. Her eyes were unfocused, looking at something else, far away. Finally, she nodded. "You think this will work?"

"Yeah, I do. I think it's the only thing that will work."

"I wasn't talking to you." Lara's eyes flicked to Riley.

"I do," she said.

Lara muttered, "Fuck," under her breath. "I thought we were stupid for following you," she said finally.

"Yeah, I'm sorry about that. I was going at this thing all wrong.

When we were in Denver, I ran into an old friend. Oana Constanti-nescu. One of the few people in this world I could trust. She got taken in by Q. She's a believer now, working with those monsters on a new Business Plot. Helped put a fascist in charge who reports directly to Irving Quackenbush. Oana. Of everyone in the world, it couldn't be her too. She was the final straw. She was supposed to be too smart...and that's it, right there. This idea that there would be people too smart to get caught up by this memetic virus, when it works on the precise holes that evolution left in our brains. It can get *anyone*."

"Your plan won't stop that."

"It'll put the fear of god into the ones using it."

Lara sighed. "Fine, I'm in."

"Yeah!" Hasim said. "I'm in. Obviously. I was hoping you were in, but I didn't want to jinx it."

"Hey, so I did want to thank you for flying Pud back. I know that couldn't have been easy," I said.

Lara frowned. "I didn't do that."

I looked to the others. They shook their heads. "Well, that's weird."

"He's a spirit guide. Eventually that's gonna sink in. Now, that whole plan of yours sounded sweet, but you left out one thing. You never said where you were going to find these people."

"They have a New Year's party every year in the same spot. I know you've heard of Bohemian Grove."

chapter
twenty-one

BEFORE I EXPLAIN what Bohemian Grove is, I should explain that conspiracies aren't really what they look like in the popular imagination. Hell, that's the whole point of this sad and sordid tale.

When you ask your average person to imagine a conspiracy, they tend to picture men doing shadowy things in darkened basements. Maybe they're in robes. They're definitely toasting "To Evil!" and the liquid in those goblets is probably blood. And okay, sure. Sometimes this kind of thing does happen, but we're all faintly embarrassed when it does.

Conspiracies look more like a bunch of rich and powerful men drinking together and shooting the shit. Business doesn't even have to be discussed directly. They might hint at it here and there, set up meetings for later in the month, but it's the hanging out that matters. It's powerful men reaffirming their social connections with each other, and if half a million people die somewhere in the world so these two can make a few extra bucks, why the hell not? That's what so many of the amateurs get wrong. It's definitely what all the suburban moms and dads who got sucked into QAnon never understood. These aren't cackling monsters gleefully torturing babies to drink their literal blood. They're boring old men out to make money. Evil happens simply because it's more profitable than good.

I think that the vast majority of the world isn't ready to accept that level of sociopathy. It's more comforting to believe your suffering is caused by malice rather than indifference. When he wasn't being horribly racist, Lovecraft got some stuff right.

In the popular imagination, Bohemian Grove is where a bunch of wealthy men—and let's be honest, for most conspiracy theorists, the *Jewish* part is at least implied—pray to Moloch out in the woods to reaffirm their dominion over the world. And yes, they have a giant demonic owl statue, but it's like that horse in Denver. You're already making a connection between the two, but remember, that's evolution talking. And evolution still thinks your number one concern is cave bears, so what the hell does it know? Sometimes a statue is just a statue.

Bohemian Grove is the wilderness getaway of one of the most exclusive clubs in the world. The kind of club where being the president doesn't guarantee you membership. The Grove accepts all kinds of members from the merely obscenely wealthy to the Pharaonically rich, and from the alpha male to the alpha male with raisins. The place looks a bit like a summer camp, built around a lake near Monte Rio, about seven hours north of Los Angeles. Different "camps" were scattered around the compound, each forming subgroups for the larger one. In practice, these looked like clusters of log cabins festooned with hammocks and outdoor grills. Security is good, and if you're still wondering which company provides it, you haven't been paying attention.

Irving Quackenbush was what they called an Old Guard member. The inner circle of the inner circle. It was my understanding he ran his own camp on the compound called Duck Soup. Cute, right?

Most of the festivities at the Grove were in the summer, as befitting its status as a summer camp for psychopaths. Plus, the weather in central California that time of year is perfect by any rational metric. The Old Guard liked to have a New Year's Eve celebration too, and Quackenbush attended every year. No way he was going to miss it when his evil plan was coming to fruition. The "To Evil!" would be implicit.

The Belle's nuclear power plant hummed as we burned up the Five. We pulled over twice, the first time at an outlet store to pick up our costumes. I chose a black suit with black Chucks for my feet like the old days. Plus, I always wanted to be buried in black.

"Don't take it off at the first opportunity," Lara groused.

"It's the last suit you'll have to buy me. Promise."

The second stop was at a diner, where I cleaned up in the bathroom. The man looking back at me in the cloudy mirror was a wraith. Bruises circled one eye, gummy cuts crossed every bone in my face. There was more gray in my hair and beard than I remembered. I'd say the suit made me feel better, but it didn't. It made me able to pretend, which would have to be good enough.

I returned to the car, where my companions were eating their meals out of styrofoam containers. We would have eaten inside, but that hardly seemed fair to Pud, who was enjoying his rare steak and runny eggs in the company of friends. I slid into the driver's seat, and Riley handed up a container with my burger and fries.

Hasim, in the backseat between Lara and Pud, gestured thoughtfully with his pulled pork sandwich. "Hey, you guys ever heard of *My Friend Frank*?"

I turned partway around, "Where is this coming from?"

"Just something I was thinking about. You know, you go into the den of the big conspiracy, you start thinking about all the other weirdness in the world."

Riley poked her fork into her Cobb salad. "Wait, I think this was a creepypasta. Like...you only ever see one episode?"

"Yeah!" Hasim said. "They only made one episode, but they made it for like seven years and nobody noticed. That's why when you watch it on reruns it's only the one."

"That's not what it is," Lara said.

"Why isn't it streaming anywhere?" Riley asked.

"Technology ruins every good ghost story," I said.

Lara sighed. "Here's the real story. *My Friend Frank* ran from 1974-1981. They made over a hundred episodes of the show. It's not streaming because the network doesn't really own the rights. The creator retained them probably for the reason the show's famous with our set. Because the thing is, it's got some kind of spell over it."

"It's like Hasim says. You only see one episode," I said.

"How is that possible?" Riley asked.

"If you turn the show on," Lara said, taking a forkful of Belgian waffle, "you only see the episode you've already seen. You can never see more than one episode of *My Friend Frank*."

"What if you're with someone else who's seen a different one?"

"The TV craps out, or some emergency broadcast cuts in. Sometimes a real emergency has to happen. It's dangerous to fuck with a spell like that."

"What's the show even about?"

"It's a little like *Perfect Strangers*," I explained.

"I've never heard of that show."

"You're a child." Riley stuck her tongue out. "Okay, so there's this guy who moves into a building in New York."

"Chicago," Lara said.

"I thought it was San Francisco," Hasim said.

"Glah!" Pud exclaimed.

"Some big city. He meets these kooky tenants in the building he lives in, and they're all friends with this guy Frank. Frank is definitely not normal."

"He was supposed to be an angel or Elioud," Lara explained.

"I always thought he was an alien," Hasim said.

"I feel like they kept it vague. But who knows, we've only seen one episode each and it wasn't like TV back then was beholden to continuity."

"Stradivarius was," Lara insisted.

"Who?" Riley asked.

"J.M. Stradivarius, the creator of the show. He was a sorcerer. I can practically guarantee it. No one makes as many oblique references without meaning to."

"Could have only been references in the episode you've seen," I pointed out.

"You ever watch Nick at Nite?" Hasim asked.

"Sure," Riley said. "I used to watch *I Love Lucy* with my sister."

"*My Friend Frank* was more like *Taxi* than *I Love Lucy*. Oh, man. We used to love *Taxi* at the Assassin house. Remember that episode where the wrestling dude gets everybody high? Best episode of anything ever."

"So how does this thing work? You only see one episode?"

"No one knows how it works," I said. "Lara would tell you that it's a spell that Stradivarius put on the show. Hasim would tell you...I don't know what Hasim would tell you."

"God's will, baby!" Hasim crowed.

"There you go. I'd tell you it's an elaborate coincidence that our minds ascribe special significance to."

Lara snorted. "This Scully motherfucker would tell a spirit guide to his face that he's just a cheesy special effect."

"I lead a gray existence," I allowed, taking a bite of the burger. "Point is, once you see the show, no matter how, whatever episode you saw that one time will be the one that's on whenever you somehow catch it again."

Riley frowned. "Yeah...that happened to me with *Malcolm in the Middle*. Seemed like every time I turned on the show, it was the one where the dad rollerskates."

"Yeah," I said. "I've seen the Chinese restaurant episode of *Seinfeld* a jillion times. *My Friend Frank* is like that, only more so."

"That's weird. But what's the big deal?"

Lara scooted forward in her seat. "Because the episode itself is important. Whichever one you see is the one you *had* to see."

"What do you mean?"

Lara shifted uncomfortably. "Okay. Well, I saw my episode one night after an op. He and I," she gestured at me, "were preparing a ritual site for the Society. It was the usual shit they make the initiates do, prepping the ground beforehand so the bosses can cast their spells in peace. We spent all day and half the night painting symbols and cleansing the space, and I'm used to this kind of bullshit from back when I served, but I've been out five years and maybe I got a little lazy. I get home, and my whole body aches. I'm exhausted. I settle down on the couch in my shitty apartment in Highland Park, drinking the shitty beer I could afford back then, and I turn on the TV. And here's this cheesy old sitcom from the '70s. The whole thing is about how a trans person moves into this building—it was the '70s, so they don't get everything right. Lot of confusion between being gay and being trans back then. I was bracing for it being a hell of a lot worse, but it's pretty sensitive for what it is. A little preachy, but people need that from time to time.

Anyway, the story is about how the tenants are uncomfortable around this lady, and then this guy Frank shows up."

Lara's tone turned thoughtful. "Frank is the most cis vanilla motherfucker alive, and he reminds me of him." She pointed at me. "In the show, Frank is the only one who isn't weirded out by this trans lady Cindy. Treats her like he would anybody else. The other tenants? They don't know what to make of her. They're wondering if they should try to get her to move out. They're talking it over at this party, and Frank walks in. They tell him what's up, and he says, about Cindy, 'It's okay to be that way.' Says it just like that, like the moral of an *Afterschool Special*. And it's cheesy as fuck, but it was exactly what I needed to hear. All the other tenants, they realize they were wrong, and accept Cindy into the community. So like a week later, I'm alone with the most cis vanilla motherfucker in *my* life, and I take the plunge. I come out to him. First person I ever did."

"What'd he say?" Riley asked.

"He fucking told me he likes *Farscape*." She shook her head, smiling at the memory.

Riley looked at me guiltily. "I don't know what that is either."

"Yeah, you don't have to," Lara said. "Anyway, here I am breaking into Bohemian Grove with him."

"Wow."

"I never knew that," I said.

Lara shrugged. "We never talked about *My Friend Frank* before."

Hasim leaned in. "Mine was the one where Marc—he's the main dude—he's turning thirty. Only they say it 'The big three-oh.' Just like that, through the whole thing."

"Yeah, that used to be a thing," I said. "I think it might have even been clever once."

"Anyway, it's one of those old plots where a character thinks everybody's forgotten their birthday, but it's actually because all the other characters are throwing a surprise party. They used to have that plot in every show. But here, there's a twist. Frank *notices* that Marc thinks that he's been forgotten, so Frank goes and tells him. He's like, 'Hey, we're doing a surprise party. So act surprised.' Marc is psyched, and he buys like a shit-ton of booze. He starts a pre-party and by the time he's ready for the *actual* party, he's so wasted he can't even stand up. The next day, Frank's all, 'Don't drink if it's not fun anymore.'"

"Is that why you quit drinking?" I asked.

He laughed. "Nah, I didn't listen until I'd seen that thing like ten times, and figured out I had a problem all on my own, and then one night I turn on the TV, there's the show and of course it's the same episode. That's when I got it."

My laugh turned into a grimace as I clutched my side.

"Huh," Riley said, squinting at her phone. "The IMDB has zero information on this show. No episode details, and like one person in the cast. The guy who played Marc. Looks like he had a small career in the '70s, but *My Friend Frank* was the last thing he ever did."

"Fits," I said. "I wonder if he's still alive. You want answers, he's the man to talk to."

Hasim shoved me. "Come on. You heard our episodes. What was yours about?"

I chewed on my fries thoughtfully. "Eunice—she was the blonde with the toy poodle—moves out of the building, and they give her a going away party. There's this weird shot...you know how the hallways are painted to look like river banks, and there's that dirty blue carpet running down the center?"

Lara frowned. "The hallway doesn't have carpet."

"Sure it does," Hasim said. "Marc was passed out on it. It's this Persian deal."

"Well, in this one, it looks like a river. Anyway, Marc goes, 'I hope that's not the last time we see her.' And Frank goes, 'She's always going to be with us. Think about her when you need her.'"

"What's that supposed to mean?" Hasim asked.

"Beats me. Let's get back on the road. The Bohemians are waiting on us."

chapter
twenty-two

IT'S PRETTY hard to beat Northern California for natural beauty, at least for a couple more years before climate change-fueled megafires turn it into Fury Road. Redwood forests, majestic, mysterious, and impossibly green butt right up against the blue Pacific and rolling Mediterranean hills dotted with vineyards. It's a place built for the kind of leisure only elderly Europeans can imagine and soulless plutocrats can afford. Bohemian Grove was right at the locus of the transition from the Naboo-like environs of the Central Valley to the Endor-expanse of the Pacific Northwest, a short ways north of San Francisco and west of Santa Rosa. The environs of the Grove bear a passing resemblance to summer camp movies, but those were mostly shot in New Jersey. Here, the trees are bigger, more ancient. They don't give a damn what we get up to. As far as places for this whole thing to end, I could have picked worse.

We made great time, humming along at ninety most of the way, only slowing when we saw a cop. Conversation trickled to a stop after the diner, and by the time we closed in on the Grove, everyone had retreated into themselves. Running the plan over in their heads, or maybe finding something to distract themselves from that very thing. Hasim toyed with one of his blades, his eyes light years away. Lara stared out the window, drumming her fingers on the car. Riley tapped away on her laptop, her glasses showing only bright squares of light. Pud slept curled up between Riley and me.

We passed into the forest, the trees closing in around us like in a fairy tale. The difference was that I knew who the Big Bad Wolf was, and Grandma had already been eaten by a memetic virus, not to belabor a metaphor. We had our silver bullet locked and loaded, but a small doubt wormed into my mind. If you're gonna shoot the Big Bad Wolf, best not miss. At least the moon wasn't full. I don't think I could have taken that level of portent.

About a mile out, I pulled over among the ferns that grew wild on the edges of the road. "Come on, pal," I said, touching Pud's shoulder.

"Glah?" The chupacabra lifted his head, blinking his baleful red eyes.

"It's time."

He smacked his lips and yawned, displaying the impressive fangs that were about to do some work.

"Good luck, cutie," Riley said, scratching his head around where an ear would be. He leaned into it, one leg quivering. When she stopped, he shook himself out and followed me onto the road.

I knelt by in the gravel and pointed into the woods. His breath smelled like eggs. "Okay, buddy. The Grove is a mile or so in that direction. If you hit a lake, you've found it."

"Blerg," he said thoughtfully. Then he put one of his talons on my shoulder, and looked deep into my eyes. His were crimson with vertically-slitted pupils, so I will admit to a certain atavistic terror in the moment, even as I had long since accepted Pud as part of the gang. He patted my shoulder almost like a person. "Glah."

"Anybody with a gun, anybody with an earpiece, got it? Be careful, stick to the dark, one at a time. As many as you can."

Pud purred as he leaned forward and touched my forehead with his. Then, in a burst of animalistic speed, he took two loping steps into the dark, threw his arms wide and caught air. Then he was only a silent shadow in the night forest. I slid back into the car and shut the heavy door.

"How Batman was that?" Hasim said admiringly.

"I don't think Batman ever drank the blood of his villains," I said.

"I might like Batman if he was a vampire," Riley said.

"You don't like Batman?" Hasim was horrified.

"Rich white guy who beats up women he labels crazy? Not so much, no."

"He beats up dudes too!"

"Most of whom are queer-coded."

I stared out at the night in horror. "I never thought of Batman like that."

"Poison Ivy is the real hero," Riley said with some authority.

"Yeah, that tracks," Hasim said.

I wanted to sit in the car and have a Batman conversation with my friends more than anything in the world. I could still walk away, right? Pud was out there, sure, but that's what chupacabras did. They hunted.

"B? You okay?"

"I'm good," I said, starting the car.

"Good," Lara muttered. "I didn't want to do this Tarantino shit. We got a job to do."

The country road had sprouted traffic, an orderly line of catering trucks. I pulled off the road a final time, and Lara, Hasim, and Riley got out. All three were in black slacks, white shirts, and bowties. Riley carried a bag under one arm.

Lara paused at the door, her face cloudy. "You're up to this, right?"

"Don't worry about me. Just make sure Riley's free to do what she has to do."

"If this works, we're not going to be the most popular people."

"So? What else is new?"

It seemed like she was going to say something else, but she didn't. She went out the door, and if everything went as it was supposed to, it would be the last I'd see of her. I was held together by spit and bad intentions, but I'd keep for a night.

The gate looked like the front of a summer camp. When you got down to it, fascists were always in a state of arrested development. Hitler made people call him Wolf. The KKK had ranks that would make your most fervent D&D player cringe. Fascists spend their whole lives being terrified, so they want to go back to a time when they felt safe. They build walls and put men with guns on them and then call each other Dragon and Cyclops. Fucking nerds.

The gate was made out of logs, with a carved sign arching overhead declaring this BOHEMIAN GROVE. The guardhouse was done up like a log cabin. I was really hoping that the guards would be dressed like Jason Voorhees or at least camp counselors, but no such luck. The security guy looked like he should be tracking Laurence Fishburne through a cyberpunk dystopia. His suit fit well enough that I could barely spot the bulge of the hand cannon resting under his arm.

"Card, sir?" I handed over the card Riley had made blind, and in a rush. It would be a bluff getting him to accept it, but that was the one thing I could still do. He squinted at it in confusion. "I've never..."

"No, you haven't," I snapped with rich guy impatience. "Scan it and stop wasting my time."

He retreated into the guard house with typical fascist subservience, returning a moment later. "Mr. Quackenbush, I'm so sorry. I've never seen you at the Grove before."

"First time."

"Are you okay, sir?" He searched my face, clocking that I looked like I'd just gone ten with a bear.

"First rule is you don't talk about it."

His eyes widened, then nodded. "Mr. Quackenbush—your father Mr. Quackenbush I mean—is hosting the party at the central lodge," he said. "Take the right hand road and follow it until you see a large building by the lake. If you see a giant owl statue, you've gone too far."

That was pretty good advice. If you're ever in a situation where you see a giant owl statue, you've definitely gone too far.

"Thank you," I said, taking the card back from him. That would be the first piece of good luck of the evening. I hoped it wouldn't be the last. Riley made a few educated guesses, specifically that the Quackenbush clan had so many failsons and failgrandsons that you could pick almost any white-enough sounding name out of a hat and the rank-and-file would accept it as genuine. So long as I was dressed well enough and entitled, of course. I was Marvin Quackenbush as far as the gate guard was concerned. Irving's son by way of his second trophy wife, a Lithuanian model who had one hit dance single about twenty-five years ago. Credit where it's due: it's not the worst song I've ever heard. Hell, she'd done more good for the world with that song than any Quackenbush had. I was singing it under my breath as my car crackled along the dirt roads.

Other roads snaked out from the first, and occasionally through the trees I glimpsed collections of log cabins. Duck Soup was one of these. Curiosity nagged at me, but I didn't have time for an exploration. It wasn't long before I spotted the main lodge, a Viking-style cottage that could have comfortably birthed an Abe Lincoln kaiju. Other cars, luxury models, white catering trucks, and a single party bus were parked in the small gravel lot out front. I backed the Belle into a space and sat silently behind the wheel. A last moment to put everything where it needed to be, mentally speaking. Finally, I pressed a kiss into my first two fingers and touched the steering wheel. The Belle was a hell of a machine. I slipped the keys up under the visor and got out.

Ant lines of caterers, dressed in white dress shirts, black slacks, and bowties moved from trucks to the interior. I could have slipped in with them no problem, but I wanted to make a splash. That's what I was. A distraction. I straightened my suit. If this was going to work, I'd be playing it McQueen, but I felt more like Super Dave Osborne.

Security loomed in every shadow, muttering into wrist mics as they walked the perimeter. This many VIPs, even in a place as ostensibly safe as this one, meant they were on edge. One slab of brick stood in the lee of one of the smaller cabins. I watched a black shape crest the top of the cabin and descend on him like Dracula on a Victorian virgin. The man never managed to scream.

I made for the main lodge. This party was legendary in the Information Underground. It was the kind of place where the real movers and shakers went. Rumor had it that this was where Quackenbush and his ilk set the agenda for the coming year. If the secret world could be steered, this was where it was done. If all went as planned, I'd crash them into an iceberg.

I opened the door to the main lodge. A cadaverous man who was far too tall for it waited behind the counter of the cloakroom. "Good evening, sir," he intoned. "First visit to the Grove?"

"And last," I said to him.

"Welcome, sir."

As I stepped into the main lodge, a jazz orchestra started up. I know about as much about jazz as I do about nuclear fission. All I know is that both are about the noises you're not making. The orchestra was gathered at the far side of the room, beneath the taxidermied head of the biggest deer I'd ever seen. It looked like something that should be in a Miyazaki film, symbolizing the inherent good of nature, now shot, mounted, and still. Long tables, as if set for feasting Norsemen, stretched out on either side of a dance floor. A chandelier, impossibly fancy and putting an exclamation point on the Grove's rustic kitsch, dyed the air a thin yellow. A full bar took up a big section of one wall. Lara stood behind it, mixing drinks with attentive professionalism.

Caterers circulated throughout the room with plates of hors d'oeuvres and full champagne flutes. The guests came in three varieties: the elderly plutocrat set that used to run the world, the slightly younger breed of tech-fascist drunk on memes and ketamine, and women who couldn't be older than nineteen, shrinkwrapped in glittering gowns. They circulated just like the hors d'oeuvres. I scanned the crowd, hunting for my quarry.

"I told you to go home." Those Romanian vowels laid over the tiny voice still lacerated my soul. I swallowed the hurt, put it with all the others. Wouldn't do to break down again. I turned and found Oana Constantinescu had approached completely silently and was now looking up with a stern and faintly disappointed expression, like a hobbit teacher whose student had forgotten one of the two hundred words for potato. She had packed her small, powerful frame into an evening gown. Her hair was up in a high bun, and diamonds sparkled on her ears and neck. She looked incredible, but I wasn't going to let that distract me.

"You had to know I wouldn't."

She threw a glance behind me, and a frown ghosted over her features. She stepped forward, taking my left hand in hers. A bit over a foot separated our heights, so she couldn't comfortably get her hand on my shoulder, settling for my bicep instead. While I would have loved to cradle the small of her back, I had to make do with her shoulder blade area. And then we were dancing. I let her lead. It was my first time dancing with a real-life Olympic gymnast after all. Oana's grace was tempered with power, her body a ball of rubber bands ready to explode in every direction, and only she could control it.

"You have to go," she murmured. "I can't protect you if you stay."

"Who said I needed protecting?"

"Everything about you." Concern filled her eyes. The presence of a human emotion hurt more to see there. If she was truly gone, I could justify thinking of her as an enemy. But enough of Oana still existed. She cared. I couldn't think of her as an enemy, even if we were enemies here. The truth was, my emotions were a stormy sea. Might have had something to do with...everything.

"You could always walk away."

"What are you here to do?"

"Oh you know me. Going to throw the ring into Mount Doom and topple the evil empire."

She held me a little tighter. Oana is terrifyingly strong; I've seen her crack walnuts in her hands without thinking about it. "I told you before that you don't know what you're doing."

"Oana...what I'm doing will seem like insanity to you. We don't really live in the same reality anymore, you and I. Can you trust me that I do know what I'm doing?"

"Why do you know what you're doing and I don't?"

"Look around," I said. "You're the only woman here over thirty. Hell, you're the only woman here over *twenty*."

"Sex work is work," Oana said.

"You'll get no argument from me, so long as everyone's consenting and can consent. Some of these girls look a little young."

Oana's jaw muscles bunched up. "They're not my business."

"You're going to look the other way."

"These men are fighting the real pedophiles. The real monsters."

"Look around, Oana!" I whisper-shouted. "This is what pedophilia looks like with the rich and powerful. They aren't cackling and fucking babies, they're indulging in the same sickness in our whole culture, the one that the best parts of V.E.N.U.S. fought against. The obsession with youth and innocence and inexperience. The implication that the best sex you can have is when your partner is scared and confused. It's fucked up, but it's harder to recognize because we're all complicit in it. When there are no real good guys and everyone is sort of bad, it becomes real easy to imagine monsters so you can sleep at night."

"You need to do your research."

"You need to open your eyes. If you want to fight pedophilia, human trafficking, all that, I'll help you. *But that's not what these men are doing.*"

"What are they doing, then?"

"Kirk Shelley. Oh shit, there he is." The Nazi hadn't spotted me. He was chatting up one of the young women who wore a look on her face like Counselor Troi hearing about Riker's newest space VD. "He's a literal Nazi. He wants to kill all the usual suspects, and let's not forget for a second that includes Slavs."

"You were a Nazi," she said simply.

"I worked for them. I took their money. I was never one of them."

"That's splitting hairs and you know it."

The worst part was she was absolutely right. I'd never had a single conviction I didn't sell for money. All those monsters I talked about? Well, I'd worked for them all. Sure, Quackenbush used me but the truth was I'd worked for him knowingly. Him and Kirk and so many others who would have had suites in Hell if only we lived in a universe with some sense of justice.

"You're right," I told her. "I'm trying to balance the scales."

"That's what Kirk's doing."

I held Oana as we danced. I didn't want to let her go. "Can I say something to you?"

"Sure."

"Remember when you and me raided that Little Green Men base out in the desert?"

She smiled. "That was fun."

"It was. Since that night you've been my friend. You're always gonna be my friend. If you ever change your mind about all of this stuff, I'm not going to make you feel bad. I'm not going to laugh at you, and you know I can't judge you. I'll just be happy to have my friend back, who fought aliens and sang along to Boston and talks like teenaged Dracula."

She held me tighter. "You can still leave."

"So can you."

We let go, both of us knowing, I think, that it was time. We were heading in different directions, and that was the end of it. She looked up at me with grief in her eyes. No other way to look at a dead man who used to be your friend, I guess. She probably saw a mirror image in mine.

"Tell Quackenbush I'll be at the bar."

I left her on the dance floor and sidled up to the fake pine log bar. Eyes were on me now. More of the guests realizing that like the old song went, one of these things was not like the other, one of these things did not belong. Meant that I was locked in. Big talk in front of Oana, sure, but once I knew, really knew for certain that I couldn't run, my bowels turned to ice. Without looking at Lara, I said, "Old Fashioned."

She built the drink without even a nose touch to confirm we were in cahoots and slid it across to me. It was damn good, smooth as candlewax and sweet as warm honey. Lara always knew her way around a bar.

"Mr. Blank, what a pleasant surprise." Irving Quackenbush, flanked by his pet Nazi Kirk Shelley, stood only a step away from me. His reptilian eyes glinted in the soft light. Kirk sidled around behind me, his hatred hot on my neck.

"For old acquaintances, right?" I asked, raising my glass. "I don't have any acquaintances older than you."

"Amusing. I'll admit that you've piqued my curiosity. Why are you here?"

I peered through my drink. Though the booze made this place look more preserved in amber, a more natural state for it. "Do you know what Shub-Internet is?"

"A particularly virulent computer virus that a few superstitious souls worship as a god. You attempted to steal it out of a US government facility."

"That was fun."

"It was also treason."

"Come on, Irv. You did a coup on that same government. Now's not the time to be throwing stones."

"What about Shub-Internet?"

"A friend who's a lot smarter than I am explained Shub-Internet to me. It's a worm," I said, wagging my finger, "but it doesn't behave like a normal worm. It's a lot more aggressive about the data it eats. And sure, it can be choosy, but when you've been starving it for years, it gets a lot more indiscriminate. And this is the important bit: Shub-Internet is *ravenous*."

Quackenbush watched me keenly. He was savvy enough to know I was getting ready to drop a beat. Or, considering his age, I was ready to have the bassoons come in on a contrapasso. "You didn't *attempt* to steal it. You succeeded."

"Took some doing, but yes. We chopped it up and that friend I mentioned assembled it on a laptop on the drive up here. Seven hours. What else was she gonna do? I Spy is only fun for like an hour, tops."

"A digital attack," Irving said, as though he were choosing what sort of wine would go with his komodo dragon steak. "You're threatening me with cyberterrorism."

"Threatening? Oh, goodness no. I'm not a thug. Threatening means that there is something in Heaven or on Earth that would stop me. I just have the—call it brass, call it goddamn common courtesy—to tell you to your face what I'm doing to you."

He smiled, but I swear I saw a tiny bit of fear peeking around the smug. "A desperate attempt to regain your former mystique, Mr. Blank?"

I spotted Riley through the crowd. She had returned from her errand. Not just the most important part of the plan—the entire linchpin. Meant Hasim and Pud had cleared her enough of a path, and my favorite techno-witch had gotten her Elder Sign on. It was time to grandstand a bit, to show these fascists who was really in charge. To put the fear of Blank in them.

"Mystique? I don't need that. Goes away awful quick and it won't put food in your belly or a roof over your head. No, I'm here for *you*." I grinned, putting the drink to my lips. I wanted to pound it, set up another, but I needed my head nice and clear. "I'm here to turn your name into a way to describe the state of being broken in half in the most humiliating way possible. To be at the two-yard line and succumb to firehose-like incontinence."

Kirk's fingers curled over my shoulder and pulled me away from his boss. I shook him off me with force I didn't know I could still summon. By now, the orchestra's sound had died, and more of the guests were turning to the only show remaining.

"You're trying my patience, Mr. Blank," Quackenbush said, but he was bluffing with a jack high, and I think he knew it. Somewhere in his bones, he knew it.

I put a little lung into my voice. I was addressing Irving, but it was more of a speech than conversation. This was for everyone's benefit. "You know why half the internet is porn? Because that's what Shub-Internet likes to eat more than anything else. While it was locked up in the—" I just barely caught myself from saying D.U.M.B. "—facility beneath Denver International, no one was feeding it. They let a god starve. Do you know how stupid that is? All it wants to do is eat, and it's not so picky anymore. It'll eat anything. And the funny thing is, these days everything is digital. Property records. Bank accounts. Identity. So I decided to feed someone to it. An entire digital life down the gullet of a god. You know who I picked, Irv? You. In the time you've spent talking to me, I've erased you. You don't exist anymore."

Quackenbush snorted. "You can't simply wave a magic wand and release this creature into my accounts."

"Sure I can. All I needed to do was bring it here. Go on. Check your accounts if you don't believe me." And there was the bait. If he didn't take it, I was bluffing. If I showed even the slightest bit of need, he would snatch it away from me. I had to fake a confidence I forgot the feeling of. I thought of Hasim's hug on my return. I thought of the look on Riley's face just before she ran from the angry mob. I felt Lara's eyes on me now. And I looked away from Irving, savoring the best Old Fashioned of my life.

Quackenbush removed the phone from his jacket. I watched him out of my peripherals, staring at me, trying to pierce my cloak. The opening riff of "More Than a Feeling" echoed through my imagination.

Quackenbush barked out a laugh, a single "Ha!" to let his contemporaries know that he hadn't been bested. "My accounts are fine, Mr. Blank. Every dollar, present and accounted for. I don't know why you thought it would be a good idea to come here and play this ridiculous game, but it's over now. Mr. Shelley—"

"What you said in Denver was dead on," I interrupted. "I thought about it a lot. Didn't have much else to do, what with falling apart and all. You told me it didn't matter if I somehow scrubbed Q from existence. The damage was already done. You were right, of course. Damn near broke me to accept it. It made me realize something. You can't delete an idea, but you *can* delete a man. I might not be able to do a damn thing about the monster, but I could still burn Dr. Frankenstein's castle to the ground."

"Didn't you hear me?"

"Check again," I said, and this time the confidence I projected was real. Riley explained that much to me. The first time he accessed his accounts, Riley would reroute him to Shub-Internet. The god would do the rest, hungrily reaching down avenues of digital information and relish every last byte. I smirked. "Humor me."

"Mr. Quackenbush, I can take him outside and put two in his head."

"Not yet, Mr. Shelley. I want him to see his defeat. I want him to know that the entire purpose of his life was only to enrich me."

Quackenbush produced his phone, tapping at the screen. His face dropped as he watched the information appear. "No. This isn't possible. The accounts are *gone!*" More tapping. "This is a trick!" More tapping. "You can't do this!"

"Sure I can. In point of fact, I did. Gotta admit, feeding the man behind Q to the god of the internet is pretty poetic, right?"

"And now I imagine you're going to kill me? You have some legion of assassins ready to storm in here?" Quackenbush demanded, his voice high and reedy.

"Why would I kill you? You're an elderly man without any money, citizenship, or health insurance. America will kill you dead without me lifting a finger." I leaned in close to him, but spoke nice and loud. "It's the world you made, fuckstick. Live in it." I laughed. "Or don't. I guess that's the whole point."

"I still have friends. Family."

"Friends?" And here I really started projecting, putting all that drama club in high school to good use. The whole room needed to hear this. "You don't have any friends. Your family hates you. You have people who would exchange favors with you. Same story with everyone here. You foster a culture of every man for himself because you think you'll always be on top, but now you have nothing to offer. You live in a transactional world and I took away every last piece of currency. You're alone, Irving. You're as alone as any man has ever been. Just like you wanted."

Now I swept the crowd with my gaze. I felt like a revivalist preacher, issuing rolling warnings of hellfire, but the devil I was scaring them with was me. "And here's the part that involves you all. If anyone, *anyone*, tries to help Irving Quackenbush...give him money, a bed for a night, a single *saltine* to eat...and the same thing is going to happen to you. You try to use the government you bought? Same thing will happen to you. Do anything other than retire quietly, and the same thing will happen to you. If you so much as try to help a friend get elected to a school board, I will ruin you. I will ruin your family. I will ruin your friends. I will ruin your *legacies*. I will burn you the fuck to ash and I will salt the Earth on top of you." I lifted my glass in a toast. "Happy New Year."

Quackenbush's hands quivered. "You did this."

"Goddamn right I did."

"I have one question. What's to stop me from killing you?"

I grinned at him. This was the one part of the plan I didn't tell the crew. I fed them some line about running when Quackenbush was distracted, and I think they believed me. I can be pretty convincing when I'm trying to set up something I want. "Absolutely nothing. You're just curing the cancer of a dead man."

"Kill him," Irving said.

Carbon steel against fabric whispered behind me. Kirk could finally get his revenge for those two years in the pen. I'd have preferred my murderer to be someone else, but I'm pretty sure you didn't usually get to choose those.

I suppose if this were that kind of story, I'd have heard an agonized *"No!"* from Lara. Since this is Lara we're talking about, instead she gave only a whispered, "Mother*fucker!*" And look, I was kind of glad that would be the last word I'd ever hear. Shot dead with the best drink I'd ever had in my hand and the Cadillac of swears in my eardrums, facing an enemy I'd just wrecked. Yeah, it could be worse.

Of course, that's not what happened. The gunshot went off like thunder, fading into a high-pitched whine. At around the same time, something shattered, and cold, stinging liquid splashed across the back of my neck. That sting would continue to bother me. Not the hole by my left shoulder spreading a stain of claret across my shirt. That didn't hurt at all. But something on my neck felt like a sliver.

My legs were far away from me, and it became hard to balance. I caught myself against the bar, but there was no strength in my arms. I was deflating like a lawn decoration being taken down the week after Christmas, losing integrity and falling to the floor in a plasticky lump. Lara slid over the bar, a bottle in each hand. Kirk hit the floor behind me, his head soaked in liquor and blood, his eyes rolling back like he was trying to catch a glimpse of his frontal lobes.

Black wrapped around the borders of my vision. I fancied I could make out tentacles in there, as though Shub-Internet had wormed into the inside of my skull. There would be peace in that. The god could delete all the data in my life and that would be the end of it. If anything remained, it would be an urban legend. A cryptid maybe.

But there was no peace. Rough hands gripped my armpits and the brush of arms, clothes, and the occasional shock of something wet. No, not arms—branches. Pine needles raked my face and the pungent scent permeated my senses.

I opened my eyes. Shadowy shapes struggled in the dark around me. I was being carried, but I couldn't tell by who or what. Fires burned around a colossal owl. I thought I should probably ask him what to do, but he'd just send me to a rose bush and some rats. He loomed as big in my mind as he had when I was a kid. The owl is a symbol of death in some cultures, right? That sounded right.

Pop-pop-pop echoed over the lake somewhere behind me. My neck hurt, and I wanted to touch it and maybe pull the splinter out, but I couldn't really move my arms. They were being held, and losing air fast.

There were voices too. Panicking voices.

"There's too much blood!"

"Dumb motherfucker should know better!"

"Dude, hold on, you can hold on."

"Glah!"

You know, the normal kind of stuff. I heard those voices, but I couldn't attach significance to them. I felt like I should know who they were talking about, but I couldn't come up with the answer.

Then I was lying flat, my head pillowed on something soft. Wind touched my hair. Maybe a hand. It was a hand. Riley's. Why was it so red? "You're gonna be okay, B." Riley said. Her glasses made her look like an owl.

"Take me to Nicodemus," I murmured.

"It's all right, you're gonna be okay. Stay here, all right? Stay here."

Pud Galvin rested his head on my chest, his talons gripping my hand as he lightly chewed my fingers.

It would have been a perfect way to finish things, except for the stinging in my neck. I suppose to be perfect, you needed that one bit of imperfection. I closed my eyes. Riley called to me, but I was so very tired. So I slept.

twenty-three

I'M THE NARRATOR, though, so you know I'm not dead. It's not like I was telling the story from the other side of the veil or something. If I had died, the story would have ended mid-sentence, and that never happens. So, spoiler alert, and I'm sorry for any consternation.

I woke up staring at an intricate ceiling, like the kind of thing that should only be in a European church. The light in the room was dim, and later I'd find the source to be an antique lamp on a table next to me. My neck didn't hurt, but it was stiff. I was sitting up. My whole body was made of lead, but my head felt like a balloon ready to float off of my neck. For a brief, disorientated moment, I thought I was underwater and I tried to thrash my way free, but the pain exploded from my chest and I saw that I wasn't being drowned. I could breathe. I was safe.

I was covered in bandages. They were close and sticky, like a terrible thundershirt. Most of them webbed over the worst pain, the ache bleeding through my chest from a point not too distant from my heart. Another covered my neck, yet another the bridge of my nose. Maybe there were more. I couldn't tell.

With some small amount of struggle, I noted that I was in a room whose tasteful antiques demanded that it be referred to as a *bedchamber* and never by the vulgar *guest room*. I reclined amongst fat pillows and blankets, feeling more than a bit like a badly injured dumpling. A bag of clear liquid dripped into my arm, and the faint floating feeling said I was getting the good stuff. That was when I noted that despite that, and the professional quality of the bandaging, I was definitely not in a hospital. Good thing too—I couldn't afford one of those.

A snore cut off with a snort turned my attention. Lara slept in a chair by my bedside, a Márquez paperback tented on her chest.

I don't know if it was good timing or if he was somehow watching, but the door opened. The man who stepped in was big, with thick lumberjack arms and a noticeable belly hanging over the waist of his jeans. His shaved head glowed under the light. His black beard was neatly combed and shot through with gray. He pulled a syringe from the pocket of his cardigan.

"You're awake," he said, keeping his voice down.

"Where am I?" My mouth felt like I'd been licking the desert.

He injected the syringe into the port on the underside of the bag. "For the pain," he said. "You were in pretty sorry shape, even before a gunshot brushed your heart."

"Brushed my heart?"

"Quite literally. You've got a hell of a scar."

"Tell me about it."

"And that's on top of everything else. Three broken ribs, too many sprains to count, a concussion, malnutrition, some light pellagra, ergot poisoning. Your liver's not in the best shape either."

"I get it."

"I've never seen anything quite like it. You look like you've been in a car accident that lasted years."

"Something like that."

"You're not quite out of the woods, but the fact that you're awake is a good sign. You're going to have to start taking care of yourself."

I didn't know how to respond to that. Fortunately, Lara saved me by yawning awake. "You don't have to be quiet. I'm up."

The doctor—that's the only thing he could be—smiled at Lara. "I'd give you the same advice I'd give him: Sleep is your friend."

"I might even listen."

"How do you feel?" he asked me.

"Thirsty. Hungry. Tired."

"Good. I'll get you some food. It'll be Campbell's. Hope that's all right. I've got you on a multivitamin. Your body was deficient in...pretty much everything. As for something to drink..." He nodded at a full pitcher of water by my bed.

"I'll get it," Lara said. "I gotta talk to this one. Could you leave us alone?"

"Yeah," he said. "It's good to see you." As he walked out of the room, one of his hands trailed, and Lara caught it, putting it to her cheek. The momentary caress was a level of intimacy I'd only ever had with one person. I was only beginning to think that I might deserve to have it again, but the impulse was too big to have.

"Thanks, Graham," Lara said. Then he was gone, and I was alone with Lara. She stared at me, her expression not quite loving and not quite angry. Finally, she poured me a glass of water, dropped in a straw, and held it so I could drink. "Dumb motherfucker. I should kill you myself."

I drank deeply. The water restored some pliancy to my tongue and beat back the headache gathering behind my eyes. Tasted like life. "Be my guest," I said.

"I'm not gonna sit here and lecture you. If you'd have trusted us, we could have gotten you out. Hell, we *did* get you out." She worried her bottom lip between her teeth. "Except you didn't want to get out, did you?"

I looked away. She was right, of course. It had been in the back of my mind since the beginning. Right the wrong I had done, go out in a blaze of glory. That way I wouldn't have to look at the world I'd made. Cleaner that way. "No, I didn't."

"Do you want me to forgive you?"

"I don't know."

"I can't." She shook her head. "Not because I'm holding what you did against you. I was hurt when you told me that you were responsible for what was happening to my life, yes. I didn't know how to deal with that, because you've always been safe. Then all of a sudden you weren't. But I watched you try to fix it, to balance it out. You had some drama queen freakouts along the way, sure, but you tried. Harder than I've ever seen anybody try to fix something." She paused, making sure I heard what she had to say. "I can't forgive you because you're the only one who can do that."

"I don't think I can."

"You're gonna have to figure out a way, because I don't like it when motherfuckers try to kill my friend, even if said motherfucker *is* my friend. Got it?"

"I got it."

"Next time, I want you to trust me. And if you can't trust me, trust Hasim, or Riley. Shit, trust your spirit guide. All that mystical power and you were gonna throw it away on a Nazi's bullet."

"Okay, Lara. I hear you." I swallowed. "I don't want to die."

"Good."

"Not anymore." We sat in silence for a time, the words hanging heavy between us. Finally, I couldn't help myself. "So, Hasim, huh?"

"One date, which we didn't get to. You got a problem?"

"Not a single one."

"Good."

"Lara? I'm tired. I'm gonna rest my eyes, I think."

"Long as you want. I'll be here."

I blinked. I swear it was no longer than that. The room was bright, sunlight pouring in from the open window. Beyond, I caught a glimpse of blue sky.

"There he is," Lara said.

"Dude! You're alive!"

Startled, I winced in preparation for my injuries to pinch me. They did, but not as badly as they had. Hasim was suddenly just *there,* leaning over the bed. He wrapped his arms around my neck in a bear hug.

"Ow."

"Sorry. Just thought you were a goner is all." He moved away, and I blinked in the bright light. "My mom's gonna be so relieved."

"It hurts to laugh," I told him.

Riley stood at the foot of the bed, smiling. Pud perched on an armoire, preening his wing flaps. The gang was all here.

"I'm glad you're not dead," Riley said, giving me a far gentler hug than Hasim had.

"What happened?" I asked.

"We dragged your dumb ass out of Bohemian Grove with Quackenbush guns on our asses," Lara said. "Got to that Martian ride of yours and burned rubber out of there. Graham's a friend from way back, so I brought you here. Amount of blood you lost, we didn't have much choice, especially because we figured that a hospital would be too dangerous. You were about a quart low in the blood department."

"I begged him to take my blood," Hasim said. "But I'm the wrong type."

"Got a couple pints of me, I'm afraid," Lara said. "Topped you off with some of Riley."

"Thank you. Both of you."

"Happy to," Riley said, touching my foot.

Lara looked to Hasim. "Did you find anything?"

"Oh yeah. There's a contract out on him," Hasim said. "Sorry, dude."

I shrugged. "Wouldn't be the first time."

"You," Lara said to Riley. "What do you have?"

"You mind?" Riley asked, patting the bed. I shook my head and she hopped up, opening a laptop. Pud soared from the armoire to land on the bed between Riley and me. I stroked the chupacabra's bristling fur and he made happy sounds. "I have good news and bad news."

"Good news!" Hasim crowed.

"Irving Quackenbush hasn't been seen since the Grove. I think we might have actually got him. Quackenbush Security is in the process of being stripped for parts by other corporate raiders and of course the extended Quackenbush family. It isn't pretty."

"We put a lot of war criminals out of a job," I said. "God knows what they're gonna get up to now."

"Think fucking positive," Lara said, lightly hitting my good shoulder.

"Bad news is, it looks like they didn't listen to your warning. The coup's ongoing at every level. You have standard smalltime grifters—influencers and the like. You also have the larger conspiracy platforms still riding that wave, and the number of politicians running for and elected into public office who are still dogwhistling to it keeps going up."

Hasim, Lara, Riley, and Pud all looked at me. No, not at me. *To* me. A horrible realization dawned over me like the first rays of sunshine that set Dracula on fire.

"Did you mean what you said?" Riley asked.

"About fucking anyone who tried this shit," Lara expanded.

There it was. A choice. I'd done it the one time and it damn near killed me. There was more work to be done. My fuck-up hadn't been cleaned up yet, and unlike when this all started, I had friends. Maybe the best ones I'd ever had. They wanted this; it was there in the lights in their eyes. More than that, they wanted *me.* I was part of the team, an Assassin, a white witch, a brilliant cultist, and a murder monster.

And me. Mr. Blank. One more hill to climb, but it didn't seem so daunting anymore. I didn't have the strength now, but I didn't need it. They had it, and I could lean on them, and when I was healed, I take my turn as their rock. We'd summit this thing together.

I turned to the smartest person I knew. Hope bloomed in her eyes as she recognized my expression, a puckish, heroically malicious glint over the prospect of returning some pain to the men who gave it without so much as a thought. "Riles, pick one of these assholes. We're gonna break him in half."

She broke into a wide grin. "Already picked him out, B."

Riley had a damn PowerPoint prepared. She pulled it up on her machine, giving us the news on a fascist piece of shit that was about to have the heavens fall on his hateful head. A plan was already germinating in my mind when Graham came in with a tray of soup and buttered bread. The food put a little strength into my limbs and the emotion surging in my body was unfamiliar. It took me some time to understand that this was the edges of joy.

My third life had come to a close. The fourth was just beginning.

And it was going to be *fun.*

acknowledgments

Every book has a long path to publication and this one is longer than most. I initially wrote this in the early days of 2021, when I was grappling with a sense of guarded optimism. Things have changed. My optimism is less guarded and more bruised and wild-eyed.

In 2017 I informally retired the Blank series. Conspiracies weren't fun anymore, if they ever really were. But then something happened. Conspiracy theory went extremely mainstream and I realized I had a hook. I tried to dismiss it, but it wouldn't leave me alone. It ended up merging with another idea I'd had for a Blank book, which was a heist into Area 51 that would bring back a rogue's gallery of supporting characters from previous books. I took some material from the first try at a third book in the series (now formally relegated to the multiverse) and the result is this.

The first people I need to thank are my publisher, Candlemark & Gleam. They're under new management, but the support has not changed. They've been my favorite press since the first Blank book was signed almost fifteen years ago. They're still the best.

Much of the inspiration and research for the book came in the form of podcasts. I've been a loyal listener of QAA (formerly QAnon Anonymous) since 2017 and this book would not exist without their informative, quirky, and hilarious reporting on the all-devouring conspiracy of QAnon. To Travis, Julien, and especially Jake, thank you. And there's a signed book in it for you.

I want to thank my editor Julie Hutchings. I owe you from the thing with the guy and the place and I'll never forget it.

And of course, I want to thank all of my readers. Without you, I'd be ranting on a street corner, which would be terrible for my blood pressure.